W9-BZW-038

May December Souls

$\mathcal{H}$e is wearing a classic pair of black dress pants and a crisp, clean ivory white shirt that buttons all the way up to that dark, long neck of his. He looks very *GQ*, like he just stepped from the pages of a magazine. Not at all hip-hop or too youthful. He is mature beyond his years, maybe by a few years, maybe even more.

As I sit down, I look around the bar area and notice a few people staring at us, or him, or me. My mind starts running away with me about what they could be thinking. I am certain I overhear one girl whispering, "That must be her son." Another man says, "I wonder what he sees in her." The lady sitting next to me looks me up and down and I smile. She leans in to ask, "Where did you get that top? I bought one just like it but it's long-sleeved, and I couldn't find one like yours."

I reply in relief, "I bought it at Charlotte Russe. They have other colors also."

Just then the bartender asks if we'd like anything. I order Alizé and Malik snickers for a minute. He then orders Hennessey and Coke. And the bartender asks a very predictable question:

"Can I see your ID, sir?"

By Marissa Monteilh

HOT BOYZ
THE CHOCOLATE SHIP
MAY DECEMBER SOULS

ATTENTION: ORGANIZATIONS AND CORPORATIONS
Most HarperTorch paperbacks are available at special quantity discounts for bulk purchases for sales promotions, premiums, or fund-raising. For information, please call or write:

Special Markets Department, HarperCollins Publishers, Inc., 10 East 53rd Street, New York, N.Y. 10022–5299.
Telephone: (212) 207–7528. Fax: (212) 207-7222.

May December Souls

a novel

Marissa Monteilh

HarperTorch
An Imprint of HarperCollinsPublishers

This book was originally published in 2000 by 4D Publishing Paperback Fiction.

This is a work of fiction. Names, characters, places, and incidents are products of the author's imagination or are used fictitiously and are not to be construed as real. Any resemblance to actual events, locales, organizations, or persons, living or dead, is entirely coincidental.

❦

HARPERTORCH
An Imprint of HarperCollins*Publishers*
10 East 53rd Street
New York, New York 10022-5299

Copyright © 2000 by Marissa Monteilh
ISBN: 0-06-050280-0

All rights reserved. No part of this book may be used or reproduced in any manner whatsoever without written permission, except in the case of brief quotations embodied in critical articles and reviews. For information address HarperTorch, an Imprint of HarperCollins Publishers.

First HarperTorch paperback printing: January 2005
First Avon Books trade paperback printing: March 2002

HarperCollins®, HarperTorch™, and ❦ ™ are trademarks of HarperCollins Publishers Inc.

Printed in the United States of America

Visit HarperTorch on the World Wide Web at www.harpercollins.com

10 9 8 7 6 5 4 3 2 1

If you purchased this book without a cover, you should be aware that this book is stolen property. It was reported as "unsold and destroyed" to the publisher, and neither the author nor the publisher has received any payment for this "stripped book."

This book is dedicated to my mom,
Jacqueline Gail Land,
the original Diva and
the classiest woman in the world.
You are the wind beneath my wings.
R/I/P 8/17/99

Acknowledgments

I THANK THE LORD each and every day for the many blessings in my life. He has proven that once you make up your mind to take one step, He'll take two. The lessons learned during this process have proved invaluable.

I'd like to express special appreciation to:

All my children—Adam, for being my spark, my constant reminder that I should take time to laugh. The fact that you are now six foot plus should finally remind me that you are no longer my baby, you are now a young man. Ron Jr., for being my rock, my center, the voice who always tells me that things happen for a reason, and the one who always looks at the bright side. Your positivity, giving nature and spirituality prove that you are headed for greatness. Nicole, my oldest and only girl who is now a woman, for being my sister-friend, confidante, and shopping companion. You know that I love big Darrien and little Darren like blood. The three of you make the perfect family.

For this publication, I'd like to focus on all of the following people whom I did not know one year ago. What a difference a year makes:

The first readers who expressed such deep appreciation of my hard work. Avis Wilson and her son Aaron, who took the time to send my first E-mail review, Sabrina Williams who sent me my first "fan" letter, Lashanda Kinsey whose appreciation of my work reminds me why I write in the first place, Daniell Robinson who, after reading my book, was inspired to take a major step toward contacting a loved one, and DeAnna Scroggins, a gem whom I consider a friend and supportive reader. And to all of the other readers who have contacted me. Your feedback really does make a difference.

The bookstores that embraced me from the very beginning. Locally, Renee and Jim at Zahra's Books-N-Things, you were the first and I cannot begin to express my appreciation for your support and love, Amira and Malik at Malik's, you know how I felt when you said yes, giving me the opportunity to see my first book on your shelves, Charles and Linda at Smiley's Books, who sold and ordered and sold and ordered again and again. And those who I've met on tour who scheduled signings and supported me 100 percent. Angela at Barnes and Noble in Alabama, William at Afro-in-Books and Things in Florida, Vidal at Mahogany in Alabama, Mutota and Fanta at African Spectrum in Georgia, Michelle at African American Book Stop, and Jennifer at Community Books, both in Louisiana, Til Pettis at Jokaes and CushCity.com, both in Texas, Kenya Erving at the CSUDH Bookstore, and all of the other bookstore owners I may have forgotten to mention.

The book clubs, the heart of the publishing business. Angel Wheeler and the Rho Zeta Omega Book Chat, Zelda Miles and the Sisters Paperback Club and Words Escape Me Summit (I fell in love with you ladies), Pamela Beck and the Cover to Cover Book Club, Andrea Ransom of Special Thoughts and the numerous other clubs who have shown interest in my title.

To a couple of people in particular whom I connected with as if we've known each other forever. Cydney Rax, who does phenomenal work with Book-Remarks.com. Our "journey" talks keep me focused. Tee C. Royal with RawSistaz.com, who provides a lifeline for readers, authors and book lovers in general.

And now it's time to talk about the extraordinary authors who have taken me in along the way. There is a camaraderie amongst authors that is the most heartwarming thing I've seen in all of my years. We all show support and love in many ways. Lolita Files, Omar Tyree, Michael Baisden, Maxine Thompson, Dominique Grosvenor, Jacquelin Thomas, Brian Egeston, Brandon Massey, Kevin Briggs and all the others.

Special love for my special friend and Starbucks buddy, Victoria Christopher Murray, who, from the moment we met in Birmingham, showed me love and understanding and support. Your willingness to listen, offer advice, and laugh has been the biggest gift throughout this entire journey. You always make me feel as though I'm never alone. You always have a similar story to tell so that I know I'm not losing my mind. Thanks, Vic.

Vanessa Davis Griggs, whom I met in Birmingham also, yet I'm sure we probably met in the nursery when we were born, or perhaps it was in another life. Either way, when I saw you sitting in the audience of my book talk seminar, I knew there was a God. You knew what it was like to only have a few participants and you took the time to show me love. I consider myself blessed to know you.

And finally, without these two people, this re-release would not have been possible:

First, to my publisher, Carrie Feron. Carrie, the first time I read your editing notes it was like food to my soul. You are so very talented and I look forward to learning even more from you in the future. Thank you for saying yes to an unknown author with a self-published title and a dream. I look forward to a long and prosperous relationship.

And to my jammin' agent, Richard Curtis. To say that you had faith in me would be an understatement. I will never forget the morning of February 8, 2001, when I woke up, turned on my computer, sat with a cup of coffee and read your E-mail. I nearly choked on my first gulp as I read your "yes" message over and over and over. You believed in my talents, you asserted your goals with conviction and you delivered. Your undying support and passion for my work and bright outlook for my future is deeply, deeply appreciated. You are a Godsend.

If I left anyone out, I'll catch you on the next one. Thank you all!

Write on!

Prologue

FOR MOST OF MY LIFE, I've believed age is just a number, however, I suppose deep down I think a man's age should exceed a woman's by at least a few years. That's how it was for my father and mother, he being six years or so older than she. Yet he left us—my mom, two brothers and me—for another woman. Not for a younger or older woman, but for a *White* woman.

For years, and still to this day I suppose, something inside of me turns into knots when I see a Black man with a White woman. But that was more than thirty-five years ago. Today, my father is still with the same White woman he left my mother for more than three decades ago. He was a musician, a saxophone player in his own group, the Chuck Malone Trio. He played in Chicago and Los Angeles, and was very well known back in the day. So you know the groupies were out in full force. Much temptation for him, I'm sure. What I'm surer of is that he gave into it. The woman he's with today was one of those groupies. I never knew him, yet I grew up imagining I did. Fantasizing what it would be like to have him at my graduations, my wedding and the birth of my children . . . only fantasies. He left me no choice other than to live with it.

But I'm older now. I will celebrate my fortieth birthday this December. Even though I'm the very age I considered ancient when I was a teenager, I find myself single and alone at times, yet not lonely. I desire the love of a man, yet I don't crave it. I've learned to love myself more than I could ever love any man. I've also just lied to myself about these thoughts. I still haven't quite gotten it right.

Maybe because I was abandoned by my father at the age of five and never learned to experience the beauty of unconditional love from a man, maybe because my mother told me "all men are the same, if they put a paper bag over your head, they wouldn't know the difference," maybe a combination of so many reasons. I've been independent and controlling just like my mother. I've had to be to protect myself. After all, I never learned the true roles of a man and a woman. I've been told I try to run things and that I'm too bossy. Hell, I say, "If you don't like it get to steppin'!" That's been my attitude. But just before they could get a chance to leave me, I'd leave them first, just so they couldn't pull a "daddy" on me. I vowed to never be abandoned again, yet I kept picking the very men who earn an "A" in desertion. The wild, reckless, charming, humorous, good-looking, outgoing, well-known lover boys possessing the personalities of politicians. I've dated movie stars, sports figures, broadcasters and senators. Men just like my father, masculine men who are in control. Men who I can get and leave, turn out and leave; I am the leaver, no longer the leavee.

When I was twelve, my mother remarried a man who was much younger than she. It wasn't until later when she got sick and we took her to the hospital that we learned her true birth date. Little did I know my stepfather was seventeen years her junior. He was much more of a brother to me than a father because of the age difference. In his thirties, he moved from his mother's house and right into my mother's house. Without children of his own, he lacked fatherly skills, but he was always there . . . for my mother.

I was twenty years old and five months pregnant at my wedding reception. That wasn't the oddest issue. The big secret was why my supposed new husband did not make it to the church or to the reception at my mother's house to celebrate the private wedding that was to have occurred earlier that day, but did not. I smiled and greeted guests in his absence, took pictures and accepted gifts, all the while keeping my gray silk jacket closed in front of me as I tried to hide the obvious bulge in my abdomen. The entire time I thought, should I send all of these gifts back later, or just keep them and send thank-you notes or turn off the music right now and expose my secret—my supposed husband-to-be's mother threatened suicide if he went through with the wedding, so he didn't show up. To this day I don't know how I got through it.

At one time he was truly my best friend. We

met when I was fifteen and he was fourteen. I was a little more than one year older than he was, but he'd always tease me when at times my birthday would come and I'd be two years older. We eventually got married after our daughter was born. She attended our small church wedding when I was twenty-two. Wedding pictures prove his mother never smiled the entire day.

You see her problem was I am not Creole, my hair is not "good" enough, my eyes are not light enough and I am not Catholic. I didn't know how to make gumbo or jambalaya, and the color of my skin was too dark. Even though in school my friends called me high yellow, I wasn't mixed, I guess. But my husband loved me no matter what, and the more my in-laws despised me, the more he adored me. He was the one man I knew would never leave me . . . but eventually, he did. The Lord took him home nine years ago today.

It's interesting that I married such a frugal, devoted, spiritual, good man when deep inside I had all the makings of a woman desperately looking for her father. To me, my dad was an irresponsible, abusive, saxophone-playing, womanizing dog who never showed his face yet managed to find out where my brothers and I lived through the years so he could anonymously leave a bat, ball and doll in our car at Christmastime. He sent a few cards every now and then, but with no return address. The mystery man who lived in the same city I lived in was sending the message that I wasn't good enough to even bother. One day, I have to ask him: "Why?"

1

"THE MALE AND THE FEMALE ENERGY, just like the yin in Chinese dualistic philosophy, the passive female cosmic principle meaning feminine, the shade. And the yang, the active masculine cosmic principle, the sun or light. The principle that there must be a Fred Astaire and a Ginger Rogers in each and every relationship, one leading the dance wearing pants and the other carefully and submissively following each step while wearing the flowing, sheer, sexy dress. Gay or straight, this must happen for there to be a peaceful coexistence through the experience we call—love," proclaims Dr. Singer, an outspoken love specialist who conducts weekly relationship seminars in the grand ballroom of a local hotel. My girl Carlotta kindly suggested that Ariana and I attend this week to learn how to meet and marry the man of our dreams. But I hope we're not wasting our time or else Carlotta will be dreaming of how she used to have her two front teeth.

"What the hell did she just say?" Ariana asks me, looking as confused as all get-out. "I think this chick just said we women need to be the shade of a man's light and I'm not having it. Let's go."

Dr. Singer, a middle-aged woman with what looks to be a copper- and rust-colored Dolce & Gabbana pantsuit, continues to strut down the aisle toward our row and stops beside me, placing her hand on my shoulder.

"There is a feminine energy. This energy follows the lead of the masculine energy *if* the feminine likes the direction in which the masculine is going. The feminine has the veto right *to feel* and *not want*, whereas the male energy has the right to *think* and *want*," Dr. Singer says, as if she can recite this in her sleep.

"I'm a-*thinkin'* we need to get out of this place! We've fought for equality for too many years to be set back to being led like the women in China who submit to their men!" Ariana's skeptical remark is loud enough for Dr. Singer to overhear as she takes a step toward her.

"That's the problem, ma'am. Too many of us women want to go to war, open our own doors, and be equal because we've fought for women's liberation. Yet we still want men to understand our feelings about why we're mad because they don't pull out our chairs, initiate phone calls, commit to their word, fix our cars and send us flowers. We can't have it both ways! We have castrated men by wanting it all. We can't have it all. You can't be respected *and* cherished, you must choose one—which do you choose? Please stand."

A confused Ariana springs to her feet and asks, "What are you talking about?"

"What I mean is, do you want to be cherished for your *feelings* or respected for your *thoughts*?"

"I want to be respected period!" Ariana states with a head roll.

"Okay, then you're masculine. So go ahead and find yourself a feminine energy person who will respect you."

"I don't want a feminine energy person, you mean like a wimp?"

"See, now that's another problem. Liberated women want to run the show and then label the feeling men who want us to take the lead as wimps. Then we ask why he lets us walk all over him when all he's doing is following our lead."

"Look, I want a man who is strong enough for me to put my big, strong head on his shoulder, yet who won't beat the shit out of me for having an opinion."

"Okay, then you want a masculine man, right?"

"Hell, yeah, masculine, I don't want a fag! I won't follow any man. I'll be beside him fifty-fifty," Ariana says, as though she already has it all figured out.

"Well, wouldn't you rather be on a pedestal? You may be seated." Ariana slides down into her chair with a look of disappointment. "See, I don't think you're getting it. Let me try to clarify this for you. Masculine and feminine is not about sexual gender, it's deeper than that. It's energy. Two gay men still need a masculine and a feminine, as well as two gay women. Donald Trump brings the masculinity, Marla Maples brings the femininity, maybe Oprah Winfrey is the masculine and Stedman is the feminine, it's all about who wants to lead and who is willing to allow them to lead."

"I think someone needs to tell her Marla and the Donald broke up a long time ago," Ariana whispers to me.

I answer for the group. "Ma'am, I think what she's saying is, we're not willing to give up being respected. I demand respect above all else." The audience applauds.

"Well then, I suggest you go find yourself a nice vagina you can lead and live happily ever after," Dr. Singer replies, giving me a look of severity combined with jest.

Ariana struggles to keep a straight face as she snickers out loud.

"Excuse me?" I ask as I am both puzzled and insulted.

"What is your name? Please stand up so the people in the back of the room can see you."

"Mariah!" I answer as I stand cautiously, turning toward the rest of the audience members.

"Mariah, you can't have it all, my dear. There is a way to be feminine enough to attract, negotiate and disagree with a masculine energy man, which sounds like what you want. If you have the time, I can teach you how to relate to the men who will cherish you and in return allow you to feel respected. They will give to you and you will give back. You won't be paying their rent, acting like their mother and butting heads with them by emasculating them. You will learn to accept being respected at work, and by your children, but when you get home, you will let your hair down and allow your man to be a man, pamper you, protect you and give to you. If he's a real man, he'll get his pleasure from pleasing you. If he keeps you mellow, you'll keep him mellow. If he's a boy, he'll want *you* to give to *him*. It works, if you'll just give it a try. Respect, after all, is very overrated. I know Aretha sang about R.E.S.P.E.C.T. when you were growing up, but C.H.E.R.I.S.H. is much better, I promise you. Now, are you in a relationship?"

"Yes, I have a boyfriend."

"Are you the masculine energy?"

"Meaning?" I ask, seeking clarification.

"Meaning, do you lead the dance? Do you decide where the two of you will go for dinner, pick the movie as well as his clothes, decide what to do on holidays, correct his thoughts, direct him when he drives, pick the what, where, who, how and why?"

"I have at times."

"Has he enjoyed your lead?"

"No!" I answer without hesitation.

"Is he feminine or masculine?" she inquires.

"I believe he's masculine."

"Okay. Well, since you're both masculine, if you don't learn when to follow and when to lead and you both end up leading at the same time, it will be chaotic, head-butting drama. How long have the two of you been together?"

"A little more than seven years," I reply as the ladies sigh in amazement.

"And where's the ring?"

"I don't have one yet. He's not ready."

"Honey, excuse me, seven years is six years too long. You should have negotiated a contract by now because you're giving away the cow and the milk and the whole damn dairy and he knows it. Do you want to get married?"

"Yes, eventually," I reply in honesty.

"Well, you have to know what you want in order to know where you want to go. Stick with him and you'll eventually die single. Please do this for me," Dr. Singer says as she plants her feet firmly on the floor and bends her legs slightly, knees touching. "Put your knees together like this and *just say no*. Don't let him in. There's an entrance fee and it's a ring. Refuse to give away free sex without requiring him to place value upon you by showing his intentions first. You are a virtuous woman, not a sex toy. Remember that: *virtuous*."

"You mean I can't sleep with him?" I ask, seeking permission.

"You can sleep with him all you want, I don't care, just don't let *it* in. Do you get what I'm saying? It sounds like you've bonded to a penis attached to the wrong man. The only way to know is to detach and negotiate for what you want. In the end, you just might have to decide to move on."

"But I love having sex with him!"

"And I'm sure he loves sex with you even more, because it's free! It's time for him to hire you as his wife so you can state your occupation as *I fuck my husband* on your tax return. At least then you'll get some benefits. Is he at least a giving man?"

"Not really. He's quite selfish at times but I'm trying to be patient hoping he'll change."

"Change. Oh, here we go," she says, switching the microphone into her other hand. "You'd have better luck changing the weather or expecting Bill Clinton to be a monogamous man. Mariah, that's a pretty name. You know better than that—you look like a bright lady. Listen, are you willing to hand him the bill?"

"What bill? He doesn't owe me anything," I say in his defense.

"Oh, he owes you the virtue you deserve, he owes you an investment in your future together and he owes you the cherishing you've missed out on for seven years. Most important, you owe it to yourself. So you'd better know you deserve it."

"Well, I want to help him work through his issues and help him learn to take the next step when he's ready. I don't want to pressure him."

"Wow, you're not only masculine energy, you're also his mother. This is going to take work. Then keep screwing him for another seven years and do away with the marriage notion, or think about perhaps letting go and finding a sex-only partner who will physically service your masculine energy every now and then for another seven years. But don't let that new partner fuck you too often or too well or you'll bond to that penis also. Ladies, repeat after me, *oxy-tocin*." The audience slowly repeats the word as they look around at one another with a question-marked smirk. "Look it up in the dictionary. It is a hormone which is produced when we are getting laid, when he's inside of our bodies; it is like a drug, it bonds us to ugly men, poor men, criminals, old men. It is secreted into your brain when you're being fucked well. You'd better know about it because it can ruin your life! You see, we release this hormone called oxytocin when we're sexually aroused. I call it *the love hormone*. The more often you have sex—enjoyable skilled sex, not the so-so take it or leave it kind—the more deeply you bond. One week you could care less what he's doing on a Saturday night, and two weeks later, you're driving by his house at three o'clock in the morning to see if he's home. Maybe the next day you'll quietly sneak up from his bed after a wild, passionate night of lovemaking just to check his caller ID box to see whose number shows up. It turns us into crazy girls, so, ladies, *be careful who you let in!* I cannot stress that enough. Now, do you have any more questions, Mariah?"

"Yes," I reply just as this is starting to make sense. "How do you de-bond from the wrong penis?"

"It takes a good eight weeks of no contact whatsoever, and then add another two years to finally get him out of your system. It's difficult. It's like an addiction because you have to de-bond from a penis similar to when you de-tox from cigarettes, alcohol, drugs or anything else, but it can be done. And while you're doing it, you date up a storm and stay as busy as possible. Even subtle contact, which allows you to see, smell, hear, taste or touch him, or *it*, and you'll have to start all over again. Or, the other option is to just fall in love with someone else. I'm sorry to say, but it is true that the absolute best cure for one really is another, but by falling in love with yourself first, hopefully that *another* will be you! Now let's give a hand to Mariah for sharing. You may be seated," she says, directing her hand toward my seat.

The audience applauds.

I idly take my seat, realizing big tuff Miss R.E.S.P.E.C.T. Mariah has actually opened up her stubborn and narrow mind long enough to get the message. Dr. Singer is right, I am sexually addicted to a little boy who expects me to give, and yet he also wants me to be Ginger Rogers and follow, or else!

"Excuse me, Dr. Singer. What do you call a man who is both masculine and a little boy?" asks another woman.

"A narcissist! He has excessive admiration or love of himself and only himself. Ladies, run for the hills! He'll make you even crazier. His penis is usually larger than his ego and his tongue—*if* he's in a giving mood, which is rare—could lick a cat clean . . . yours! Now that's it until next week, people. Thanks for sharing and please remember you can buy a copy of this week's lesson on videocassette. Thank you so much for coming."

As everyone applauds and begins to disburse, Ariana and I gather our purses and jackets and head for the door.

"You didn't really buy that crock of bull, did you, Mariah?" asks a disbelieving Ariana.

"Ariana, please! Me? Shit, I'm not *even* ready to give up my thoughts. I speak my mind and whoever doesn't like it can kiss my butter-pecan booty, okay?"

"I'm feeling you. That was a waste of ten dollars. She's the reason why men rule the world and women earn lower wages than men do. What a joke. I'm going to give Carlotta a piece of my mind. Just because she got engaged, does she actually think this woman is the reason why? Please!"

"Well, I heard she dumped him already. All she wanted was the ring."

"Oh no, I didn't hear that one. Come on, Mariah, let's go for a drink. It's comedy night at the Leimert Club and I'm all ears."

I glance at my watch. "Girl, I'm going to Kareem's house to get laid. I'm out."

"Okay, Miss Oxytocin! I'm going home to look up that crazy-ass word in the dictionary. And then I'm going to call Carlotta to get the 411 on this breakup after I curse her butt out for telling me about this cult meeting. Oxytocin . . . I'll call you tomorrow. And get some for me too! You two greedy freaka-zoids!"

2

KAREEM'S TOFFEE-BROWN-PAINTED BEDROOM IS filled with the scent of Butt Naked incense. The gold and chestnut velvet comforter to his California king-size bed is invitingly pulled back to expose the jet-black satin sheets and extra large feather down pillows enveloped with gold satin cases. The pillows are scented with the Strawberries and Cream fabric softener that drives me wild. Across the bed Kareem has laid out a cherry red lace bra and G-string nightie set along with my four-inch pumps, trimmed in soft red feathers of course. Above the bed, as well as on the wall, there are mirrors, mirrors and more mirrors to please the voyeur in him, or should I say in us. Those intoxicating Black Love fragrant candles are burning. It's a red-light special-get-our-groove-on night in his typical bachelor-type spiderweb. The soft blue and gold lights from the aquarium set the mood as the movement of the tropical fish mesmerize and hypnotize me into relaxation as if they're in on the seduction. And let's not forget the X-rated tape in the VCR entitled *The Chocolate Milk Lady*. It's hard to hear the audio over the volume of the Barry White music in the background. This particular cut is called "I'm Gonna Love You Just a Little More, Baby."

"Take off your brassiere, my dear," Kareem says in a slow deep voice.

I submit and respond, "Yes, Big Daddy!" as I undo the hooks and slide my bra down from my shoulders to my waist and toss it over the bed-post.

"Oh, baby girl, run those long nails along my back."

I'm sporting bright Corvette-red, three-inch-long, fake curved nails. The next cut is entitled "I've Got So Much to Give."

"And I want to give all of it to you, baby! Have you been a bad girl?" he asks with naughty intentions.

"You know it, Papa," I moan in response as familiarity prompts me to softly draw his tongue into my mouth for a sucking that will surely send blood pumping down south in preparation for our hot-buttered session. I gaze into Kareem's sexy, intense, squinted brown eyes as his pupils instruct me to part my long legs and arch my pelvis toward him for submissive entry. He moves my G-string to the side and quickly discovers that even without the oral, I am thoroughly juiced up as he immediately locates my familiar entry with his middle finger. He parts my throbbing opening to test for readiness.

"You are soooooo wet, aren't you?"

I affirm in agreement with a girlie sigh as I gently reach for his already stiffened KJ—Kareem

Junior—and he reaches for his box of purple glow-in-the-dark condoms.

I beg, "Oh, baby, I need to feel you inside of me now!"

Kareem slides my lace G-string down my hips to my ankles, only to toss it who knows where. He rotates his body to lay upon mine. I wrap my already quivering legs around his massive back in acceptance of his next move. His pronounced, more than adequate member teases the vicinity of my love in a torturous fashion, eliciting even more urging from my womanly hips for intercourse. He steals my breath away while he tightens his taut, firm gluteus and guides himself to join my arousal. He moans in response to the familiar wet and warm, snapperlike sensation. After all of these years it still fits like a glove. I find myself tightening up and relaxing at the same time. Before I know it, his thrusting is aiding the release of my explosion into ecstasy as only Kareem can do.

I give way to a loud, deep groan as he instructs, "Yeah, take it all, baby, with your greedy ass!" This must be the love hormone.

The clock reads 1:30. "Are you a freak?" He removes himself mid-stroke and mid-groan to turn me over and back me up. I'm in full view of the porno flick shot of the threesome Jacuzzi scene. I arch my bodacious booty and brace my upper body with my sweaty and fatigued elbows. I bury my face in his puffy satin bed pillow and find myself engaging in pillow sucking and biting as a result of his full and deep penetration. My hips are shaking for continuation and begging for more rearview pleasure.

It's 3:07. "I know you like it when I spank that ass!" In the full-length closet mirror I can see my rear end bouncing like a stripper at Fat Fanny's. I glance back toward him to look into his eyes with a slick, professional, you-can-have-it-all glance as I watch him work it. Now it's 4:56. "You are my freak, let me see you work those hoe-titties!" Kareem demands while I lean upward and squeeze them together for his viewing. He once again gently removes himself and lays on his back under me while I lightly tickle his thighs with my nipples and move upward so that I can squeeze my ample breasts around KJ and watch his tip thrust in and out as if it is searching to secure itself in the warmth of my bosom. I stretch my body upward to lay upon his chest and straddle him. Now I am in control. Suddenly he grabs me around my sweaty waist and tosses me once again onto my back. The missionary at this point surely means he is about to get his serious thrust on. His eyes demand a mutual glimpse of my undivided attention while he stares me down within an inch of the tip of my nose. He forcefully demands an apology from me for being disobedient and talking shit last week during an argument.

"What were you trying to do? Let someone else in my shit, huh? You know I will fuck someone up."

I mumble a muffled response—"No. I'm sorry, baby"—and turn my head to the side in shame to divert further scolding. Before we know it the night has slowly slipped into daybreak.

"Oh, shit, the sun is coming up. I've gotta get home before Chloe and Donovan wake up," I say in a panic, no doubt the guilt of a true nymphomaniac being serviced. I motion for Kareem to pull out as he reluctantly falls to his back in frustration while I stumble around in search of my dress and panties.

"I was just about to get off, Mariah!" he exhales.

"Why is it that it takes you all night?" I ask while wiggling my hips into my undies.

"You know you're much more cooperative when you're horizontal. I wish I could keep you in bed. You're like a different person, not giving me any shit," Kareem says as he walks to the bathroom with a still erect organ and a big greedy Kool-Aid smile.

As I grab my shoes from downstairs, I notice several ladies' business cards and phone numbers on the bar. One is even from a girl I know and she knows he's my man. In the bathroom I see long hairs on the floor, obviously not mine. My natural plaited twists wouldn't shed any strand longer than three inches. Besides, it's the wrong color, too light. Oh hell, I don't even know why I'm checking. I guess that's another symptom of oxytocin bonding. I've got it bad.

"Bye, baby, call me later! Next time I'll pull out that orange 'man in the boat' dual massager and dildo you keep beggin' for," he yells. He doesn't even bother coming downstairs to walk me to my car, and I don't even ask him to. I'm too used to it to give a shit.

*   *   *

I PULL INTO THE LONG DRIVEWAY of my sand-blasted pale peach- and cream-colored apartment building in West Los Angeles that leads to my two-car garage. My three-bedroom apartment is the top rear unit of a four-plex. What I like most is the huge backyard with more than enough room for Donovan's basketball hoop and my antique wrought-iron patio furniture. I even have room to plant my flowers when I get a moment to relax. It's like therapy to me. My neighbors are cool but we don't really look out for each other like back in the day. I'm quite sure they don't even know I'm getting in so late, or should I say, so early.

I tiptoe into the house and quietly slip into bed so as not to awaken my teenagers. It's six-fifteen and Donovan will be up by seven. I doze off within zero-point-three seconds. It's that after-sex deep dead sleep.

"Mom, I'm leaving now. Should I take the bus?" asks Donovan as he startles me.

"No, baby, I'll take you." Another statement made out of guilt. Maybe he knows I just got home. I'm sure he heard the floor creaking while I was sneaking in, or maybe he woke up at three in the morning to use the bathroom and passed the open door to my bedroom leading to an unslept-in bed.

Suddenly I find myself driving with one eye open, the whole time yearning to be reunited with the pillow. I glance down at my pinkie finger and notice I still have one false nail that I forgot to take off. I slyly remove it and slip it into my purse while a quiet Donovan is looking down at his notes from English class. He's so damn handsome. My baby is only sixteen years old and he's nearly six-two already. He even wears a size thirteen shoe. Donovan is very muscular, like his dad, who passed away nine years ago. He's not bowlegged like his dad but his build is very similar. He's actually named Donovan Jr. It was a great decision to name him after his dad back then. I had no idea that name would mean so much to him, living on as Donovan Pijeaux in his dad's honor.

How I allowed him to pierce both of his ears I'll never know. He has this dark, curly hair from his Creole background. He also has his dad's eyes. They were the deepest blue I've ever seen on a black man. Donovan's are greenish-gray. The girls love it unfortunately. They treat him like he's Deion Sanders or something, poor kid. He's a much darker complexion than his dad, even darker than my complexion is. His sister got all the "light-skinnedness" of the Pijeaux. Unfortunately, the trendy bug has bitten Donovan. He likes Nike shoes, shirts, shorts or whatever to match or he's not cool. Too much of my income has been spent on Hilfiger, Polo, Fubu and Nautica. It was never like that when I was growing up. We'd get a pair of Jordache jeans from Zody's and we were set. A pair of boat shoes and maybe a cool jacket, no brand-name labels were necessary, or maybe that's because I was L-7, or as they say, "square."

"Hiiii, Donovan," a group of White girls sing in unison when he steps out of the car. He's far too cool to actually say more than two words back to them. He lifts his head and quickly replies, "Sup?" I think *sup* means what's up, abbreviated for the Y2K. He's too cool for me. I dare not ask for a kiss any longer or rub the back of his head as he gets out of the car. He'd rather die on the spot.

"Have a good day, Donovan. See you later!"

"Okay." He grabs his Adidas bag, shuts the door and walks away far too slowly for someone who's probably late for class. Donovan does not have a care in the world. The other kids speak as they walk by. The guys give him the new high five called daps or a pound, I'm told. Kinda like the Black handshake we started back in the seventies.

IT'S WEDNESDAY MORNING and I'm forty-five minutes into my return to postorgasm sleep. I receive a call from my agency to work at a movie studio for a few days. I would give anything to turn it down, but Lord knows I need the money. I stumble out of bed wishing I could afford to refuse the assignment, knowing I'm going to be good for nothing today, hoping whoever it is that I'm working for only has me sitting in one spot answering phones. Today, I cannot handle anything deep like redlining documents or anything legal. They'd surely tell me to go home with my love-hangover self. The coffee lover in me sips away at a total of four cups as I get dressed. I think I'm addicted to the roasted hazelnut flavor with French vanilla creamer. Today I'll double up on the crystals, hoping for a caffeine fix.

I kiss my daughter, Chloe, good-bye. She's eighteen years old and just finished her first year in junior college. But now it's time for a summer job to pay for her hair salon visits, nail appointments, pedicures and stuff. With all we've been through together, I'm just glad to have her home. She's on her way to go sign some papers for financial aid.

We wave good-bye and pull off at the same time. Damn, I'm so proud of her. She's just been accepted to Cal Berkeley now that her grades have improved. She's very good at math and hopes to one day become a CFO for some Fortune 500 company. It was a struggle but she's on her way. I always pray that she forgives God for taking her daddy and leaving her here with me.

3

IT'S SUMMERTIME AND STICKY HOT, hotter than July as they say, and unusually still. So still it appears the wind has silenced itself to a hushed calm whisper. It's Hollywood and most of my days are spent in its fast-paced, glamorous enigma. To live here can be rewarding to some, destructive to most. I just sort of ended up here.

I was born and raised in Los Angeles, however, my purpose for working in Hollywood is purely coincidental. I'd been in retail for many years and one of my customers was the head of the production division at a leading film studio. He convinced me to give up my $24,000-a-year stressful, demanding, unrewarding job, double my salary and become his secretary—or assistant as some say. After a few months of prodding, I agreed.

After working for him and then moving on through the years, I found myself some ten years later still a *secretary*. How scary that word is now that I find myself getting older, awakening from the complacency of my careerless job and coming into the "Is that all there is?" thought pattern.

So I've given up on full-time assisting and

signed with a temporary employment agency so as to free up a few days a week. The free days are left open to explore other career pathways—acting, broadcasting, my own business, writing, something that is *not* nine-to-five. My agency knows I'm only available two or three days a week to fill in for other secretaries who are taking sick days. I'm not available for vacations, maternity leave and all that long-term madness that would force me to commit and become distracted. Oh hell, I'm now known as the worst four-letter word in the entertainment industry, a *temp*.

I'll be working for Sarah Dunlevy, a senior-level executive in the home video department whose assistant is away at a three-day training seminar. This female executive is known to have difficulty keeping assistants because of her demanding and rude ways, so I'm told. I used to work for *the* toughest boss in the entertainment industry back in the late eighties. There's nothing she could ever do to live up to that experience. Sometimes my agency tells the executives whom I temp for the name of my previous boss and they are no doubt impressed. Sarah is no different. As I meet her for the first time, she is sweet and almost too respectful to me. She relaxes and so do I.

Sarah is White with a Coppertone tan and flawless skin. She's kind of plain with an average height and build and I'd say she's a fairly casual dresser; wearing a simple black pantsuit and a black tee with flat black loafers. Her hair is a sugar cane shade, short and straight with wispy bangs. She's makeupless, not even lip gloss.

Within a few hours of the first morning that I work for her, I hear two voices on the other side of the partition. These workstations are cubicle setups and there is absolutely *no* privacy. I try not to listen, but it is impossible not to. Two women are talking about *him*.

I overhear one woman say, "Honey, this brotha is like Adonis, so *finnnneee* he makes you wanna cry!"

I laugh to myself at how fucking silly they are and I keep working.

Throughout the day I meet a few coworkers. Most of the assistants are female. These are young women who are just starting out as secretaries. And they make it known that they are just passing through on their way to bigger and better things. One girl named Robin tells me, "When I'm your age, I'll be doing a lot more than this shit, no offense." I explain that I took none while my right hand tightens into a fist as I walk away.

That afternoon my boss calls me into her office to tell me she needs a series of videocassettes to overnight to Chicago. She tells me to check with customer service to see if we have any on hand. The representative who normally works in that department is on vacation and I'm told to see the intern who is filling in for her. As I walk out of her office, on the other side of my partition I see a head. It is a big, bald, very dark, smooth, perfectly shaped, Michael Jordan chocolate head framed by two of the most perfect ears I've ever seen. I'm thinking I'd like my inner thighs to get to know what those ears feel like. My dirty mind quickly becomes silent as he turns toward me and I see his glorious face. He has large, deep brown eyes with long, thick eyelashes like Ahmad Rashad, full outlined kissable lips like Tyson, a perfect, chiseled nose like Rick Fox, and flawless, silken skin like a baby's ass. I stare for the longest three seconds of my life. My mouth is drooling and that's not all. I sit down immediately so as to be at a lower position to cease this vision before I say something stupid. All I can think is he must be very tall for such a full view over the cubicle, and this must be the Adonis these suddenly not-so-fucking-silly girls were talking about.

I stand up again and he is gone. I quickly and awkwardly sit down and once again hear one girl on the phone asking for her friend Reikel. "Girl, he showed me his modeling pictures he took on the beach last weekend. I think he wants me badly!" Just then, my boss asks me if I've checked on the videos. Of course I tell her I've been trying to locate the extension number to customer service. She insists that I go down the hall and ask for them and let them know this is a rush request.

I walk down the hall toward a barely opened office door ahead of me. The name outside reads ROCHELLE WASHINGTON. As I knock, a deep, slow voice says in response, "Come in, it's open." Familiar words from my mouth I'm thinking, being as hornified as I constantly am. I grab the knob with my right hand as I push the door open farther and step in—it is the rest of the body that belongs to the head from heaven. Mr. Adonis looks up at me and then looks me down and looks me up and then looks somewhere around my belly-button area and asks, "How tall are you?"

I try to swallow my saliva quick enough to answer, "Five-ten. My name is Mariah."

At a cool, leisurely pace, he stands up and says, "Hello, Mariah. My name is Malik," nodding his head in affirmation of our greeting.

I lift my hand to rub my sweaty forehead and turn to the side with a nervous twist, then pivot, only to notice he is now in full view of my Mae West-size booty and taking complete advantage of the sight.

I turn toward him and reply, "Hello, Malik. It's nice to meet you."

He swaggers his way around his desk and looks me up and down again while his thumb and index finger stroke his stubble-free, virgin-to-a-razor chin. Can his mind possibly be as filthy as mine—imagining the frontal standing position?

"Well, I suppose you're filling in for the person who normally handles customer service requests?" I ask.

"Yes, I'm a temp of sorts filling in for Rochelle this week." I'm thinking to myself, if she only knew what she has in her pants this week, lucky and unlucky.

"I'm also a temp. I'm just filling in for Sarah Dunlevy's assistant for a few days." As I explain to Malik exactly what it is that I need, as far as videos are concerned, he turns around and opens a file drawer with listings of videos, quantities, locations and so forth.

"It looks like we have a few left in the vault

next door. I can get them and bring them to you, unless you want to go for a walk with me," he suggests with a glow in his eyes.

"I can walk," I respond, feeling extra stupid. He holds out his hand for me to exit first. I can feel his eyes once again checking me out as if he has X-ray vision. I then step out of his office and turn toward him with a Naomi Campbell runway spin as I motion that I will follow his lead. Maybe this is the lead Dr. Singer was talking about. I'm thinking this view I could live with. And boy, can he walk. He has this sensual, smooth timing to his step like the left foot gets just a little more time on the ground than the right, and his arms cooperate with his legs like they are in on the stride, not like a pimp walk, but like, "Yeah, I've got it goin' on and somewhere to be when I get there."

He slows down to walk beside me while he gives me a little background information on his reason for temping: "I mentioned that I'm sort of a temp because I'm interning here. I'm originally from Harlem but I'm in Los Angeles for this summer program and then I'll resume my studies at Syracuse University. I consider myself very blessed."

Blessed you are, Super Man. I am immediately slapped into reality when he says college. What did I expect with skin like that and the fresh smell of a Similac and Coolwater combination? Get a grip, girl. You're old enough to be his mother. Yeah, but the thought of breast-feeding could never be so divine.

"You're in college, huh?"

"Yes, this could be my final year. I've been on a five-year ride for football and eventually I want to go pro," he explains as we step stride-for-stride.

"Then you are to be congratulated for getting an education. I'm sure you're working hard on and off the field."

"I'm an honor roll student, so I guess you could say I'm working hard," he admits with a humble shrug of his shoulders as we approach the video vault.

"I'd say so."

I am torn between the question of the obvious age difference, and what the heck I am feeling that is making me act like a teenager—goofy, tongue-tied and sweaty again. Yet the freak in me was saying, "Girl, work this 'cause you a bad ma'ama jamma—turn him out, turn him out." The mother in me has visual flashes of my daughter on *Ricki Lake* claiming that her mother is dating someone her age, and the mature woman in me is saying, "If you don't cut this crap out and get those damn videos from this boy, you'd better!" I bet this boy gets his stick dipped more than Jiffy Lube.

I suppose the mature woman in me wins over, so I say, "Malik, I have a daughter who's about to leave for college up north. Perhaps you can tell me about how the internship program works?"

Oh, why did I say that? He stops in his tracks as he opens the vault door and raises his full, sexy, bushy, curious eyebrows and those Maybelline-quality eyelashes and turns directly toward me. He is again close enough for me to smell his scent. It is clean and pure like he has soap on a rope hanging from around his neck. I pause and look into his eyes with an innocent gaze and turn my ear toward him in anticipation of what he is about to say.

"You have a daughter about to go to college?" he asks, looking puzzled.

"Malik, I have three children, two boys and one girl, and yes, she turned eighteen years old in March."

"Excuse me, ahh, Mariah, but that just cannot be. I know you didn't give birth to anyone eighteen years ago. You must have been nine years old."

"You're very sweet, but I was not nine."

"Okay, you must have adopted them or they're your stepchildren, right?"

"No, Malik, now all of this is very flattering." If the word *hot* is not written across my forehead, then perhaps the Cherokee-red tone of my cheeks is a dead giveaway. "But I am obviously not as young as you think. However, it's very nice of you to think I do not look my age."

"My opinion is you look tight. I need to see some ID," he quips.

I laugh and some of the tension from the initial attraction is disjoined for a moment.

"Malik, at some point I need to get these videos in my hands before my boss comes down here looking for me, even though I've enjoyed the experience and the flattery."

"I'm sorry, I totally forgot what we are in here

for, but damn, my mama doesn't look like you. If she did, I'd have kicked many a brotha's you-know-what. I know your sons' friends make excuses to come by your house."

As we both walk toward the video shelf, laughing and keeping one eye on some part of the other's something, one of the girls from down the hall walks in. "Oh, are we having a good time or what? What did I miss?" she sarcastically inquires.

"Nothing, Brenda," Malik responds through a half chuckle. "We were just telling jokes."

"Just jokes? Clue me in. I like hearing jokes," she remarks with cynical jest, placing her hands on her hips.

"Brenda, have you met Mariah?" asks Malik.

"Yes, I saw you earlier today. I understand you're only going to be here a few days, right?"

"Yes, just until Friday," I answer softly, checking out her possessive intentions.

Malik hands me the videos and winks at me as our hands briskly rub against each other.

"I must get back to my desk, thanks so much, Malik. Take care. Nice to meet you, Brenda."

I turn to walk out and I feel both of them staring at me, sensing completely different thoughts in each of their minds. Both basically with a fuck-you type of theme.

I don't really recall walking to my desk. I just sort of arrive. I'm taken back to when I was in high school and had a crush on Dennis Wallace. This is the same sort of feeling. The feeling we lose as we get older and jaded and afraid of being hurt. It's the feeling that some feel when they claim love at first sight. I suppose I've felt sort of a crush for the first time in twenty-five years. Not a fatal attraction crush, more of a forty-year-old teenage crush with the wisdom and erudition that warns, stay away. I put my head down for a minute to replay the video in my head of Malik looking me up and down. It is erotic and X-rated and forbidden and nasty. It is the type of look I can accept from a forty-five-year-old man, but never receive. It is soulful and curious and virginal and perverted all at the same time. It simply turned me on.

I feel a tap on my shoulder and turn around to see my boss behind me.

"Thank you so much. You look tired and flushed. Do you want to go to lunch now?" she asks as I hand her the videos.

"No, I'm fine. I probably do need a bite to eat. I didn't have breakfast this morning and didn't get a whole lot of sleep."

"Okay. Go to lunch whenever you'd like and we'll send the overnight package later this afternoon."

She places the videotapes on my desk along with some brochures and a cassette from a dictaphone.

Sarah says, "I've dictated the cover letter to go with the tapes. And the one-sheets I have on my desk need to go also. But go ahead and leave when you're ready. I hope you feel better."

"Thanks, I'll just go now. See you in an hour," I reply, getting up from my desk.

She's so nice. I can't believe she's been labeled hard to work for. I find her to be very sweet.

My pager goes off. It's a voice mail message from Kareem. He says he's going to be spending the weekend with his family. They are in town from Chicago. After all the years I've dated him, I've never even met them. I pick up Sarah's extension and dial his number.

"Hey, yeah, it's me, now what's going on?" I reservedly ask.

"Hey, Vanessa Del Rio, how ya doin'?" he comically inquires, only I'm not amused.

"What's up, Kareem?" I ask plainly.

"Mariah was on fire, my little sex kitten. Damn, girl, how do you spell *insatiable*? You made my toes curl. I had Bambi, Trixie and Loveliness in my bed all at once last night. Takes a hell of a nigga to handle you and I accept the challenge. Anyway, like I said on your voice mail, my family is in town and I'll be spending this weekend with them. I'm just letting you know ahead of time."

Once again, he's not even going to invite me to meet them. After seven years I'd hoped maybe now that they're in town, he would invite me.

"Are you letting me know ahead of time so I can make plans to meet them?" I ask, already knowing the answer.

"Now, don't start with me, Mariah. Don't trip, girl. You know no one brings their mates to these things, it's just family."

I feel in my gut that he is once again ready to use my comments as ammunition and as an excuse to hurry off the phone so that I won't ruin *his* weekend with my "bullshit!"

"Baby, next time when they book more rooms at the hotel you can come," he says at a rapid pace. "But for now, I have to go because I have another call coming in. Gotta go, bye!" He quickly hangs up.

I'm not surprised, just tired and disappointed in myself because he knows the same thing I know. By Monday evening we'll be boning each other and somehow the thrust will surely erase my memory. Maybe.

In my heart I've always believed that when he travels alone or attends family events alone, he brings someone else, just wants to be available to meet other people, or simply doesn't want to be bothered. Bachelor extraordinaire, I suppose. But either way, I'm always home like a good girl, being a good mom, and catching up on weekend responsibilities.

4

I SLOWLY WALK TO THE COMMISSARY, THINKING about Kareem and wondering about myself. Why do I allow so many fears to encompass me? I am afraid to fly—airplanes terrify me. It's a simple word called *gravity*. I resist change and I rarely take chances and throw caution to the wind. One of my biggest issues has been trying to find Daddy through my relationships with men. Now it appears I really have found him in the form of a six-foot-nine, unavailable, popular, selfish, ex-basketball player who always gives me the impression it's all my fault that he's either gone, or that I chase him away. Stop searching for Daddy and find a real man.

As I take the gardenlike sidewalk stroll from the home video building to the commissary, I pass the guard gate. I see Brenda, third in a line of cars preparing to exit the lot. She is driving a brand spanking new, shiny, ebony black Range Rover, and Malik is in the passenger seat.

Brenda has got to be barely twenty-three years old, muscular-looking like she works out constantly, flat-chested with that big old sista onion.

Gotta give it to her. If her personality was as big as her ass she wouldn't be half-bad. She wears her hair like Aaliyah did, swept over her right eye and applies that dark lipstick and onyx-toned makeup like the young people wear. And worst of all, she has her own office. Driving a car like that, she's got it going *on* and her *on* is all up on my *on*.

They are obviously going off-lot for lunch. As the gate raises up and the freshly detailed Rover pulls through, I can see Malik's left arm stretched behind the headrest of her seat as he waves to the guard with his right hand. Their watercolor smiles indicate that both Brenda and Malik are humored by something. As they drive out toward the street and make a left turn, I turn away and then look back and turn away again, shaking my head.

For some reason, I'm putting a lot of thought into what is very apparent. They are very friendly with each other, and if they don't have a thang going on, then one surely wants to. I've been called naive and unsuspecting many times but this is just one example of me trying to see things for what they are before they hit me over the head. Why do I even give a damn anyway and why am I putting all of this thought and energy into it unless it means I am interested? Or could I be . . . jealous?

I sit down in the commissary and order the Wednesday meat loaf, mashed potatoes and veggies. Not that I need the calories, just that I am hoping it is close to the way my mom used to make it. I suppose my waistline is the furthest thing from my mind at this point. Being tall and more than one hundred sixty pounds doesn't really concern me because people say they can never guess I weigh so much. I mean the whole idea of the tall beauty contestants and models weighing one hundred fourteen pounds always makes me laugh. If I weighed one hundred fourteen I'd look like I was on crack or something. My face would be drawn, my arms are already thin, and my legs would be way too scrawny.

No, my main concern has always been BTT—booty, tits and thighs. The typical body of a Black woman, yet it's always a struggle to not go over or under my weight. I can't say I've had any complaints about my weight. Men have enjoyed my attributes on an intimate level, and more important, I've enjoyed their enjoyment, if you know what I mean. At this point, my body is the least of my troubles.

So here I am in deep thought about my man who has once again put me aside while he does his thing. When will I no longer allow this to happen, and when will I learn to place my focus upon myself first?

As I stand up to remove my tray from the table, I look across the room and see two of the other assistants sitting near me. One of them waves and motions for me to come join them. I decline and say, "I must get back. My hour is up." These are the two girls named Tanya and Robin who were gossiping about Mr. Adonis, and that is something I don't want to get involved in. I am too old for that type of gossip, just as I am too old for Mr. Adonis.

I return to my desk and finish up the day without really putting my mind into my work. Most of the afternoon is slow, few phone calls, and I did end up sending the overnight package to Chicago.

As six o'clock approaches, the private line at my desk rings. I decide not to answer it because I have instructions to let the calls for the permanent assistant go to voice mail, so I just let it ring. Suddenly as I gather my belongings and prepare to say good-bye to Sarah, I see that head again over the cubicle wall, moving toward me.

He comes around to my desk and says, "Good, I thought you left for the day. I called but you didn't answer your line."

"I don't answer that line, but I did hear it ring," I say while the vibrations from my heart's palpitation are rising to my throat.

"I never answered your question about the internship programs and how they work so you can help your daughter."

"Oh, that's right, I forgot all about it. Don't worry, I'm sure the colleges will have counselors who will inform her. Thanks anyway."

I find myself sort of distant, either taking my negativity for the day or my premature jealousy out on him, which would mean I am definitely not being very nice. I know he can sense it.

I turn and walk to the door of Sarah's office and ask, "Sarah, is it okay with you if I leave?"

"Sure, I'll see you tomorrow, right?" says Sarah, standing up to gather her notepad.

"Yes, I'll be back in the morning," I reply.

"Thanks for everything; you did a great job," she says as she walks out to go to one final meeting downstairs.

"Are you sure you don't need me to stay?" I ask just in case.

"No, I'll be in this meeting for a while. Go ahead and leave." She turns to Malik and says, "Hi, Malik. Is everything working out okay?"

"Yes, Ms. Dunlevy, I'm learning a lot and am meeting nice people. Thanks for asking."

As she walks away, he says in a baritone voice, "Nice people like you, Mariah."

"Thank you again, Malik. I'm going now. My son has a track meet and I don't want to be late."

"Really? What does he run? I ran the hundred and two hundred."

"I'm quite sure he runs the two," I answer as I shut down my computer.

"If he ever needs any advice I'd be glad to talk to him. I had the fastest time in the state when I was in high school." I'm thinking that must have been yesterday. "How fast is he in the two?"

"Malik, I'm not sure, but thanks for the offer." And then I say it, "How was your lunch?"

"Fine, I just went to Pink's, and how was yours?"

"Fine, just couldn't resist that meat loaf; you know how it is when something is not good for you but you eat it anyway." He has no idea I'm exhibiting signs that Michael Douglas had to deal with from Glenn Close in *Fatal Attraction*. The question goes right over his head. "Well, good night. Have a good evening and I'll see you later."

"See you tomorrow, right?" he inquires, seemingly anticipating an affirmation.

"Right, you will. Good-bye."

He just stands there watching me walk down the hall and this time I'm not in the mood to work it or whatever. I just walk—even though I know I want to stay and talk and look into his Ahmad Rashad eyes, I walk. I come to the end of the hall and I turn around to see if he is still looking and I see that silly girl Robin, standing on her tiptoes over our shared cubicle wall talking to Malik as he is looking down the hall at me. I turn the corner realizing she probably overheard our conversation. As innocent as it may have sounded, she surely knows that he or we or I have a heightened sense of curiosity or something.

I SUPPOSE IT WOULD BE NICE if my boyfriend Kareem were to show up in support of Donovan. He gets along with all of my kids because he's like a big kid himself. After all, Donovan asked him to come and somehow he runs faster when Kareem comes to watch. He plays basketball better, football better, everything better when Kareem takes the time to check him out. But once again, he had something else to do. Or he's probably mad at me as usual, but who gives a shit. I've had it with him turning his own guilt around on me as if I have the problem. Being a no-show is not proving his point. It is only showing Donovan his true colors. He is one tired brother.

Anyway, the meet usually lasts a few hours but when it's your child it doesn't matter. His events are always first and last, so I just brought a book on breaking into broadcasting, and of course one must have a booty cushion. I'm good to go.

By the end of the meet, my son's relay team comes in fifth out of seven teams and he came in second place in the two hundred. Before I know it, it is nine-thirty. My voice mail pager is as dormant as an overdue library book. It hasn't gone off once. I guess Kareem is still pouting.

Donovan and I enjoy a quiet, home-cooked meal together. My daughter left a note that says she has gone out and my youngest son is at his dad's house. See, he doesn't live with me during the week, only every other weekend. He has a different father from Donovan and Chloe. His dad moved up north and got married last year. He feels it is better for Kyle to go to school up there. After months of aggravation and thought, I agreed. I've been through a lot since Donovan Sr. died and the thought of a father who is around and wants to be involved can only be an advantage to Kyle. That's something that Donovan and Chloe are not allowed because their dad died when they were only nine and eleven.

Donovan and I say good night to each other. I am so proud of him. As I close my door to get ready for bed, he knocks. "Mom, what happened to Kareem? Was he there today?"

"He couldn't make it, but you can tell him all about it. He'll try next time, okay?"

"What happened to him?"

"He'll have to let us know. He probably got caught up at work."

"Okay, Mom. Well, have a good night."

"I love you!"

"La-u-too," he admits with a firm hug.

Oh, it's cool to say that now that no one else is around. But does he have to make it sound like one word? Either way, it's the sweetest sound I know and the best love to feel, the love from your children.

He closes the door and once again I have just made excuses for Kareem. My child is caught in the middle of my on-again, off-again relationship. What kind of message am I sending to my son? That he's not important enough either? When Kareem is in my life, he's in my children's lives, and when he flakes on me, he flakes on them. I understand his flakiness, but my kids shouldn't have to get caught in the middle. My God, their dad died. The premature death of a parent has got to be the worst form of unintentional abandonment that anyone can experience.

I believe Chloe was hit by her dad's death the hardest. After all, she was Daddy's little girl. She idolized him as her hero and then as soon as she hit puberty, he was gone. Just as she started to get her preteen bearings, she had to come to terms with the death of her source of protectiveness, support and strength. One day he was driving her to school, singing songs and reciting psalms from the Bible, and the next day he was in the oncology ward of Torrance Hospital suffering from leukemia. No matter how many conversations you have with your children in an attempt to brace them for the realities of a terminal disease, there is never an easy way or a nontraumatizing way to discuss the fact that a parent is dying. I do not believe any of us ever really thought it would happen until he took his last breath and went home to be with the Lord.

I always tell her she is the physical evidence of the spiritual love shared between her dad and me. Chloe looks just like him. She is so beautiful. She could be a model if she wanted. She's thin and has the longest legs I've ever seen. Her big eyes are like those of an innocent deer. She is just like him in every way. She is quiet at times, has an intense giving spirit, and she is very loyal. When she was born, some people actually came to the hospital to see what color she would be. I overheard one girl who was looking through the viewing window say, "Give her a few days, she'll look like a nigga." Pubic stitches and all, I had to be held back from kicking her ignorant ass! It breaks my heart to know that as African American people we do that to ourselves.

But today, here she is, eighteen years old and still high yellow, as we say. We don't turn colors like chameleons, after all. In school, some girls would tell her she thinks she's cute. I tell her that only means *they* think you're cute, so take it as a compliment. When she was a baby, I'd push her in the cart at the grocery store and people would ask, "Is this your baby?" Oh, that used to kill me. A talent agent once told me years ago she was too light to be considered for Black auditions. Believe me, being light-skinned is not the prize, it shouldn't even be an issue. She's even been told she has "good" hair—whatever that means. All I know is, she didn't get my hair. But I'm proud of my naturally curly, nappy, kinky do. I'm happy to be nappy, as they say. I hope that one day she'll know how truly beautiful she is. For now, I don't think she has a clue. She says she has absolutely no booty whatsoever and wants one like my side of the family. Honey, be careful what you ask for, you just might get it. After she has a few kids, I picture her in the waiting room of a plastic surgeon asking for liposuction to reduce her backside. Yeah, that ass does run in my family, it'll be knocking on her door real soon. And some titties, too!

5

I DECIDE TO TAKE my routine soothing bubble bath. This is my second most favorite tension-relieving activity. To be honest, it's not like I take long, hot baths to get clean. I just love to luxuriate my body, mind and soul. I kinda see it as a way to make love to myself. I light my frankincense and myrrh incense along with six or seven aromatherapy ginseng candles to stimulate my mood and emotions. I pour a generous amount of Sand and Sable bubble bath and fill the tub with steamy-hot water all the way to the top. I slowly lose my towel to the floor, raise one leg to cautiously point my toes into the hotter-than-hot water. This is my first temperature check to give me permission to take the next step. My wide hips shield the view of my legs and I bend my knees in surrender to lower the rest of my body into the indulgence. Every time the water cools off, I add more hot water until it's steamy like a smoldering Jacuzzi. My daughter bought a comforting sea-foam-green bath pillow for my birthday, which I slowly lean back upon as I beg this sensuous moment to take me away further than Calgon ever could. I pamper Mariah, I spoil Mariah. My oldies radio station is playing the Stylistics, "You're as Right as Rain," and the Whispers, "Say Yes." The most inspiring song of this relishing experience is the Ohio Players, "I Want to Be Free." To top it all off, they even play the song Kareem dedicated to me last year, the Blue Magic cut, "Stop to Start." No lie! Do you ever, brotha! You only stop so you can check out some new honey and get some time away from your woman. You only stop so you can dip your stick into something you found physically attractive because you want to know what it feels like, not spend the rest of your life with, just toy with and bring around your friends to flaunt so they can say, "Man, you hitting that?" That makes you a big man, to be an old playboy. Well, I peeped the meaning of that song. One day, starting all over again will happen about as easily as a snowstorm in hell.

After a while I raise my soothed body out of the water and check myself out in my full-length mirror. The candlelight is kindly flickering and flattering my good parts as the last of the bubbles slowly glisten and drip down my abdomen and along the sides of my thighs. Those are the two parts that need more work than the others. Years ago I got a tattoo of a saxophone over my left breast. I decided to get it over my heart in honor of my father, who played the sax. It's now a little lower than it was years ago because my breasts have given way to gravity, but they're still pretty firm, just a little more southerly. In most cases if you're a forty-year-old mother of three and you deny that you have cellulite, stretch marks and/or varicose veins, you're lying. I think we women notice it more than men do. The slightly faded stretch marks on my stomach serve as evidence that I've borne a few children. And then there's the upper thigh, which I'd like to just cut right off. Oh, to be a straight-up-and-down woman with no hips; to me, this would be a dream. That's enough—I'll just limit this mirrored vision to a frontal view and skip the view from the back.

I take my sexy ass to bed and within minutes I am out like a light, like a match, like Ellen, like . . . well, I doze off quickly.

It must be two-thirty in the morning and the startling ring of the telephone wakes me. I jump and snatch the phone from the receiver in a paralyzed state, yet conscious enough to pray that nothing is wrong with anyone. It wasn't *him*, it would be too much of a surrendering gesture for Kareem to place a call and apologize. It is my on-again, off-again actor friend whom I play around with when my main man decides he needs some space and pulls that rubber band act. After all, isn't it true that every woman needs a man she can call when her main man ain't doing her right? He calls every now and then to test the water and see if I'm lonely and horny and mad enough at Kareem to deal with him. He is once again making a booty call, yet he never admits it.

He always asks the same questions, "Is everything all right, do you need anything, is everything cool?"

When my answer is no to the do-I-need-anything question, he knows I'm back with my man. But the reason he's creepin' so late is because he's married, and I know it. We just don't talk about it.

"Hey, boo. No, I'm fine. Thanks for asking."

"Okay, no problem, I was just checking."

I tell him I'll talk to him later and we hang up. I have to laugh; this man is a cutie, great face, built to last and he talks like LL Cool J. He's from Philly and knows every damn song from the sixties, seventies and eighties like it was yesterday. That's a trip because he wasn't even born until maybe sixty-eight himself. He's a nice guy, believe it or not, but I know if I was available I'd deal with him even less. He'd surely put an oxytocin helpin' on me and break my heart. I refuse to be like my best friend, Violet Crenshaw, and fall in love with a married man. But my actor friend is cool, I guess. He knows where my heart is. I think he must really see me as a freak. Oh well, hell, I am. But I'm into hot monogamy, not hot infidelity. Call it what you want. This too cannot last much longer.

I get up to use the bathroom and check to see if my Chloe is snug in bed and she is. I'll miss her when she goes off to college in August and then she'll be living on her own. I kiss her forehead and go back to sleep.

I never call Kareem because he always accuses me of doing a bed check when I call late. Anyway, I'm still pissed at his triflin' ass. How many *f* s are in triflin'?

* * *

THE NEXT MORNING I take my son to school and head for work. My pager goes off. It's Kareem. I am determined to let him have his space until Monday. Once again I'm hoping he will see the light and become less selfish and *change*—not! As Dr. Singer says, I'm too bright for that.

I ignore his page and proceed to walk to the home video building. I see Sarah walking upstairs.

"You know, Mariah, the girls in the office are giddy over Malik, and believe it or not, if I were thirty years younger, I'd be under his desk."

I laugh in agreement. "Yes, he is a very handsome boy!"

"Was he asking you out last night? I mean I'm sorry if I'm being nosy or crossing the line, but I think that after all these years I know the look on a man's face when he's interested."

"No, he wasn't."

"Well, if he does, I say go for it. If you're not taken already."

"Actually, I do have a boyfriend, so I'm not available. Look, I appreciate you asking, but I usually don't talk about my private life at work. I hope you know what I mean."

"Me too. Actually people know very little about me except for the fact that I'm a bitch."

"Oh, yeah, Sarah, I've noticed. You put the *b* in *bitch*."

"Funny—just shows you, you can't believe everything you hear."

"My mom always told me to believe half of what I see and none of what I hear."

"Good advice."

"Why is it they never call a strong man a bitch?"

"That's a whole other subject, has something to do with our place in society; I guess I'm out of place. You know I looked up the definition of bitch on my computer. It defines it as a demanding woman, slash, bad situation. Isn't that a trip?"

We proceed to head over to the office. I just know Malik is down the hall and that's a real turn-on of anticipation for me. I'm feeling much better today and now I actually feel kinda bad for being so distant toward him yesterday. I head straight to the kitchen for my usual dose of morning caffeine. While I pour my coffee, Robin and Brenda come in. They are very quiet as they sit down behind me and begin whispering.

"Hello, Brenda. How are you?" I inquire out of maturity.

"All right, what was your name again?" Brenda asks smugly.

"Mariah."

"Isn't that the name of someone who comes and saves people or something? Oh, I'm sorry, that's a messiah, right?"

"Pardon me?"

"Oh, nothing. By the way, you have a run in your stocking," Brenda says, snickering.

"Thanks, I'll see you two later. Bye, Robin."

"Bye," Robin says, probably embarrassed by her friend.

I smile at Brenda with *no* reciprocation. Hell, I don't have time for this bullshit. This is exactly why I don't want an office job. Women are so fucking petty and mean to each other.

I walk back to my desk by way of Malik's office and the door is closed. I find myself back at my desk looking up his extension. I expect him to answer but I get his voice mail instead. His voice is deep, similar to that of a baritone and slow like he is just too cool to even be bothered by this corporate bullshit. His tone is that of a man at least in his thirties.

This is Malik Tolliver. I'm out today on business. If you need assistance please call Brenda Wilson on extension five-one-four-one, or leave a message and I'll return your call as soon as possible.

I hang up, slightly bothered. Okay, I'm very disappointed. I suppose subconsciously I was looking forward to a game of cat and mouse. I was even in the mood to be the cat. But it won't be happening today. It will be a long one.

My mother-in-law has left a message on my voice mail regarding a family picnic in Santa Clarita. She wants to take Chloe and Donovan for the weekend. Of course she doesn't invite me, which is cool because I never socialize with the Pijeauxes anyway. And I think they are the phoniest people I've ever been around in my life. The most love she ever showed for me was when I was pregnant with *her* grandchildren, especially when Chloe came out with a light complexion.

I decide to call her back and tell her I will check

with the kids and get back to her later in the week.

"Good-bye," I say as we end our conversation, and of course as always, always, always, she just hangs up without saying good-bye. It drives me crazy, and from what she would tell you, that wouldn't be a long drive.

Sarah asks me to have lunch with her and I agree. She takes me to the exclusive Mr. Chows restaurant in Beverly Hills. We lose track of time and end up dining for three hours—probably a result of the wine we ordered. I have several glasses of an Italian wine called Moscato. It's like a smooth sweet Asti-Spumante champagne without the bubble. The best darn wine I've ever had in my life. By now I'm feeling pretty good. I actually open up to her more than I usually do with people I work with. I decide to tell her about the reasons why I temp part-time and what I want to do with the rest of my life, probably the biggest dream of all, becoming an entertainment news anchor.

"What steps are you taking to get there?" she asks, circling the rim of her wineglass with her index finger.

"I went up north for six months as a news reporter. It was part of a training program, but it only paid five dollars per hour. I couldn't survive on that. I'm starting to think maybe I decided to get into the business too late. I never knew back in high school that I should have even considered broadcast journalism. I went on to get a finance degree from San Diego State University and then became a manager in a retail store. I did that for nearly ten years until Allen Goldwyn hired me. I then decided to go to UCLA at night to take different broadcasting courses. Eventually I got my certificate. I even worked for a television tabloid news show as an interviewer. People have always said I look like a news reporter or anchor, except for this hairstyle. I've done some bit freelance jobs, and also traveled a few places to interview with television stations, but I experienced the casting couch thing when news directors put you up in the same hotel they're staying in, things like that."

"Think about it—why would a news director who lives and works in the same city be staying at a hotel?" she asks while nibbling on the last few crumbs from our onion loaf.

"Co-ink-key-dink, right? Anyway, nothing panned out. I've also done some commercials and print work. I've played everything from a teacher, to a business executive, to a nurse and mother. Even had a part as a news reporter on *Power Rangers!*"

"Wow, *big time*." The waiter brings our barbecue chicken salads. "May I have more dressing, please?" she kindly asks.

"They had me sporting this conservative Connie Chung wig for the shoot. Maybe I'm not putting myself out there enough. But I'm going to hang in there because it's not over until you win, right?"

"That a girl! And scratch that notion that your hair is too radical. That could end up being your claim to fame—sort of a calling card. I can relate, because like you, I also started as a secretary and accepted one of the couch offers ten years ago when I was in my late thirties."

I'm thinking to myself she doesn't look that old as I pretend I'm not doing the math in my head. "Similar roads, but yours has ended up paying off for you. I mean you're a successful female in a 'good old boy,' male-dominated business and you're kicking ass and taking names," I state while evenly pouring the last bit of chilled wine into each glass.

"Well, it's that bitch reputation that has gotten me where I am. But like you said, would a man be called the *b* word for doing the same thing? I don't think so. This chicken is excellent," she exclaims while wiping her mouth with her fancy linen white napkin.

Again, my pager goes off. Once I realize it's Kareem, I start to wonder if I should begin to share that whole story with Sarah, and then I realize he doesn't deserve her time and I don't need the stress.

We leave feeling good; not tipsy, just good.

Later that day back at the office, Sarah explains that she's leaving early. "I'm going to see a man about a dog."

"What kind of dog?" I ask her.

"Mariah, you mean to tell me you've never heard of that before? That means get some stuff, you know, some tube steak, Oscar Mayer woman."

"Oscar, oh, my goodness. That's a new one and

much more than I need to know," I say, taking a seat in front of her oversized cherry wood desk.

"See, you act all pure and naive, but I'll bet you're a real hell-raiser!

"Not!"

"I need some release and so do you; you'd better get some yourself. I'll bet it's been a while."

"I guess that's what they call 'love in the afternoon,' and I heard what you said. No comment."

"It's this afternoon or never. His wife won't let him out at night," she tells me while grabbing her sable-brown briefcase.

"Sounds like a dog to me. Been there, done that."

"I don't doubt it. You can leave too if you need to. Those cobwebs start chafing after a while."

"Sex is one thing I'm not lacking. Good-bye, Sarah!" I say, standing up to exit her office with her.

"See you tomorrow." She walks away at a hurried pace while I close her office door.

SUCKER THAT I AM, I decide to go ahead and return Kareem's page, determined not to go even if he invites me and not to allow him to renege on being a jerk.

"What did you do last night?" he asks as if he has a right to. Obviously he's feeling guilt over whatever or whomever he did last night.

Softly and quietly I answer, "Oh, nothing."

"How was Donovan's meet?"

"You would know if you'd been there, Kareem."

"Okay, so you're still pissed off about this weekend? Damn, I can't have a full day of pleasure and peace without ending the day with shit from my woman. I don't need this. Now, let's start all over. How are you?"

Oh, hell, excuse me, was I not being feminine? Was I leading again? Let me follow this one and see where the hell it takes me. "Just fine, Kareem."

"That's great. Now I'm going to Wesley's Fish Shack to get some catfish for you and the kids tonight. Will you be home by eight?" he inquires with a combination of nerve, bossiness and misplaced thoughtfulness.

"Yes, Kareem, fine. And eight is absolutely perfect. What a grand idea," I say sarcastically.

"Good girl. Now I've got to go. See you then."

"Good-bye, see you then and have a good day."

Aahhhh! I want to fucking scream. Dr. Singer probably has her wimp-ass man of a husband tied up in her basement, or maybe he ties her up in the damn attic. This will never work. How can two people continue to just sweep the dust under the rug? The crap is never dealt with. Issues that are not resolved are not forgotten and eventually rise to the surface. How can I continue to allow him to make me feel responsible for being hurt and misunderstood by him? If he were a real man, wouldn't he want me to be happy instead of me always pleasing him? Well, I guess that's the sign of a little boy. My mom always said a little boy becomes a man when he gets his pleasure from the happiness he brings you; a little boy stays a little boy when he gets his pleasure from the happiness you bring him. But I suppose in his own way he believes fish dinners are pleasing to us, so optimistic little me continues to give him the benefit of the doubt. But the doubt is snowballing.

6

AT SIX O'CLOCK, Sarah's line rings. It is a deep, seemingly excited voice asking, "May I speak to Mariah?" he says, sounding as if he's trying to catch his breath.

"Speaking."

"It's Malik. I rushed home to catch you before you left."

"I'm glad you did. I was just about to forward the phones. Are you okay?"

"Oh, yeah, I'm fine. I had an orientation meeting for a mentor gig I'm involved in through the studio. Next week I'll be going to a few local high schools to talk to young football players. It's pretty cool."

"That's positive, sounds like you're very involved."

"I suppose so. I was calling to ask you something."

"Okay, what is it?" I'm holding my breath and hoping he'll say something I'll probably have to reject out of common sense or maybe he is going to ask me how to spell a word, or what to get his mom for Mother's Day, or what is my sign, but I wish he would go ahead and ask.

"I've been thinking ever since yesterday, would you be open to the possibility of maybe talking sometimes away from work? I mean, I think you're a nice person and I enjoyed talking to you and I sort of feel like I could learn a lot from you. I'm asking would you consider calling me after Friday? Do you think we could be friends?"

Friends! Now there's that word. Here I am developing a friendship with a kid who sees me as someone he could learn from. Does he mean what so many men mean when they say let's just be friends, when what they really want is to rock your world? Or friends like the TV show, and we all know what that means. Everybody's doin' everybody.

"Friends would be cool, Malik, but it would probably be expensive due to the bicoastal thing. You are leaving in two weeks, right?"

"Right, I mean we could write each other letters and E-mail, or you could call me collect, or . . . I just want to get to know you. I'm learning to open myself up to receive the things that will create the experience I want to feel. I say we open up and get to know each other."

Be feminine; follow the lead if you like where he's going. "Sure, Malik."

"Well, how about if I give you my number tomorrow?"

"Okay. You're coming into the office, right?"

"I wouldn't miss your last day. You just make sure you come in, Lady Temp!"

I assure him, "Oh, I'll be here. So I'll see you in the morning. Have a good night."

"I'm glad I caught you. Be good."

"You too!"

Okay, now, tomorrow I'll get his number and we'll talk on the telephone late at night, run up phone bills, write letters and become fucking pen pals. Not exactly what I had in mind.

AS USUAL, Chloe is on the telephone and Donovan is in PlayStation mode.

"Did you finish your homework?" I ask Donovan.

"Yes, Mom."

"Let me see it!"

I know good and damn well I couldn't correct that stuff if my life depended on it. The math is too new, the history is too old, the geography is too far away and the Spanish is too foreign. Hell, I can't remember half the shit I learned in high school and that was twenty-two years ago, let alone what I learned last week. My memory bank is like a Rolodex that won't flip anymore. It's a good thing my daughter is around to look it over. I just check dates and make sure it's complete and act like I know what I'm looking for, really only noticing maybe some sloppiness or bad grammar. I know he's not fooled again.

BY EIGHT O'CLOCK, no Kareem and we are getting hungry. By eight-thirty, I page him and ten minutes later he's at the door.

"Why did you page me? You knew I was on my way over," he replies with irritation written all over his face as I open the door.

"Just trying to get a gauge on how far away you were. Donovan started to zap a frozen lasagna dinner."

He ducks his head to accommodate his six-nine frame as he steps through the doorway with four bags of fish dinners in hand. Kareem is slender, long and strong all over. His features are fine, his lips are plump and his eyes are sexy. You could say he looks good with his graham cracker complexion. I can attest to the fact that the myth about big hands and big feet is true. Maybe that's one reason why he's so out there. Perhaps the attention from curious ladies is just too intense to ignore.

Chloe hugs Kareem tightly. They have an agreement that if she gets into Cal Berkeley, he will stop smoking. Tonight we all smell cigarette smoke just like all the other nights. Chloe gets on him; he jokingly denies it and then goes out on the balcony for some fresh air. She takes the telephone and the fish dinner into her room and closes the door as Donovan goes outside with Kareem to tell him about the track meet.

"It was so cool, I ran the second leg and I caught up with this real quick guy from Alta Loma, but the third leg was weak and we just couldn't pull it off."

Kareem maturely talks to him about the old adage "It's not whether your win or lose, it's how you play the game." "Just do the best you can do, and it sounds like you did. That's all you can ask for."

The three of us eat at the table and discuss our

day. Kareem is the only man they've really bonded to over a long period of time other than their dad. It's these times when I yearn for this side of him on a full-time basis, but it would involve change. That word again. That is something he should not do for me, he must want it for himself. It is apparent that he does not want us full-time.

"See, Donovan, I was leaving the office in time to catch your meet when I forgot I had a client meeting at seven and it ran a lot longer than I thought it would. I knew you would tap into what we talked about last week. Just keep doing your best."

"And did my mom tell you I came in second in the two?"

"No, she didn't. That's great. Now wait, don't get a big head!"

Donovan and Kareem laugh as they get up to go into Donovan's room to play video games. It's an ongoing competition that seems never-ending.

"Baby, get me a drink!" Kareem demands as he walks away.

"Okay!" I answer as I walk to the kitchen to grant his wish.

He takes the drink into Donovan's room to play like a big kid. I'm prepared to tell him I don't like that because it sends the wrong message. He isn't playing bid whist with his other old playboys. This is a teenage boy who is impressionable and who is looking to him by example. I decide to wait until Donovan and Chloe go to sleep to discuss it.

I spend a moment on the phone with Ariana to pass the time as Kareem and Donovan play. "Mariah, I looked up the word *oxytocin*. It is genuinely in the dictionary; it says, *an oxytocin pituitary hormone; small oval gland attached to the vertebrate brain whose sections control the endocrine gland*. It also mentions something about a uterine smooth muscle. You can actually have a hormone bonding rush from an orgasm."

Before long, my *love hormone* Kareem and I are in my room. The house is quiet. He begins to light up a cigarette with one hand and shakes his glass with the other. As the ice cubes slosh about he asks, "Can I have another fill up? And hey, where's that X-rated tape we didn't finish watching last time? Pop it in the VCR. Tonight I'm going to cash in that head rain check," he demands as he plops down on the bed and stretches out on his back.

This time I'm not in the mood to follow.

"No, I did not offer you a rain check and I'm not going to pull out the dirty tapes tonight, Kareem. And you know I told you about lighting up in this house, not to mention drinking in my son's room."

"Oh, damn, it must be that time of the month," he comments to shift the blame on me.

"No, it's not, and you know I don't like freaking when they're home."

Even though by now they're used to him sleeping over. They obviously know we're getting busy. We just keep it as quiet as possible.

"Then let's go to my house."

"Were you drinking before you got here?"

"Just a couple of beers at the Leimert. What's up with you?"

"I'm going to leave it alone, Kareem. Let's just try and have a good evening. I've already said what I needed to say."

Just then as I'm taking off my dress, I notice the run in my stocking and I'm sure he notices it, too. The run begins toward the inside of my crotch and runs down the inside of my left leg.

"Who's been trying to finger you today?" he asks while glancing at my leg.

"Oh, you're really tripping tonight."

"Turn around!" he says as he grabs my arm and yanks me around. "And what is this red mark on your elbow? Is that a rug burn?"

"Oh, please, don't start this madness tonight. You're trippin'," I say, pulling my arm away from him.

"Oh, if I had that shit on me, you'd be all on my case. Remember the time you actually accused me of having kissed someone because I had gold speckles on my lips, but I can't say a damn thing to you, right?"

"Kareem, I am not in the mood for this. Why is it that you always start shit with me before you go out of town or leave to do something on your own? You need some psychological help on that. It gets real tiring."

"Yeah, well, I'm tired of my woman thinking that just because I'm busy one night she can sneak out and get her freak on with somebody on a damn rug. Or was it today at work? Maybe the man you're working for this week."

"You're getting loud, I'm going to do you a big favor and say this—"

"What?" he interrupts as if he is not clear.

I attempt to harness the volume of my words but the intensity of my anger somehow overrules. "And I know it will only give you the ammunition you need to get mad and stay away so you can screw up, but you are not more important than my children and you are surely not more important than me. Now get your Newports and Tanqueray, and go home or wherever, but get the hell out of here. And thanks for the fish!"

"You're the loud one. No fucking problem. Good-bye," he belts with a cigarette bouncing in his mouth, blinking from the smoke rising to his eyes as he zips up his pants.

He quickly closes my bedroom door and leaves. What a shame that deep down inside, a part of me wants him to hug me tightly and apologize and beg me to let him fix whatever I'm feeling. It doesn't happen.

I check on the kids. They are either sleeping or pretending to be.

I take the phone off the hook and lay across my charcoal comforter, ripped panty hose and all, as I fall asleep in a pool of tears. I love that man so much, but that kind of self*fishness* will never turn into self*lessness*. Not soon enough for my taste. Once again a great evening turns bad. And I didn't even get any lovin'.

7

I AWAKEN TO SWOLLEN EYELIDS and postseafood morning breath. My daughter appears extra-kind this morning. She brings me my morning coffee made just the way I like it, with my creamer and three teaspoons of sugar. We always joke, *Give me coffee and no one gets hurt*. This day I know she overheard Kareem's premature exit. She offers to take Donovan to school. I thank her and they leave.

Before I know it I'm back on the studio lot at my desk headed for more coffee in the break room. This time I purposely avoid walking by Malik's office, hoping maybe if I wait until he comes around later the swelling around my eyes will have faded.

As I make it back to my desk, I hear Robin and Tanya talking on the other side of the partition again. "So what if they are seeing each other, I don't care. I'm not her friend anyway," Robin says.

"Well, we do party away from work and that would be fucked up," Tanya admits.

"I don't see a ring on her finger or his, so I say

he's open game. But come to think of it, he hasn't tried to really get with either one of us. Hell, he might be a faggot! Do you see how his mannerisms are like fem? And he's too sweet and nice," explains Robin.

Tanya replies, "Girl, why does every man who doesn't pinch your ass have to be gay? Being sweet and being gay mean two different things. Besides, he plays football. Football players are not gay, only basketball players."

Now once again these two are creeping up on fucking silly. I am not trying to hear it. Obviously they are talking about Malik and Brenda. I decide to interrupt their stimulating convo.

I suddenly yell, "Robin, do you have any tampons? Can I have one if you do?" I proceed to the other side of the partition to eyeball them and apologize for the personalness of my needs, "But I'm just ill-prepared, can you help a sister out?"

"Girl, please, you'd better check out the machine in the rest room and gather up a quarter. I can't help you," Robin exclaims, on the verge of sounding irate.

"I understand what that's like but there really is a machine in the ladies' room," Tanya says in a helpful tone.

I smile at both of them and walk away. I just know I hear Robin say, "I didn't know women her age still had periods. Doesn't menopause or whatever normally make a visit by then?"

Robin laughs and Tanya walks away with a chuckle.

Mission accomplished. I broke up their gossip

scene for the morning and gave Robin something else to talk about.

I take the long way around and end up back at my desk. Sarah sneaks in, looking ever so chipper.

"How was your evening, Mariah?"

"Don't ask. I'm sure it wasn't as good as your afternoon. Is that what the smile is all about?"

"Maybe so, maybe not. This time I have no comment. But isn't it a beautiful day in the neighborhood?"

"A beautiful day to be neighborly."

In unison, "Would you be mine, could you be mine?"

"You know, I'm enjoying this assignment. Are you sure your regular assistant is coming back?"

"Maybe so, maybe not."

Sarah's line rings. "Sarah Dunlevy's office," I answer. "May I ask who's calling? One minute, Celeste." I turn to inform Sarah, "It's Mr. Miller's assistant, Celeste." Mr. Miller is the studio chief.

"This is Sarah. Okay, I'll hold. Hey, Tom! What big meeting? Regarding what? And you need my expertise? Well, why didn't your assistant notify my office prior to now? Couldn't it have been E-mailed into my schedule, especially if it involved home video? Tom, I am ill prepared and I do not feel comfortable. But I'm . . . Tom, fine, good-bye," Sarah says as she hangs up in irritation.

"Is everything okay? Is there anything you need?" I ask.

Sarah storms by me with an ink pen, a blank notebook and a blank face. In a breeze, she is gone.

Her line rings again. It's Malik.

"Can you please come to my office for a moment?" he asks.

"Well, just for a minute, but I need to be here to answer the phones. It's kind of not a good time."

However, it is better than the alternative. If he comes to my desk, I'm quite sure the little girls will get an earful. I forward the phones and go.

His fragrance is drawing me to his door like a magnet. It's kind of a peppery, mellow, macho, manly, masculine, mango, musk type thang.

As I walk in, he closes the door behind me. I look at him and nervously inquire, "What type of cologne do you wear?"

"Joop," he whispers in an enticing tone.

I reply, "It's nice on you," as I stare at his generous lips.

If ever there were a heterosexual, sexy, fine, masculine man, this is it. He actually makes me feel butt ugly standing next to him. He smiles in slow motion, exposing those pearly white teeth I'd missed before. What could be better than dark skin and ivory white teeth? He licks his lips as he hands me a small envelope. I look down at the envelope, and in dark brown ink, bold italic print, it reads *Mariah*.

"I hope you don't mind. I just had to let you know that I want to get to know you, from the neck up. With all due respect and admiration, Mariah, I want you to look at this and remember me as a man whose soul crossed paths with yours and connected one summer. The vision of you will be forever in my mind and I want to be forever in yours. I'm just glad we met," he proclaims.

"No, no, no, no, I don't. That's very sweet, but what is it?" Why am I stuttering?

"Open it," he kindly says as if to encourage my next move.

I open the envelope and slowly pull out a handsome, sensual, shirtless picture of Malik on the beach, sitting on the rocks, staring into the deep orange majestic sunset. He's wearing casual cream-colored warm-up pants and brown Birkenstock sandals. His rippled chest is glistening as the rays of the sun dance across his skin. Damn, he has some big-ass nipples! Anyway, I flip it over and the back reads *You've Got a Friend*. In my head I hear Roberta Flack and Donny Hathaway singing every word. It also reads *Forever, Malik*. As well, he has written three telephone numbers below his name.

"This is a great picture," I say as I look down at the body on this man. "You should think about modeling because you've definitely got the look." I glance up at his face while placing the photo back in the envelope, then removing it again and once more looking down at it. "I really appreciate you confessing your desire to get to know me better 'from the neck up.' I don't know what to say, but to be honest, you don't even know me." I suppose I'd better look at him from the neck up. I look into his eyes and smile in appreciation. "Thanks."

"Mariah, this may sound crazy or dumb, but from the moment I first set eyes on your face"—

uh-oh, now I'm hearing Roberta Flack singing "The First Time Ever I Saw Your Face"—"I felt as though I knew you from somewhere before. It's scary but so beautiful. There's something in your eyes and I've never felt this before, I've only heard of it. When you told me about your kids, I longed to meet them. When you left my presence, I longed to experience your energy again. It's like you're magical and I want you to know what I'm thinking." He crosses his arms as if he's said something he'd been wanting to get off his chest.

"The bottom line is, what would we really have in common? Not to mention the issue of the obvious age difference. There are so many things you've yet to learn that I've already experienced, and things you do know that I've forgotten," I reply in an attempt to sound interested but not motherly.

He rotates his body and walks toward his desk, faces me and takes a seat on the corner. "That's just what I mean, Mariah. I want to talk about where I'm going and where you've gone and what I should know and what I shouldn't want to know."

I cautiously step closer to him, standing in between his legs. "Malik, this is very deep, and I know you're sincere, I really feel that. But I don't make new friends easily. I have a full life filled with kids and responsibilities that keep me busy. And I have a boyfriend, I think!" I take a passive step backward, exhaling as I again glance down at the words on the back of his picture.

"Oh, you do?" he asks with curiosity.

"Yes, Malik." I reply as if I'm not proud of myself for admitting it and regret the fact that I have one.

"Well, I suppose he wouldn't appreciate our conversational bonding?" he inquires as he stands up and takes a seat behind his desk.

"It's not about him, really. All I know is, if we are connected spiritually or any other way, it's deeper than the both of us are. I do believe our meeting is no coincidence," I claim to reassure him.

"I agree," he says, leaning back in his chair.

"So believe it or not, I do understand the concept of spiritual transitions. Malik, I really like you and I thank you for the picture. I will treasure it always because you put so much energy and thought into it. I also appreciate your honesty in expressing your thoughts so openly. It's nice."

"It's called communicating, Mariah, and I want to communicate with you. I want to listen to you and hear you. It's rare that women thank men for their thoughts and time. That's maturity and appreciation expressed through words. That's why I want to get to know you."

"Okay, Malik, let's cut to the chase here," I say, leaning over his desk. "Are you looking for some older woman, younger man thing? Because if you are, just tell me."

He stands up and leans in even closer, placing his palms flat on the desk. "Yes, I'm looking for Mariah and Malik, M&M, that's all. Nothing else, for now! And if that means you're older and I'm younger, then so it is."

Taking a deep breath, I am impressed by his maturity and self-assuredness. I step away, finally placing the photo in the envelope and holding it to my chest with both hands. "Malik, I'm going to go back down the hall now, but I'm sure I'll see you before the day is over."

"How about lunch?" he asks, coming around the desk to approach me. "I actually found out that today is my last day too. I'll be in L.A. for two more weeks. This mentor thing has replaced my internship. Two weeks less money, but I'm cool. Let me take you to Roscoe's. Please?"

"Okay, what time?" Feminine response.

"You let me know when you're ready and we'll go. Can you drive though? I don't have a car today," he admits.

"Sure. I'll buzz you later, my friend!"

He moves past me to open the door to accommodate my exit and says, "Thank you!"

Thank you. A man is thanking me for letting him take me to lunch; what's this shit? As I walk out I look down to stare at his picture again, obviously led by the second pair of eyes on the top of my head. Sarah is still in her meeting and thank goodness she is. I feel like I've just been in a trance and need time to snap out of it. I immediately pick up the phone to call Violet, my girlfriend I've known since elementary school. She always accepts all parts of me, freaky or motherly; she never judges me. And right now I need her ear badly.

For a moment I almost forget that my cubicle is in earshot of Miss Telefax, Telephone, Tell a

Friend so I get up and go into Sarah's office and close the door.

"Violet, you won't believe this. I met this young, and I do mean young, guy at work. He's interning and will only be in town for a couple more weeks. He wants to get to know me better and he just gave me his friggin' picture. Girl, he is so good-looking. He makes George Clooney look like Pee-wee Herman."

"Okay, what do you think he means by wanting to get to know you better? And he's only in town for a short time too. Have you lost your mind?" she asks as if she already knows the answer.

"Vi, he's sincere, I just know it. He kinda thinks we're soul mates."

"Soul mates. How can your soul mate be young, and I do mean young, as you say? I thought we were going to start choosing men with our ears, not our eyes?"

"I believe that's exactly why I'm attracted to him, by what he says."

"Don't tell me it's not because he's fine. And if you are really listening to what he is saying, you'll run for the nearest exit with your dress up in the air."

"Vi, I know you don't want me to get hurt, but I'm not talking romance, just . . ."

"Just what? You already joked that you're in need of a thug in your life. You always say you could have been hanging tight with Tupac, drinking Alizé and screwing all night long." Damn, I can't tell her anything.

"He is not a thug, far from it. He has kind of this *GQ*, hip maturity. He's actually a very deep man."

Just then Sarah bursts into the office and starts cursing at the top of her lungs, throwing her pen and pad at the wall.

"Vi, I have to go. I'll call you back when I get home." I quickly hang up and attempt to console Sarah. "What's wrong?"

"I've been fired, Mariah, that's what's wrong. Fuck them, I'm not waiting two weeks. I'm calling my attorney and getting the fuck out of here now. Calling me to attend a pretend meeting and setting me up like this. Even my immediate supervisor was in on this bullshit."

"Sarah, why?" I inquire in amazement while picking up her pen and pad off the floor.

"Mariah, just go home. I'll sign your time card until six o'clock. I've got to make a phone call to my lawyer and I'm out of here."

"Can I at least help you pack?"

"No, I don't want any of this shit. I never brought any damn pictures anyway. Just my briefcase and my fucking plant. Shit, shit, shit! Please go, Mariah. And leave your phone number for me before you go. Now, I need some privacy, please. Thanks for everything." She closes her office door in front of me.

I complete my time card and slip my phone number under her door, all the while thinking about how totally fucked up they are for treating her like this. I mean, I know there's two sides to every story but to call a mock meeting and set her up is really low.

I haphazardly find my way back to my desk to find a memo on my chair addressed to the department from Brenda. She is notifying us that she planned a lunch for Malik today at one o'clock at the Studio Grille. I immediately dial his extension.

"Malik?"

"I was going to buzz you. I don't want to go to lunch with the department," he says, sounding disappointed.

"Well, if you don't mind me saying so, you should. You've known them a lot longer than me and it is your last day."

"Mariah, please come with us," he says as if to beg.

"Something just came up over here and I have to leave anyway."

"Is there anything you want to talk about?" he asks in a curious voice.

"No, I'm just going home early."

"Mariah, please call me this weekend and let me know what's going on. And if you change your mind, you know where we'll be. At the Studio Grille."

"Okay, I'll remember that. Have a great lunch."

"Talk to you this weekend, right?"

"Right."

I HEAD HOME knowing it's too early for my son to be out of school. My daughter's car is in the garage. As I walk in, I hear a noise in her room. I walk toward her door and knock lightly as I open it. There is a man sitting on the edge of her bed and she is under the covers looking as though she just woke up. He looks at me as guilty as a convict.

"What's going on?" I scream.

They both just look at me like dummies as I grab him by his shirt.

"Get the hell out of my house," I yell at the top of my lungs.

He slowly and coolly walks by me toward the door, hunched over with his pants sagging down to his damn knees. Thank God more boxer shorts are showing than booty. I scream at him, "Boy, you need to be at the mall buying yourself a damn belt, you fool! You'd better get your ass out of here. If my husband were alive he'd kill you!"

As he walks out I realize she is the problem, not him.

"What were the two of you doing, Chloe?" I ask while standing over her bed.

"Nothing, Mommy, I swear."

"Then why are you still in bed?"

"He just came by to talk," she mumbles, trying to sit up yet still managing to wrap herself in her sheet.

I bellow in a clamorous voice, "Talk on the phone, Chloe, not in your bedroom in my house. He looked at least twenty-eight years old. What kind of man would come to your room in your mom's house in the middle of the day? I can't believe this. Is this what you do when I'm at work?"

I storm out, ranting and raving as she says only I can do. Raving to the point where I'm sure she probably wishes I'd just spank her like I did when she was younger and get it over with. That would be much less painful than my mouth.

I walk in her room again and see a brown paper bag on the floor near the bed. I pick it up and look inside. To my surprise I find two empty bottles of Snapple and an empty condom package. I flip out!

"Get your butt up and get dressed. You are about to get the hell out of here!" I yell in bottled-up frustration and shock while I storm out of her room and across the hall into mine, slamming the door and reaching for the telephone.

Times like this I wish I could call my mother but instead I call Violet and she begs me to calm down. "Look, she did get accepted to college, she's trying. At least he wore a condom! And damn, Mariah, they were drinking Snapple, not Old English! Take a deep breath and try to get away from her until you calm down."

"Vi, I've had it. After all, she barely graduated from high school. She's run away twice, and there have been too many other problems to mention. I knew she didn't want to really go off to college. She was only getting away from me. And you know what? What kind of example am I? I'm unable to get away from a losing relationship myself."

"Then why are you so angry, Mariah? Think about what you just said and cut her some slack."

"Violet, I've got to go." I hang up as if I have an attitude with Vi also.

I run for the door and hop in my car. I drive and cry and drive and cry. Is she my mirror? Is that why it hurts so badly? Is she looking for love from her dad in men just like I am? Why is this affecting me so deeply? Am I failing at motherhood *and* relationships? And why am I forgetting the sex I had in my mom's house with Chloe's dad when we were in high school? We just never got caught.

For a long time she used to think her dad was an angel who was sending me messages every time she would do wrong so I would catch her. And I often do. At this moment I pray he will stop sending me those messages. I'd rather not know.

I stop at a pay phone. I figure now is as good a time as any for the kids to be with their grandmother. "Mrs. Pijeaux, it's fine if you pick up Chloe and Donovan tonight." I actually see this as another blessing. "That's fine, eight o'clock? Okay, they'll be ready, good-bye," I say.

Click. No response.

8

I WAVE GOOD-BYE as my mother-in-law pulls off in the same old dingy white Volvo that Donovan Sr. and I used to take to the drive-in movie when we wanted to get busy. Chloe avoids giving me eye contact and Donovan looks as if he's wondering why we are so quiet. Once again, he feels the tension between us.

I close the door and notice it's eight-twenty. I think I'll call my youngest son, Kyle, before he goes to bed. Maybe if I put more effort into being there for him than I have in the past, getting him through his teenage years will bring less heartache than this. He's in the seventh grade now, so he stays up until nine-thirty. Kyle looks just like his dad also. He's dark-skinned like maple syrup and just as sweet. The boy could grow up to be six-foot-ten if he's not careful. He's skinny right now because puberty hasn't paid a visit, but his appetite is on its way. He reminds me of that cutie Kobe Bryant. After all, Kyle is a little comedian and I need a laugh. The phone rings and *she* answers. She never did like me. She thinks I want her husband back—quite the other way around. But I'm civil as I ask for my son.

"Hello, this is Mariah. Is Kyle there?" Usually she says she's on the other line or he's outside playing or sleeping. She has only heard Kyle's dad's side of the story. After all, she's only been in Kyle's life for three years. During all that time he's lived with his dad. Therefore, I'm sure she sees me as a deadbeat mom. She wasn't there when I was taking care of all three kids when neither of their dads was around. She wasn't there when Donovan Sr. died and I begged Kyle's dad to spend more time with his son. She didn't see all of the years he lived with me. All she knows is that five years ago, when his dad wanted Kyle to live with him during the week and me on the weekends so I could deal with our bereavement, I agreed. Three years ago when he met her they bought a house up north. Before I knew it Kyle's dad had made plans for him to go to school out there. When I inquired as to what was going on he promised me it was a better school district and I'd see him every weekend. That changed to every other weekend because his dad wants him to play sports on some weekends. To this day he doesn't play sports unless it's during the week and I only see him two weekends a month. The situation is real fucked up. I always say I'm getting a lawyer. As of yet, I haven't. Kyle seems happy, but I know it has an effect on him. Anyway, tonight she actually gives him the phone.

"Mom, next weekend when I come home can we go to Speed Tracks and maybe stay out there overnight so we can swim at a hotel and play basketball?" Kyle is always wanting to do something that is out of the range of my budget.

"We'll see, baby. I miss you. How was your week?"

"It was okay. I have new neighbors now, so I walk to school with my friend; his name is Josh."

"Well, you tell Josh that your mom says hi. Maybe I'll have a chance to meet him soon," I suggest in excitement.

"Mom, I had a dream about you last night. You were driving me to school and we were cracking up laughing about who cut wind in the car. You were swearing it was me because you said you know the smell of all your kids' farts and then you said moms don't fart, they poot. I woke up with my sides hurting. I was in tears. Daddy thought I'd lost my mind. I could still smell the fart when I woke up."

"Probably because you laughed so hard, you cut some cheese in your bed! You are so silly," I say as we both laugh together. "That's gross."

I remember when I was little I could never say anything like that without getting popped on the head. My mom thought *funky* was a bad word. But I lighten up now because it is funny and it's a part of being human, bodily functions and such.

"Okay, Mom, I'll talk to you later. Tell Donovan and Chloe I said what's up. I'll call you guys this weekend."

"Call them at Grandma Pijeaux's house. They'll be there until Sunday night."

"Oh, you're going to be all alone. What are you going to do?"

"I'm not sure yet. I'm not used to this. I'll probably just take long hot baths and drink lots of coffee, huh?"

"That's you. One day I'm going to buy you your own Starbucks when I get to the NBA. You're a walking coffee bean."

"Love you, baby. Good night!"

Now lonely little Miss Codependent has to focus on what she likes to do. That's scary.

The caller ID box shows an unknown number as the phone rings. I answer it with cautious reservation. Part of me wants to let the machine pick it up with a message stating *I'm working on a project all weekend and unavailable until Monday morning, please call back at that time.* But for fear of it being an emergency, I don't have the nerve.

"Pijeaux residence."

"Mariah, it's Sarah." She sounds very intoxicated. "Girl, you've got to meet me out here, it's so much fun. Let me buy you a drink."

"I don't think so. I'm finally home alone for the first time in who knows when. No kids, no boyfriend, just me. But I'm glad you're celebrating in spite of those assholes. You cannot let them win."

"My day was the worst. Actually, it was a nightmare but I don't want to talk about it. Please change your mind and come out for an hour. *Please?*"

"Well, to be honest with you, my afternoon was pretty shitty too. I could stand to release some stress. And you were kinda short with me, but I understand."

"That's why I want to buy you a drink," she offers.

"It sounds like you've had enough. What are you drinking?"

"Just a few glasses of cham-poo!"

"You mean champagne? Where the heck are you?"

"I'm at the Pistachio Bar in West Hollywood near Santa Monica Boulevard and La Cienega. Come now!" she insists.

"All right, give me until like nine-thirty. Where will you be?"

"At the bar, girl! Where else?"

"What's the dress code?" I ask quickly, feeling as though she is rushing me.

"Oh please, we're not in high school. Just get your ass over here and wear whatever!"

"Okay, Sarah, what's your number in case I can't—" *Click!* "Hello? Sarah?"

I've been hung up on twice tonight. What a day!

As I pull my car up along Santa Monica Boulevard I see a line outside the bar to get in. I valet-park and approach the line. Nothing but women! I look at them and think to myself, Sarah couldn't be at an all-girl bar, but it is Pistachio. Sarah just had a piece of dick yesterday, from a dog, not a female one, I think! She couldn't be—no! These women are feminine and pretty. They couldn't be gay. Oh, shit, what the heck new can of worms am I opening now? I go in.

Right away I hear someone calling my name just as I see Sarah at the end of a long, reddish-brown walnut, countrylike bar. I walk over to her as I feel piercing stares from women as if I'm new meat, prime cut, choice USDA, Grade A fresh. I literally fall onto a bar stool next to Sarah and look her dead in the eyes. "Why didn't you tell me?"

"Because you wouldn't have come. Lighten up, Miss Hetero-dick crazy purebred."

"No. Far from pure, but definitely not coochie curious," I'm happy to inform her.

"Coochie curious? What makes you think because we're at a girl bar we have to want to fuck girls? Maybe we're just trying to get away from testosterone-ridden men for a minute," she says with breath reeking of Ketel One.

"I've had too much of a stressful day to get involved in a deep conversation about sexual preferences, and so have you. Now, let's go somewhere else!" I say while standing up.

"Sit down, please. Damn, you're really uptight. How old are you anyway?"

"Thirty-nine, Sarah!" I take my seat again, resting my elbow on the bar.

"And you've never set foot in a gay bar?"

"I went to a *guy* gay bar to attend a party for one of my male friends, but I'm used to being around a bunch of men and I'm okay if gay men don't hit on me. What am I going to say if one of these women talks to me?" I ask while looking around the cramped dark room.

"Talk back and exchange conversation and get your mind off of society's standards and make your own. It's all a part of being yourself."

"This isn't me." Neither is this Shania Twain music they're playing.

Just then a woman leans in between the two of us to order a drink. She says, "You look like an actress—that Huxtable woman . . . ahh, what's her name?" she asks with a glow.

"No. I'm not."

"Well, you sure look like her. You're a cutie patoo-tie!"

Gasp. "Thanks!"

"Can I buy you a drink?"

"No thanks, we're not staying," I say, looking at Sarah.

"Well, let me know if you change your mind, bright eyes! I'll have a Seven-and-Seven and Bailey's on the rocks," she says to the bartender.

"Sarah, I'm gonna kill you," I say as she smirks.

"Relax. Besides, I'm not leaving you by yourself and you're not going to be condemned to hell if you stay for an hour. I need your conversation and company and I'm buying you a drink."

Another lady walks up who knows Sarah. They hug and she introduces me.

"Mariah, this is my good friend Cindy. She's in the business also."

"Yeah, but not in the closet like you, Sarah. Nice to meet you, Mariah. Pretty name." We shake hands.

"Nice to meet you also. What do you do?" I ask.

"I'm a producer for *The Opposite Sex* talk show on a cable network. Can you believe it? I'm into the same sex but my show is about opposite sex relationships? Well, I believe there's a man and a woman in every relationship anyway. It's all about the role you play."

"That's deep. I guess it sort of makes sense."

Sarah tells Cindy, "Mariah wants to host a show, or something, but she's too frigid or rigid or something," Sarah says, stumbling over her words.

"Sarah, I see you've had a big jump on me with the alcohol," Cindy protectively comments.

"Let's get you caught up," she says to Cindy. She then gives me a look and tells me, "And no, I won't jump on you. What are you drinking, Mariah?"

"Alizé."

"She'll have a Goldschlager on the rocks," Sarah tells the bartender.

I force a smile, and before I know it, it's just after midnight. I actually hit the tiny, disco-lit dance floor with three other women. I do that at straight clubs with my girlfriends when I get fed up with the men who act like wallflowers, but never like this. This is free and open and without care of what the men think. I am actually having fun! But that Goldschlager tastes like mouthwash!

Sarah is talking to the bartender while I chat with Cindy. I suppose she just can't keep it to herself any longer. I overhear Sarah say, "They fired me because I'm bisexual. Those assholes couldn't stand the fact that I could probably get more pussy than they can. My performance, my ass. It's my performance in bed that keeps them up at night while they jack off in my name. Gloria Allred is handling this shit and we can all retire when I get through with them."

"Sarah, I wouldn't discuss that right now if I were you. If this goes to litigation and it turns out to be a big case, everyone in this bar will be testifying against you to get a piece of the limelight. Let's go," I say.

Sarah continues with a slow, stuttered speech, "Mariah, you're too fucking sensible to be my friend. How about being my woman? Just kidding. Now I know why they call you light-skinned black people red-boned. You look like a fucking beet." I'm turning red because I want to choke her.

Cindy agrees to take Sarah home. Obviously Cindy has been to her house before and can get Sarah settled in bed, literally.

We all offer good-bye kisses and hugs. I have a slight buzz and actually accept a business card from one of the girls I danced with. The buzz is not the reason; I actually think she's a nice person. Honestly, I am flattered.

What a night! By two o'clock in the morning I'm home and in my warm bed. No messages and no regrets about the night. Just tired as all get out. I proceed to kiss myself good night, if you know what I mean, and I'm out.

IT'S NINE-FIFTEEN on Saturday morning. Donovan calls to wake me up.

"What did you do last night, Mom?"

"Ahh, I went for a drink with a coworker. I did get in kind of late so I'm glad you woke me up. I have a lot to do today. How's Chloe?" I ask through a composed yawn.

"She's fine. She's still sleeping. But the reunion starts at eleven at Cadillac Park so I think Grandma is going to wake her up."

"Well, have fun and tell Grandpa Pijeaux I said hello."

Grandpa, my father-in-law, remarried a beautiful woman after he divorced my ex-husband's mom. Actually, his new wife is as black as the night and the complete opposite of all that Creole crap. Yeah, he went straight down south and I have nothing but love for him. We actually share similar views on his ex-wife. I'd love to be a bird in the tree and check out Miss Evilene's attitude toward the new Mrs. Pijeaux.

"Call me when you get back from the park, okay?"

"Okay, Mom. Have a good day!"

"Bye, my love."

I ARISE SLOWLY as I make an agreement with myself to walk around most of the day looking whooped. Most of what I have planned includes long overdue chores and checking out the Internet to see what broadcasting jobs are available. Maybe I'll read a book.

I decide to clean out my closet and separate clothes that need to go to the cleaners. I'll wash dirty clothes, rearrange my dresser drawers and organize my office desk files. I drudge through old résumé tapes that I need to send to television stations when I apply for broadcasting jobs. Hopefully I'll come across a few stories I've done that would serve well as a final demo tape so I can have them edited. Perhaps I'll gather old shoes and clothes to donate to my church and even rearrange my bedroom furniture. I'm on a roll! I know the kids hate being around me when I'm in this mood. It means I'm being the director, and if I'm moving furniture, they know something's on my mind.

I know Kareem has gotten through one night of his family reunion weekend. His dirty deeds are almost done. Now he'll only have to stay away until Monday. What is all of this reunion madness this weekend anyway? I mean, between the Pijeauxes and Kareem's family it kinda makes me think of my blood relatives. Wonder what they're doing today. Right now it's just my brother and me left since my older brother died. We don't have much communication with my real father. But my stepfather is always there for my mother, praise God. I suppose I'll visit my mom tomorrow after church. She suffers from Alzheimer's disease. Down south it's called senility, but I think it's the same thing. Convalescent home visits are difficult. But I can always tell my mom gets a real kick out of seeing my face and hearing my voice. That alone brings me pleasure. I cannot compare the heartbreak I feel in seeing her in that condition with the evolution she's going through at this time in her life.

As I remove my clothes from the dryer, I notice

some papers are stuck to the side of the inside
drum. I pull one slip of paper away and notice it
is the business card of my new female friend, totally ruined. Most of the print is faded down to a
blur. The other, oh my God! It's Malik's picture! It
is so ruined and wrinkled and torn that you can
barely tell it's a photograph. I felt as though the
outcome of that photo would symbolize the outcome of our friendship. Couldn't I have taken
better care of this picture if it meant that much to
me? What was I thinking? Didn't I check my
pants pockets? And why did I put it in my pocket
anyway? It's almost like when a friend buys you
a plant and you let it die. The care and attention
given sort of symbolizes and measures your caring for that person.

I scramble to glance at his perfect cocoa face
and it turns out I can see much more of him than
I thought. As I turn it over, I realize it's the writing on the back that I have trouble reading. In
particular, the telephone numbers. How will I get
in touch with him since he would no longer be at
the studio? Maybe I can write the school, but
which one? I could call people in the department,
but not the girls. My head is reeling with just how
I could be this stupid. Maybe if I hadn't been so
drunk last night I probably would have thought
to take it out of the pocket of my jeans and perhaps I could have slept with the damn thing. That
would have kept it from washing machine hell!
Mariah, you dummy!

I try to make out the faded numbers. The prefix could be 336 or 886 or 338 or 888 or . . . Oh,

hell. There are too many combinations to cover. I know the area code and I know the last four digits are 4624.

I run to the phone and dial every combination and politely excuse the call if I don't recognize the voice. After seven or eight times, I hear the party answer, "Hello, talk to me!"

I am unable to speak or hang up. It is Malik's deep, unforgettable bass voice. I just sit there feeling like *America's Most Wanted* prank caller. I put the receiver down slowly and run for my phone book. As I write the number in my telephone book, the phone rings. I quickly answer, "Hello."

"Hello, who is this?"

"Who is this?" I reply.

"Did you just call here? Maybe you had the wrong number?"

Oh no, it is him!

"Ahh, Malik?"

"Mariah?" he asks surprisingly.

"Yes, it's me. How are you?" He must think I'm insane.

"Fine, why did you hang up?"

"Well, it's a long story. I'm sorry, I didn't mean to have you call me back."

"No, I'm glad I did. Thank God for call return—or star sixty-nine!"

Shit, no joke, I'm thinking.

Malik says, "Well, maybe you'll tell me one day. I was thinking about you a minute ago. I can't believe you called, or I called, or whatever. What's up?"

"What's up? Ahh, just cleaning the house. You

know, housewife duties without the husband, I always say."

"Maybe one day you'll tell me that story too. I assume you were married once before," he inquires.

"Yes, your assumption is correct. Maybe one day I'll go into it, but, Malik, my ex-husband died."

"I'm sorry, I hope I didn't appear to be insensitive. I had no idea."

"It's okay, no one really knows what to say. If anyone had told me I'd be taking care of two kids whose father died I would have sworn they were lying."

"Two kids? I thought you had three," he says, sounding confused.

"Malik, this conversation is getting a little deep. Would you mind if we take a detour to a less intense topic?" I ask respectfully.

"No problem, actually, how about if we talk about the two of us having a meal together? No serious topics, I promise. Only happy, fun, light, nice, peaceful stuff. How about it?" I cannot refuse this offer.

"When?" I ask, thinking the sooner the better.

"Tonight! I'm free, are you?"

"Well, I hadn't planned anything. Are you talking about dinner?"

"Yes, definitely dinner. I can pick you up whenever you say," he says, sounding accommodating.

"Well, how about if I meet you somewhere?" I suggest.

"That's cool! You don't want me to know where you live or meet your kids yet, right?" he guesses.

"Something like that!"

"Okay, what time is good for you?"

"You let me know the time and place and I'll be there." Am I trying to follow?

"Wow, and you're letting me make the choice, or at least allowing me to think I am. Okay, how about seven o'clock at the Cheesecake Factory in the Marina?"

"I'll meet you in the waiting area, if that's all right with you?"

"That's fine. I'm looking forward to it," he graciously exclaims.

"Okay, see you then."

9

WHAT DO YOU WEAR when you're thirty-nine years old and about to meet a man nearly half your age for dinner? I could slip on some tight jeans and my trendy little tight T-shirt that's cut just high enough to expose my navel like the teenagers wear. But my navel is not my best feature. I'll leave that to the kids. Or maybe the baggy long pants and flowing loose top to camouflage my figure. No, that makes me look too matronly. Oh, these tight black capri pants might work but they hug my rear end like they're painted on. I could wear a long top to cover my big hips. Fuck it, I'll be daring and wear a short-cropped top, slightly low cut. After all, my new *friend* has no idea what attributes I possess. He's only seen me twice in those long temp dresses with huge summer flowers all over. Kind of virginal looking. Maybe that's why he wants to "get to know me better." Wait'll he gets a load of me! But do I want him to see all of this? Heck yes, I do! The black capri pants and my pale lavender sleeveless vest that zips. I'll leave the zipper just above the danger level. I'll accent the outfit with tiny silver angel earrings, my sterling silver bangle and my silver Prada antique-style watch. I might even get a little cute and wear my light frosted lip gloss over the sheer brown sugar shade I normally wear. The shoes will be my new three-inch silver slides I bought this summer. I'll accent my toes with Chloe's Sugar and Spice frosted nail polish. I might even sport a toe ring. My fingernails are always short, bare and natural, no acrylics for me. Besides, fingernail polish chips too often. And the fragrance for the evening is Trésor. He asked for it!

I arrive and the valet parks my car as I see Malik sitting on the bench outside the restaurant door. He quickly stands up when he sees me walking toward him.

He is wearing a classic pair of black dress pants and a crisp, clean ivory white shirt that buttons up all the way to that dark, long neck of his. He looks very *GQ*, like he just stepped from the pages of a magazine. He looks like a model, so fine and clean cut. Not at all hip-hop or too youthful. Actually I can detect a deep sense of maturity by the way he walks and carries himself. He is mature beyond his years, maybe by a few years, maybe even more.

He stops and puts out his hand. I respond as if his every wish is my command, with trust and curiosity. My hand falls limp at the wrist and my fingers dangle like a ballerina as he gently raises my hand above my head and spins me around to partake upon a panoramic view. I'm thinking, great choice of wardrobe, Mariah. He is obviously a very visual creature. I'll bet he makes love with just enough light to appreciate the full silhouette as opposed to a brother who only wants to feel his way around in the dark. I'll bet he likes soft dim lights and candles, and . . .

"Mariah, you look so beautiful, you are a sight for sore eyes. This outfit definitely has a different flavor from what I've seen you in at work," he conveys, checking me out top to bottom.

"Thanks. And you look very handsome yourself, Mr. Tolliver."

"Thank you, Ms., what is your last name anyway?"

"It's Pijeaux. Like Pee-joe."

"Different! And"—he takes in a whiff as he lowers his nose toward my neck—"you smell great!"

"Thanks again."

He nods his head in affirmation and gives me a once-over.

"I made sure our name is on the list to be seated soon. They gave me this dang-gonned pager that's suppose to go off when our table is ready. I've never seen that before, but they're so crowded and this is such a big place, I guess it makes sense."

I reply in agreement, "Yeah, I've always thought whoever came up with that idea is making some money, huh?"

"Right, right! Do you want to sit outside here and wait or sit at the bar and have a drink? It's your call."

"I'll leave it up to you." Feminine.

"Well, let's have a drink at the bar while we wait," he suggests like a gentleman.

"I hope you don't mind me asking . . . you are old enough to drink, right?"

"Yes, I am, but you're the one whose ID they'll be checking, not mine," he teases through his compliment.

As we walk toward the bar I ask, "Malik, exactly how old are you anyway?"

"I just turned twenty-one in May," he appears happy to admit.

"Wow, a newly authorized drinker, huh?" I ask.

"Sort of, but even so, I don't indulge that often anyway."

"Oh, you don't indulge, huh?"

"Not that often. Do you?"

"I have been known to get my drink on, as they say," I reply, trying to sound hip.

"I ain't mad at you."

"So what day is your birthday, May what?"

"May twenty-first."

"May twenty-first? Wow, that's my dad's birthday," I tell him with amazement.

"Well then, he's gotta be a great man. All men born on this day are some deep brothas," he jokes with confidence and sincerity.

I quietly smile as we look around for a place to sit. We spot one seat at the bar as Malik says, "Here, you sit and I'll stand."

As I sit down, I look around the bar area and notice a few people staring at us, or him, or me. My mind starts running away with me about what they could be thinking. I am certain I over-hear one girl whispering, "That must be her son." Another man says, "I wonder what he sees in her." Another says, "Well, if that's not robbing the cradle, I don't know what is." The lady sitting next to me looks me up and down and I smile. She leans in to ask, "Where did you get that top? I bought one just like it but it's long-sleeved, and I couldn't find one like yours."

As she admires my top I reply in relief, "I bought it at Charlotte Russe. They have other colors also."

"Very nice," she responds as she smiles and turns back toward her date, who is also looking and smiling. I return the smile and refocus my attention upon my date.

"So that makes you a Gemini, right?" I ask.

"Yes, it does." He reads the look on my face. "Uh-oh, what does that mean to you? Have you had past experiences with many Gemini men?" he asks.

"Only my father and my ex-husband, that's all."

"Is that good or bad?"

I explain, "Well, I don't judge everyone by that; I actually believe astrology can be accurate but mainly I read it for fun. In the case of my ex-husband, the experience was good. In the case of my father, the jury is out. But one thing is for sure, they're complete opposites."

"You know, I was reading an article in some magazine last week about astrology. One thing it stated is that most Gemini people, like me, have the gift of gab. Which I agree is true. And that we have the uncanny ability to do two things at once, which I thought was interesting," he tells me.

If I could keep my dirty mind anywhere outside the vicinity of the gutter I think I could really enjoy this evening.

He continues, "Actually, there was an interesting question in this magazine about relationship fantasies."

"Relationship fantasies?"

"Yes, I thought about it and I decided my fantasy would be for the rest of my life to be a game show and each morning I would choose a new and exciting reality from behind door number one, two or three. I'd have a car and driver at my disposal twenty-four hours a day and pillow talk would be more exciting than sex for me and my life mate. But for now, I just live my life that way. I treat each morning like a new opportunity to choose an exciting reality," he says, looking at the ceiling and then directly into my eyes.

"That's beautiful," I profess, in admiration of his creativity. "I've never really thought of that." Okay, he's a talker in bed, I've figured out that much.

"What would yours be?"

"Well, let's see." I pause for a moment, also looking to the ceiling for an answer. "I suppose I've always wanted to be in a place resembling . . . Shangri-la. It would just be my soul mate and me. No telephones and no interruptions from life and I would be in total telepathic attunement with my lover. No lying or broken promises. Each sacrificing whatever and whenever for the sake of the other. I've had dreams about that before."

"I don't think you have to go to Shangri-la for that. You can make that happen right here in L.A., if you believe," he suggests.

"Oh, I believe, all right. And being the optimist we Sagittarius people are supposed to be, I have a great amount of hope."

Mariah, you're talking too much already, I tell myself. Men like it when you listen attentively and take in all they have to say with an "in awe" type look. Be feminine and listen.

Malik asks, "Speaking of men in your life, where's your boyfriend tonight? And does he know you're here with me?"

Just then the bartender asks if we'd like anything. I order Alizé and he snickers for a minute. He then orders Hennessey and Coke. And the bartender asks a very predictable question: "Can I see your ID, sir?"

I smile at him while he takes out his wallet and hands it to the bartender in a cooperative way that's apparently respectful of the bartender's duties.

"I'm sorry, sir. I must ask anyone who looks under twenty-five," the bartender says after handing the wallet back to Malik.

"No problem."

"Really, Malik, the time to worry is when they stop asking. Like in my case," I say as if he should be proud.

"Well, I'd ask you, darling. So when is your next birthday?" he asks while replacing his wallet into his pants pocket.

"December fourth," I answer. I suppose we're about to get down to the nitty-gritty now.

"And you'll be . . . ?" he asks with a direct hit.

"Twenty-five for the fifteenth time," I answer falsely as a way to joke through the nervous reality of my preconfession. "No, I'll be the dreaded forty."

Without missing a beat he replies, "I'm sorry, but that's still amazing to me."

"It's even more amazing to me. I don't know where the years went. Last time I looked around I was your age."

"And the fact that you're single amazes me even more. I know you think I forgot, but tell me what your boyfriend thinks about this meeting between us."

Malik jumps slightly and reaches into his pants pocket as the vibration of the pager catches him off guard.

"Wow, that's a trip. I guess our table is ready. You've been saved twice," he says.

We grab our drinks and Malik pays the bar tab. We walk to the reservation desk and once again I am noticing people staring as the hostess shows us to our table.

As we prepare to be seated, Malik pulls out my chair. I notice the hostess giving him the once-over. He sits slowly as if his manly thighs are too tightly pumped with testosterone or as if his blood-pumped, diamond-cut muscles are too entirely massive to quite close his legs, or maybe another bulge is blocking the way.

"Here are your menus, sir. Your waiter will be right with you," the waitress says, flashing her pearly whites. Malik doesn't catch her flirting eye. But as a woman, I know exactly what she's thinking. I have to admire her for her good taste.

While we peruse the menus, I'm debating whether to bring up the answer to his question, but I don't want to dominate the conversation. So I'll keep my answers brief and to the point.

"Have you eaten here before? What's good?" I inquire.

"I was here for lunch recently and had the ribs. They were very good. And of course the cheesecake is a requirement."

"Is it good? I always seem to be too full from dinner to order any."

"Very good. We'll have to order some to go tonight so you can try it later."

"That would be nice." Way to go, girl; compliment your new friend. After all, men see this whole restaurant thing as an experience worthy of a grade that includes their very being. If you give it a D, they take it personally as if they owned the restaurant and cooked the food. If you give it an A, they think they're all that, or so I'm told. "I think I'll order the meatloaf," I say, trying not to sound like I'm making small talk.

"You sure like meat loaf, don't you?" he asks, peering across the gigantic menu.

"I'm telling you, it was one of my mom's award-winning dishes, and I'm always comparing it to her recipe."

"How did the one at the studio compare?"

"It didn't. It was too bland. It needed some

Lawry's or something. You know, some soul!" Although I suppose no one's recipe will ever compare."

"Yeah, it's like my mom's fried chicken. It was on."

"How long has it been since you had some? Hopefully before you came here for the summer. Does she cook upon request?"

He closes his menu and places it to the side. "Mariah, my mom died when I was nine years old. But I still remember her cooking like it was yesterday."

"I'm sorry. I didn't mean to appear insensitive."

"You didn't know, no problem. Actually I enjoy reminiscing about her and replaying those memories like videos in my head. There's nothing like a little boy and his mom."

I close my menu as well. "Just so you know, my mom is in a convalescent home. She has dementia from poor maintenance of her high blood pressure. It's very hard to see her like that."

"I'll bet it is. That must be real tough on you. Are the two of you close?"

"Oh, she's like my sister because I'm the only girl and we grew up doing girlie things. But anyway, would you say you look like your mother?" I ask, placing the topaz-blue dinner napkin over my lap.

"I'm built like my dad. But my facial features are the spitting image of my mom through and through. Actually, you resemble her. She's light-skinned and she was very tall."

Suddenly I begin to wonder if Malik likes older

women or likes me because he's looking for a mother figure, mother friend, mother role model.

The waiter approaches and begins his presentation of specials as Malik spreads his napkin across his lap as well, giving me his undivided attention. "Good evening, our specials tonight are . . ." I am lost in the conversation and Malik's admission about losing his mother . . . "Fresh salmon fillet, with capers, herbs and baby shrimp, served in a creamy white sauce" . . . My son was also nine when his dad died. How does one find the strength to go on at such a young age? I feel for him and I also feel like I want to breast-feed him right here and now . . . "Filet mignon, marinated in a light red wine with sauteed mushrooms and onions topped with yellow tomatoes" . . . Malik, I too want to know so much about you, it's as though you're thirty-seven, or forty-two or forty-six, okay, maybe thirty . . . "Can I get you anything to drink or perhaps an appetizer?"

"Malik, why don't you order the appetizer. Another drink would be fine." Feminine.

"All right, another Alizé and a Hennessey and Coke, please." He opens his menu again. "The stuffed mushrooms are stuffed with what, sir?" he inquires.

"Crabmeat!" the waiter states.

I immediately reply, "Oh, great choice, I love crab and mushrooms."

"Then we'll have one order of the stuffed mushrooms and a few more minutes to order. Thanks," he says as the accommodating waiter moves on to the next table.

What a mature way to order and close an encounter with a waiter who I wish would never come back so we can talk. "You know what, I'll have the ribs that you said you tried before and a small dinner salad with ranch."

"Do you want me to order for you?"

"Please, would you?" I respond with a smile.

"Of course I will. You know, most women would be flaggin' down the waiter, asking for a toothpick and more water and more napkins and a better table and asking why they don't have what they want and looking around the room to see who's who in this joint. That's just what I'm talking about. Older women are so classy and feminine and reserved—most older women, that is."

"How would you know?"

"I've dated a few older ladies," he admits with a sense of pride.

"Is that your preference?"

"After my experiences with the twenty-five-and-under crowd, I've elevated to a more mature age range for more mental compatibility."

"What makes you so mature?"

"I haven't figured that out yet. Maybe it's because I had to take care of myself at a young age. Also, because I don't have time to play childish games with people. I've learned that life is too short for bullshit, excuse my language," he interjects, taking a swig of straight Hennessey.

"I agree with you. Sometimes hard knocks will teach you a crash course in mortality. What's the longest period of time you dated an older woman?"

"Seven months."

"And how old was she?"

"She was thirty-four and I was nineteen. It just didn't work out. Not because of the age difference but because she was looking for a father for her daughter and I wasn't looking to replace her father. I loved her daughter because I loved her. I think I was more convenient to her than anything else."

"Oh?" I ask, slowly spreading the melted butter on two pieces of hot French bread.

Malik takes a slice. "Thanks. What about you, lady? What's the age of the youngest man you ever dated?"

"He was actually twenty-six and it was just a couple of dates. You see, I didn't know he was twenty-six. He told me he was thirty-five and one night his friend spilled the beans on him. It wasn't so much that he was younger. It was just that he lied," I admit while taking a small bite of bread and wiping my mouth with my napkin.

"Can you blame him for wanting to get next to you? He was probably intimidated."

"More like immature. Anyway, I got back together with my boyfriend. Otherwise it probably would have gone further," I say, taking hold of a cold glass of ice water.

"Okay, now we're back to this boyfriend again. Please answer me before the waiter comes back."

The waiter walks up and says, "Here are your drinks and your appetizer. Are you ready to order?"

Malik smiles and points at me as I sip my water, peering over the rim of my glass, knowing he's gonna get me to answer him yet. He orders the ribs for both of us. The waiter takes the menus and walks away.

"Why did you laugh when I ordered Alizé?" I question, changing the subject again.

"Because my friends and I say that's what the young girls order because Tupac and Biggie made it popular in their songs. Don't change the subject, Mariah, you have my full attention."

"His name is Kareem and he is spending the weekend with his family. They're in town from Chicago. He doesn't know I'm here, and due to the fact that we had a big argument on Thursday night, I'm sure he doesn't care," I assert, cutting a small bit of the mushroom and taking a bite. "This is really good. You made a great choice."

"Thanks. Kareem, is he Muslim?" he asks while preparing to try out a piece for himself.

"No, he used to play basketball and his teammates gave him that name."

"Oh, I'm sorry the two of you had an argument. I know how that can be. But do you really think he doesn't care that you're here with me?"

"Well, I suppose the truth is that I don't care. That's what's up."

"Oh snap!"

" 'Snap,' Malik, is that like 'Oh shit'?" I joke.

"No doubt!" he replies, playing along with my quip.

"Is that like 'yes'?" I ask as I pick up my drink.

"For-sho!"

"Cut it out!" I request, giggling through another sip of Alizé.

"What kind of guy attracts you, Mariah?"

"One who is intelligent," I affirm without missing a beat.

"My last IQ test was one hundred forty!"

"And funny."

"Did you hear the one about . . . ?"

We laugh out loud, only to stop in a pregnant pause. I take a big gulp this time and swallow it down as I notice he reaches his left hand over to protectively cover my hand on the table. He swirls his Hennessey in his glass with his right hand and says, "I want to give a toast to you for being woman enough to give a man his space and acknowledge his existence to another man who I'm sure you know wants to get to know you better. I see you as a good woman and you deserve the best." We raise our drinks with a solid mutual clink of our glasses.

I want to reach my big butt over the table and kiss those perfect lips just for being a gentleman. Yes, a gentleman. That's how a gentleman should communicate.

"Malik, I wouldn't praise myself too much. After all, I'm out with another man, friend or not, and Kareem and I haven't officially broken it off. And as far as whether or not I'm allowing him his space, he'd take it even if I didn't."

We talk on and on so smoothly. It's like we've known each other forever. Sometimes we just pause to shake our heads back and forth and stare at each other as if to ask why. Why is he so young, why is she taken, why is he leaving, why is she so much older?

Our dinner is served and before we know it, we are wiping our barbecue-stained hands with our napkins over an empty plate of clean bones and parsley. I am also halfway through my third drink and I'm feeling it too.

"Mariah, you haven't asked me if I have anyone in my life," he states as if he'd hoped I would.

"I've learned after nearly forty years not to assume because it makes an *ass* out of *u* and *me*, right?"

"True. That means you should ask."

"You're right because I must admit I've sort of assumed that you're seeing Brenda from work. And I've accepted the possibility of you having a woman back in New York."

"Where did you get that from?"

"Living and learning," I say, shrugging my shoulders.

"I do not have a girl back home, but I date. And yes, I have taken Brenda out. She's cool and all, but she's too immature."

"Well, what would her perception of your relationship with her be?" I curiously inquire.

"Definitely not a relationship. Just a getting-to-know-each-other thing."

"Are you attracted to her?" I ask, taking my final sip of alcohol.

"Yes."

"That's honest."

"Mariah, we all have a life, but I am single and unattached. Believe me, when a woman and I are committed, that person will know it."

"Anyway, it's really none of my business,

Malik. You can do whatever you want to do. You're a healthy, virile, good-looking man with a lot of maturity and ambition. You're what we women call a great catch," I say, tipping my empty glass toward him.

"Thanks, but some of us are in the water and some of us are in the boat. To be honest with you, I wish you were in the water with me. The ones in the water haven't been caught yet."

"Well, I could be cast overboard at any minute, Malik, or just jump ship," I point out in humor.

Again we laugh as the waiter inquires, "Will there be anything else, sir?" I hadn't even noticed that the busperson had cleaned off the table at some point.

"Anything else for you, babe?"

"No thanks, I'm cool."

The waiter hands Malik the bill. Malik actually pays with a gold American Express card—even I don't have one of those. He even leaves a twenty-five percent tip, not like those cheap men who leave five or ten, or like some, none at all. I usually end up sneaking a peek at the tip amount, which tells me a lot about a man. There have been times when I'd end up leaving the table with my tail tucked between my legs as the waitress stares us down as if to say "Cheap bastards." I've even reached into my purse to make up the difference. After that, I've gone straight home only to never return my date's calls. It lets you know how giving they are and how appreciative they are of service workers who survive on tips. A tippin' man gets an extra three points from me every time. I think a good tip is a sign of respect and appreciation for a job well done. If I could tip Malik, I would. I'm impressed already.

"Okay, now what would you like to do? It's only nine-fifteen," he asks.

I can't believe we've been talking for more than two hours. "By the way, that was great. Those were the best ribs I've had in a long time. Tasted like we were in the 'hood at Smokey's."

"You'll have to take me there one day. Oh man! I forgot to order your cheesecake."

"Oh no. That's not necessary. Where would I put it?" I ask, placing my hand over my stomach.

"Oh no, you are going to eat it tomorrow or give it to your kids, but you have to try it," he insists.

He actually calls the waiter back to the table and asks for a whole cheesecake to go. I stare at him with a "you didn't have to" look. As he captures my seductive glance, I blow him a kiss. He catches it in his hand and puts it in his pants pocket with his wallet. Just where I'd like my kiss to be, somewhere in that general vicinity. Again, why do I always turn something so innocent into something so damn dirty?

He slides a smile to me and says, "You have the biggest, brownest eyes I've ever seen. Every time I picture you in my mind, your big eyes are so overwhelming—kinda like Natalie Wood."

"That was way before your time. What do you know about her?" I ask after the waiter brings the cheesecake to go.

"When I was young, my dad used to talk about

how beautiful she was." He stands and pulls out my chair again as we proceed to exit. "He always said my mom had eyes like her. You have Natalie Wood eyes too, Mariah. Deep, dark and trusting. I believe eyes are the window to so much that is fragile and innocent. I can see deep inside of you, and my worst fear is to hurt you. A man should know he's on to something when his one desire is to make one special woman happy. That's when you know you care."

A man! A masculine energy twenty-one-year-old man wanting to protect me. But what is this fixation with his mom, or am I tripping? Damn, Mariah, his mom died. It's called respect and cherishing her memory.

He pays the valet and asks, "So, any suggestions?"

"What do you suggest?" Feminine.

"How about a movie?" He imparts his suggestion without missing a beat.

"Sure. There's a theater next door if you want to check out what's playing."

10

MALIK TAKES MY KEYS from the valet and opens my car door for me. I follow him to the Marina Theater. A new movie has just opened and there are crowds everywhere. He motions for me to park in the first space we find, and then I get in his car. He's driving his grandfather's brand-new 750i BMW. It's pearl white with palomino gray leather interior. He looks like Somebody in it. He parks and comes around to open the door for me. I have to remind myself to just sit there and wait until he comes around. It's the type of thing we women forget to enjoy after years of being with someone who doesn't take the time to treat us like a lady. But it's not always the fault of most men. We women are so damn independent and so in a hurry that we just hop our happy butts right on out before he gets a chance and then we close the door.

We actually find two seats as the movie is just starting. I don't like to talk during a movie, and I realize that seeing a movie is not such a great idea for a first date, or excuse me, a first friend meeting. But just being with him is cool. As the movie begins, I notice he doesn't chitchat loudly or annoyingly. We just sit quietly and munch on our popcorn.

There is an intense sex scene, which I know arouses him and everyone else, including me, of course. Suddenly I reach for his arm. He smiles at me and places his hand over mine.

"Are you comfortable?" he protectively inquires.

"Very much so," I answer as I look into his eyes like a kitten about to be fed some gourmet seafood treats.

As I put my head on his shoulder, I can feel his shoulder muscles ripple and tighten to greet my head. I feel like Goldilocks, having just found the right place to settle in. I then rub my hand up and down his arm. Why am I doing this? I am just reminded that this is not the body of some out-of-shape, middle-aged, lazy man who has let himself go by watching sports all weekend and drinking beer. His arms are powerful and strong. His muscular forearm is tight and forceful, shaped as if an artist has drawn him and then presented his work of art to a classroom of college students to observe in some art history appreciation class. These biceps and triceps are ripped and lithe. Undeniably he is flexing for me and it is working. Mariah, this is an athletic, brawny young man, girl. Can you hang with this or not? Perhaps I'd better check myself before I wreck myself, as they say.

He gently puts his hand on my forearm and begins to pat my skin as if to say, "It's okay, baby, don't let the ruggedness scare you." I realize the combination of his sexy aura and the mixture of cognac and passion fruit is kicking in. I quickly raise my head. I'm feeling goofy and kind of off centered. I try to focus on the rest of the movie, but the only thought I have is how I want to know him, all of him. I am no longer worried about what people think of us together. I want to experience Malik one hundred percent just because he has impressed the hell out of me. I decide I want to make love to him here and now! In my imagination I expose my thoughts to him and he obliges. He stands up and firmly pulls me to my feet, turns me around so that my back is to him, and unzips my pants and pulls them down to my calves. He slides my G-string to the side, proceeds to sit down and pulls me down to sit on his lap. Yes, for everyone to see.

"Are you sleeping? You're breathing hard, baby!"

I awaken to his voice, feeling as if I've been discovered. "No, I'm just trying to focus. I think I'm a little drunk, or buzzed as they say."

"Well, we can leave if you're ready to go."

"The movie isn't even over, Malik. I wouldn't want to miss the rest of it," I say while panting as if I'm having a panic attack.

"No, I think you look a little flushed. In my opinion you need to walk off that cognac."

"I'm sorry, I suppose I had two too many."

"Actually, you had four."

"No, I didn't," I say, giving him a light elbow to his side.

"No, I'm just kidding. How are you going to drive home?"

"Maybe we can get some coffee or something."

"Okay, where?"

"Why don't we go to my house?" I suggest as he smiles. We stand together and prepare to exit. His arm is tightly wrapped around my waist as we make our way out of the theater.

"All right, but you can't drive your car, no way."

"Malik, forget my car. Take me home, please?"

11

I SUPPOSE I'M SOBER ENOUGH to direct him to my house. The next thing I know we are in my living room.

"Where are the kids tonight?" Malik inquires.

"They're away for the weekend with their grandmother. A family reunion."

"And you didn't go?"

"No, it's a weird kind of thing I have with their dad's family. Not exactly functional," I inform him while he checks out my digs.

"What family is?"

"True. Would you mind filling two coffee cups with some hot water from my water cooler? I only have instant. Is that okay?"

"I'm cool with that," he mumbles under his breath while bouncing past me as he enters my kitchen. "You're the one who needs it."

"What did you say? I heard you," I reply as I go to my bathroom to take off my shoes, rinse my face and take a few Tylenol.

Malik yells, "And take some Tylenol or something so you don't have a hangover. You little lightweight."

"I'm way ahead of you."

I dim the lights ever so slightly as I return to the living room. Malik has already made a cup of coffee for me. I add the cream and sugar to finish the preparation.

"Maybe you can just drink it black this time. What do you say?"

"Oh, funny man, trying to sober me up?"

"I just want you to feel better. Are you usually like this?"

"No, I don't know what happened. After all, I ate a wonderful dinner first. Who knows?"

"I'd say this is a good time to try that cheesecake. I'm glad I put it in my car. I'll go down and get it. By the way, nice place. And on a temp's salary too?" he teases.

"Bye, go! And thanks."

I waste no time lighting a couple of my tall torch candles. I decide to burn some mango incense, and place a log in the fireplace. I then put on some soft music while Malik goes down to his car. The best CD I can find is Toni Braxton's *Secrets*. I feel like a playgirl setting up her nest for the kill. Part of me wants to believe getting romantic is all Malik has in mind anyway, so we might as well get it over with. That way he can go ahead and tell his buddies what it's like. Part of me wants it more than he does, maybe out of curiosity. But experience has taught me that nothing could ever come of this anyway, so what the hell. The rest of me thinks we should just go ahead and get busy and then I'll wake up and this dream will be over with.

"Nice touch," Malik says as he walks back through the door. "Smooth."

"I'm just getting comfortable. I do this for myself all of the time," I reply in obvious denial.

I take the cheesecake from him and proceed to the kitchen to get two plates and forks.

"Which way to your bathroom?"

"Straight back, first door on your right."

I cut two thin slices, already feeling a tad bit steadier than I was during the movie. I place the plates on my black marble sofa table and bring our coffee cups over so we can enjoy our dessert.

"Baby, you like angels, don't you," Malik comments as he returns from the bathroom.

"I have them all around because I believe they surround me in spirit."

"I've never seen gold angels like those, and the black angels are so lifelike. They're beautiful. Your bathroom is hooked up. Purple walls with the black rugs and towels . . . you missed your calling as a decorator."

"Actually, my girlfriend Ariana is a designer and she came up with the royal color scheme of my apartment—the blue and gold, green and gold and purple and gold. She asked me to describe myself in one word, and I said 'regal,' so she went with that."

"Regal you are. But I've never seen purple and gold walls."

"Thank you. My bedroom is actually decorated with the same color scheme."

"Oh, really?" He gulps. "Let's try this cheesecake," he suggests with naivete as we lean back on my emerald green velvet sofa.

I cannot believe I am seducing this young boy. He *has* to know what's up.

Malik grabs his fork and begins to cut his first sliver. I touch his hand and gently take the fork from him. I instructionally turn the fork toward him, raise a bite to his mouth and begin to feed him his first piece from the fingertips of an almost forty-year-old woman. Malik opens his mouth to welcomingly permit my entry. His inviting tongue greets the fork as his full Tyson lips close in to capture and admit the rich, creamy flavor. A tiny bit of the cheesecake lingers at the corner of his mouth and he brings his napkin up to take care of it. But not before I gently move in to softly exit my tongue and sweetly lick the cheesecake from the corner of his mouth. Malik momentarily closes his eyes and moans upon my touch. As he begins to open his eyes he glances toward my mouth shyly and I whisper, "Umm, that is the best I've ever had."

With quiet and innocence, Malik implores, "Can I have another piece?"

I purr an ultimatum. "Only if you'll kiss me."

I drop the fork to the floor as Malik tenderly raises my chin to summon my face ever so close to his lips. Instead of kissing my lips he raises his mouth, slightly lowers my chin, begins kissing my big Sade forehead, and then carefully makes his way down to my eyebrows and down my nose. It's as if he's making love to my face. He teasingly avoids my mouth, travels down to my chin and then up around my ears, my ears, my ears. I gently place my hands on each side of his face and slightly back away for a better visual of this masterpiece. I desire to explore those perfect features with my fingertips. I softly touch his thick, chiseled lips with my fingertips, following every line with my index finger. I lightly touch his classic nose from the tip to the bridge and around the nostrils. He clutches my hands in his and begins to kiss my mouth. Not simply thrusting his tongue as far as he can as if he wants to win a prize for tonsil hockey. His kiss is warm and intense, sensitive and slow and mind-blowing. He uses more with lips than tongue, yet tongue too.

He then takes my hand and begins kissing my fingers, each one in order from my pinky. He licks in between my thumb and forefinger, copying oral sex. It is the most erotic pleasure I've ever experienced. He licks the palm of my hand and my wrist bone. Who'd have thought licking a wrist bone could elicit that kind of pleasure? It is like he's exploring my uniqueness and my very being. He kisses the side of my neck as if it has a mind of its own. I pleasingly respond to every inch of his wet, hot tongue as if it is searching for what lies beneath. I whimper in ecstasy upon his touch and moan in pleasure at his skill.

Just then, Malik catches a glimpse of my saxophone tattoo over my heart.

"Can I kiss your saxophone?"

I nod my head, affirmative.

Suddenly, he slowly unzips my big silver zipper and they are exposed. My breasts appear swollen and at full attention as if to say, "We were wondering when we were going to get in on the action," and my nipples are extrasensitive and suddenly as large as I've ever seen them. Kind of like I am a virgin or an old pro. Either way, I haven't known better. If I'm not ready for him now, I never will be.

I grab his massive yet soft hands as I slowly stand up and coyly moonwalk into my bedroom, gazing into his eyes the entire way. My top is unzipped and falling down my shoulders. My bra still clasped beneath my breasts. I leave him standing at the foot of my pine sleigh bed for a brief moment while I light more candles and turn on my soft lavender headboard lights. Toni Braxton is serenading us with "Find Me a Man" as I turn around only to realize he is gesturing for me to come to him. He begins to sit on the side of the bed while he folds over the charcoal corduroy comforter and sits on my fuchsia and noir Egyptian cotton sheets. He slowly lowers me to lay upon my back, carefully lowers himself to me and gently kisses the outer edge of each breast, actually just around the armpit and up to the areola. I'm thinking what experience he must have had in only twenty-one years, or what a 'ho! Or maybe he's never been compelled to explore a real woman like this before and I bring out the freak in him. Shit, I thought I'm the one who's supposed to be teaching him something new— like how we can put those green Popsicles in my freezer to great use. I should be showing him what we can do along the foot of my sleigh bed, how the tile seat in my shower can come in handy, how I can give him the butt massage of his life, how I can help him out by taking one of my nipples into my mouth if he'll take the other, what we can do with those long silk scarves in my nightstand drawer, exactly what a real striptease should be while disrobing from my Victoria's Secret hot-pink harem outfit, how he can watch me spank myself or how we can use what's in that shoe box under my bed.

He then looks deep into my eyes, bad mistake for a lady who is trying not to bond, calls my name, another mistake, and asks me, "Mariah, what's the difference between sugar and Sweet 'n Low?"

"I don't know, Malik, what?" as I giggle seductively.

"This is sugar," he moans and kisses me tenderly on my lips, all lips, wet, sweet, full, and erotic. "And this is Sweet 'n Low!"

And damn it if this giving man doesn't pull off one leg of my pants and go from my nipple to my navel to my goodie trail and beyond. I'm looking down at the top of his beautiful ebony head and I'm thinking, now this is what those ears feel like against my thighs, oh now, this is too damn smooth, smooth, smooo, smm, ssshit!

Riiiiinngggg—my fucking phone rings.

IT'S TWELVE-THIRTY in the morning. The ringer must be on the extrasensory aggravate your ass high volume level.

Malik quickly retreats and says, "You should get that. It might be the kids."

"No," I respond in a frustrated tone.

It rings three times and my message center answers it. I am relieved as I give Malik a green light look as if he should proceed. It rings again, and again, and again and . . . "Hello!"

"Are you awake?" Oh damn, it's Kareem. I hold the receiver in silence, struggling to sit up in the bed while covering my face in shame. I can hear each second pass in the exact beat of the rhythm of my heart. "Hello! Mariah?"

I clear my throat. "What are you doing calling this late?"

"Baby, I want you to come to the hotel and meet my uncle. He's a retard and he's got us talking about his ignorant ass back in the old days. What are you doing?" I glance at Malik, who is now sitting right next to me looking down at the floor.

"Kareem, I'm not going anywhere tonight. I haven't even talked to you . . . ," I say as I sit here with one pant leg hanging from my ankle, breathing at a fast-slow guilty pace, ". . . in more than two days and now you want me to come meet them at twelve-thirty in the morning after you realize there are no new women within your reach tonight. You have more nerve than . . . forget it. I'm hanging up."

"No, I want to come over. I miss you and I'm coming to get my stuff. You always said I could. I need you."

"You're drunk and I'm going now," I threaten.

"I'm on my way," he insists.

"No! Do not come here tonight. I'm not letting you in and I'm hanging up now."

I hang up, and after a few seconds I thankfully realize he does not call back. I look at Malik and say, "I'm sorry! I had no idea he would call," as I rub his back in comfort.

"Maybe it wasn't a good idea to come to your home anyway. I don't know what I was thinking."

"No, I want you here. I invited you and I want you to stay here tonight. I'm enjoying you and I want you to stay," I say as I begin to whimper.

He hugs me and wipes my black mascara-stained tears. I lightly pat the back of his head as I proceed to the bathroom to get some tissue for my burning eyes.

The phone rings once again. I let the service answer. My better judgment tells me to check the messages. There's a total of twelve from the entire evening. I skip over and save eleven of them; the twelfth is Kareem calling from his car. He's on his way over.

12

"BABY, YOU'RE SHAKING! Are you afraid of him? What have the two of you been through that would cause you to be scared?" Malik asks as he stares at my trembling, sweaty hands.

While I focus upon replacing my disheveled clothing I respond, "Yes, I'm scared of him. I'm also tired of his controlling ways and his belief that he can just treat me however he wants to. It's as though I've given him the message that *his needs* are more important than *my wants*. I'm tired of this."

"What do you want?"

I can't believe someone is asking me what I want for a change as opposed to asking me to give them what they want and be what they want and do what they want. "I want to be cherished by a man. I don't want drama. I want to be treated like a queen. I want to experience one hundred percent of myself with a man who adds to my completeness, not takes away from it. I want to be protected and loved. Love is all we're really here for, Malik; that's all we can take with us when it's all said and done. We cannot leave this earth plane with the Corvette or the Academy Award. All we have is the love in our hearts. Love should not hurt and this does."

"I've never really heard anyone put it in those terms, but I agree that the man should be the icing on your cake and not one of the ingredients, because that would mean without him your cake is incomplete. I can say one thing!"

"And . . . ," I remark as I somberly look down toward the floor.

Malik raises my chin toward his face and looks me in the eye. "I'm here, and I'm not going anywhere. No one is going to hurt you. Not tonight and not as long as I'm around."

I gaze into Malik's eyes as we sit in silence, perhaps expecting a knock at the door, perhaps expecting that one will suggest we slip out of the back door. But no one does. An air of strength comes over us that is complete and so right. We sit on the floor in a comfortable yoga position and simply stare into space. We lean into each other as I lower my head to rest upon Malik's massive shoulder. He lightly rubs my shoulder and gently kisses the nape of my neck. Out of the silence comes peace.

WITHIN WHAT SEEMS like moments, the digital clock on my dresser reads 3:15 in the morning. "Would you like some coffee?" I groggily mutter.

"Yes, please, baby. I can make it," he offers.

"Oh no, I need to attempt to stand up, stretch my legs and down a few more Tylenol anyway. Come with me?" I say, taking his hand.

We sit at my oak and white tile kitchen table sipping coffee for hours. We talk about his childhood and mine. My father as well as his father. We discuss his relationship with his grandfather, which began after his mother died. I also divulge my dependence upon my mother after my father left.

"My dad was a tenor saxophone player for his own trio at the Tropicana nightclub in Los Angeles. They called him the Crown Prince. Sammy Davis, Jr., and the Beach Boys used to come by our house when I was little. That's how popular he was back in the sixties.

"We lived in a huge three-story home in Windsor Hills. The house had a pool and a maid's quarters, a huge family room, gourmet kitchen and spiral staircase. We drove around in our brand-new, black, convertible fifty-nine Cadillac. We were rolling in the dough." Malik smiles.

"But late at night when he'd come home drunk after performing, he would yell and scream and accuse my mother of having men over the house. One night she ran down the street with a fireplace poker in her hand begging the neighbors to call the police. I used to hide under my bed or find comfort in my big brother's arms until the ringing in my ears would subside." I take a sip of black coffee and struggle to swallow as if something is stuck in my throat. Malik moves his chair closer to mine as I continue.

"My mother knew he was the one being unfaithful. She always said it was one of the girls at the club. He denied it and would leave for hours at a time while she would lie in her bed like a baby curled up in her own misery. One White woman in particular used to drive by our house when we were playing outside. She'd just park her car down the street and watch us play. I remember my mother running up to her car and chasing her away. The night my father decided to leave, he crept into my room and placed this broken heart under my pillow. I've worn it around my neck for the past thirty-five years."

Malik listens intently, looks down at my necklace. He pauses and asks, "I'm sorry to know you had to go through that. Did your mom ever have a chance to talk to him after that?"

"No. He never showed his face again for another twenty-five years."

"What did you guys do after that?"

"My mother just walked away from the house. I'm sure it was foreclosed upon. She didn't know any better. We struggled to survive. You see, she'd never worked a day in her life and suddenly found herself taking care of three children by herself. Some nights we used to go with her when she worked graveyard. We'd sleep on the floor while she'd answer phones. We moved from place to place every year or so, changing schools as often as we'd change our shoes."

"Did he continue performing?"

"No, he eventually quit the band and got a job parking cars for a valet service."

"Do you remember his music?"

"Oh yes. He recorded 'Mona Lisa,' 'Kansas City,' and a cut called 'Countdown.' He actually recorded the song 'Unforgettable' by Nat King Cole. He played a saxophone version that was beautiful."

"Is that what's up with the saxophone tattoo?" he asks as if he's putting two and two together.

"Yes."

"That's a nice tribute to him."

"You know what? All I've ever wanted to know is *why* he left. My mother has always wanted to know but never asked him. All she knew is that he left her for one of the White women who would come to the club to see him perform. How can he live with himself? How do you abandon a five-year-old little girl? I was Daddy's little girl, or so I thought."

"One day you will know why *if* you're supposed to know. Your dad's actions were part of his evolution in his life, and in the end he has to answer to his maker just as you do," he advises in a tone of wisdom.

"Has that been your mind-set as you've dealt with your dad?"

"Yes. I've had to contemplate the same questions of abandonment by my father. My father left me not long after my mom died. How does a man learn to be a man without a man around? That's why my grandfather stepped in."

"And how does a girl learn to be loved by a man without learning love from her father?"

He answers with a warm glow, "By learning to love and honor herself first. Envision yourself as that little girl who he missed out on raising. Treat yourself like you would treat your own daughter."

"That's a topic all by itself, my daughter. Sometimes I see myself in her and I don't deal with it very well. I'm very hard on her and she's turning out to be just like me. I'm all she's known and I'm not the greatest role model."

"Would it be so bad for her to turn out just like you? I don't think you're a negative role model. What matters is that you are there for her and that you're doing the best you can with what you have. Teach her the things you learn as you learn them, but put yourself first. How can others around you be happy if you're unhappy?"

I prepare to answer that question but instead reply, "You must think I'm a basket case. The typical abandoned woman who can't be happy with a good man. The type of woman who works through her crap with the dogs who are reminding her that she's not good enough to be treated like a queen."

"I don't see you in that way! I know you can be happy with the right man. Sometimes you have to kiss a lot of frogs to work through it. I've kissed a few wrong ones myself. However, I desire to be happy with the right woman as well."

I pause. "Any woman would be blessed to have you, baby."

"Any woman? How about you?" Malik inquires as he grabs my hand with both of his hands and looks me in the eye.

"How about me? How can I be happy with you or anyone right now until I'm happy with myself? How can I be a good woman until I learn that I deserve to be treated well? Only then will I learn to relax and enjoy a man. Oh shit, I have so much work to do on myself," I acknowledge as I shake my head.

"I want to be there for you while you learn it. I want to be with you, Mariah."

I feel elated and skeptical at the same time. "How do you know that? I'm nearly twice your age, I have three kids and I could never give you children. My body couldn't take it. Besides, you deserve a child-bearing young woman you can grow with," I say, almost hoping he'll prove me wrong.

"Your children would be enough for me if it came to that. For now, I just want to be in your life. I'm here and I want us to grow together."

"But just think, you're leaving in two weeks. It's not going to work," I say, tapping my fingers atop the table.

"It's not going to work if you say it's not going to work."

"I'm being realistic."

"Well, I found out something yesterday and I've been wanting to tell you all night. I found out that I have been selected as the *last* pick in the NFL draft. A pro football team has offered me a three-year contract."

I pause again. "You declared yourself eligible for the draft? You didn't go into all that. That's wonderful!" I exclaim as I raise his hands to my face and kiss his beautiful knuckles. "The last pick is just as good as the first."

"How about two hundred forty-first last?" he informs me.

"Yes, even that. Where are you going?"

"I'll be playing in Baltimore for the Ravens."

"Congratulations." I leap to my feet, leaning over to offer my support with a hug. While still seated, Malik hugs me even tighter until reality sets in. I take one step back and stand away from the table. "But this is crazy. Let's just slow down and start thinking and, oh my God. You'll be a professional football player. You can't have some older woman in your life with a high-profile career like that. You can't be serious." I approach the sink and repeatedly rinse out my coffee cup.

"I'm not worried about that. There are other concerns."

"Tell me about those."

"For one, I have to leave school one year early and my grandparents are not too happy."

"I'm sure they're not."

"And I need to go to camp and fight for a spot so I can play and make some serious money," he explains.

"Oh my God, baby, this is such great news." I glance at my wall clock in the kitchen. "It's almost seven in the morning. We've been up far too long."

"Shoot, I have to get my grandfather's car back to him by seven-thirty. He's going to church." He places his cup in the sink and replies, "I'll wash it."

"Oh please, no. I've got it. But thanks," I reply, washing the few dishes, just daydreaming through the window over the sink with my hands sloshing about in the hot, sudsy water.

Malik hugs me from behind, squeezing me around my waist. "With all of our intense conversation, I see you stopped worrying about Kareem showing up," he reminds me.

I snap out of it for a second. "Believe it or not, I wasn't *even* thinking about him. Shoot, I don't even know what day it is," I confess, wiping my hands with the dish towel as I rotate to join his hug.

"I'll tell you what day it is. It's Sunday morning."

"Oh, that means I've got to get to church later."

"How about I go with you?" Wow, two dates in a row.

"Fine with me if you don't mind going to see my mother afterwards. That's what I always do after church."

"I'd like that!" he declares.

"Neither one of us will be going if we don't get my car from that parking lot." I break from our bear hug and walk toward the kitchen door.

"Oh, I forgot. Come on, get to steppin'," he says, patting me on my behind to rush me along.

"Won't you be late getting the car back to your grandfather?"

"Baby, I'm ready when you are."

I hurriedly wash my face and grab my purse.

He drops me off at my car in the empty theater lot. I proceed to get in my car and roll down the window as he reaches his Hershey head in and says, "So where is it and what time?"

"Corner of Jefferson and Overland. It's the City of Angels Church. How's ten-thirty?"

"I'll find you. Now drive carefully." He kisses

my forehead and taps my heart pendant with his fingertips. "See you in a few."

I sit in my Honda for a moment and watch this hunk of a man walk away. He motions for me to pull off first and I oblige.

13

I'M BACK HOME in a flash and I check the messages I'd saved earlier. I have a message from Chloe at nine o'clock last night, a message from Violet, eight from Kareem and one from Carlotta wanting to gossip about the fact that Ariana is not open-minded enough to get the message about Dr. Singer's seminar. The concept of masculine and feminine is starting to make more sense to me than I was willing to admit.

I dare not lie down for fear I will never wake up. I decide to find comfort in a quick soothing bath and deep thought. By nine o'clock it's time to get dressed. I call the kids, but it looks like they've already left for the day so I leave a message. "Hello, Mrs. Pijeaux, Chloe and Donovan. I'm just calling to wish you a beautiful day filled with lots of family and fun. Call me when you return. I'll talk to you later." As I am leaving the message, a call clicks in. It is Kareem.

"Why did you leave? Your car was gone. That's cold-blooded that you left knowing I was on my way. Where did you go?"

Oh my goodness. He drove by last night and

because my car was not in the garage he left. Thank God Malik's car was parked on the street.

"Kareem, we have to talk and I mean tonight. When does your family leave?"

"Not until Monday. I'll be with them all night tonight."

"Well then, Monday is fine. Do not plan anything else. We have to get together and discuss some things," I say firmly.

"Okay, but I want to know where you ran off to last night and when did you get back home? And don't say you were at Violet's house. I know you weren't because I drove by her house too."

"Good-bye. I'm getting ready to go."

"Where? I wanted to stop by real quick and borrow your VCR before you leave."

"No! Good-bye."

"Let me talk to Donovan for a second."

"No, you just want to slip in a question about whether or not I was home last night. Besides, they're gone for the weekend."

"*What?* You've been alone since when?"

"Why is it that you always think the only time I can fool around is when they go away? Do you date me because I have kids and you know I'm not going to be in the streets all night like some single women? That's so asinine! Good-bye!" I slam the phone to end the verbal disappointment.

He calls back and I let it ring and ring. I think he feels as though he's losing control and it is driving him nuts. Control was and has been the main issue through all these years. He assumes I can't live without him. All this time I've been in limbo with him, going nowhere. I can no longer continue being a fool because I'm afraid of being alone, being abandoned or just plain old unwanted. It's driving me crazy.

I CAREFULLY and gracefully step out of my car because my navy blue pin-striped skirt is much shorter than the skirts I normally wear to service. But I am feeling a little different today, so why not? My suit is accented with a beige satin blouse with a soft feminine bow tied at the waist. My three-strand pearl necklace is in full effect as well as my small teardrop pearl earrings. These three-inch, steel-gray sling-backs have me kicking up to about six-foot plus, which is cool because Malik is definitely someone I can look up to. I turn to lock my car door while out of the corner of my eye I see Malik exiting the passenger side of the white BMW. He waves to acknowledge me and approaches with pep in his step as the Beamer pulls off.

"You look like an angel, Mariah. Now I know why you like angels but they don't have leggggs like that, girl. Where do you hide your wings?" he jokes as he peeks behind me.

"Be real." I blush.

"No, I'm serious. And thanks for letting me come with you."

"My pleasure. You look pretty handsome yourself."

Malik is wearing a wheat-colored Italian suit that puts Magic Johnson's wardrobe to shame, and a tan shirt with one of those new rounded collars accented by a silk tie that has a blend of every shade of mocha from here to Colombia. It has a slight taste of denim blue with mainly a combination of rust and ginger and caramel and cocoa berry and blackberry and copper berry and juju berry and very berry too. Now I know why they call it a tie—it ties everything together if you do it right, and Malik definitely knows how to do it right. It complements his Wesley Snipes skin and brings out those deep sienna-brown eyes with his long, sexy eyelashes. He's actually kinda pretty in a macho-stud-type way.

We walk into the sanctuary as the usher hands us our programs. I hug several people I've met over the years. Mainly friends of my mother and stepfather who have been members since the sixties. The service has just begun, so we quietly head to our seats.

Malik whispers as we sit down upon the burgundy theater-style seats, "Dang, I've never seen a waterfall in a church before." The band plays a subtle jazz groove with a gospel touch. "This is pretty cool, baby. I like it already." The reverend approaches the podium.

"Today, beautiful spirits, I want to talk about forgiveness. Forgiveness of sin is an act of God toward the sinner because to forgive sin is an exclusive prerogative of God. Jesus Christ, by virtue of His Divinity, assumed the right to forgive sin and He passed his prerogative to His church. As a church, we must continue to forgive as a divinely commissioned task. There are many ways in which a sin is forgiven. One particular way is to verbally profess forgiveness, which I'll be discussing this morning. Forgiving is making amends to an individual by way of opening your mouth and your heart to say I'm sorry, or simply saying I forgive you. It's that easy. But some of us have too much pride or we just want to be right all the time. What that does is add roadblocks along our highway of abundance and happiness. Forgiving one another for an act you consider unacceptable clears the way for your goodness. It doesn't matter what the response might be of the person you are forgiving. You don't do it for them; you do it for you! God has forgiven you in Christ, and your final action will be met by corresponding actions of God upon final judgment. In the meantime, stop living your self-made Hell on earth, and begin to live Heaven on earth right here and now. Walk the walk and talk the talk . . ." Malik squeezes my hand.

". . . And so as we go about our day and about our daily lives, let us remember to make amends and find resolution in our everyday expressions of Christ. I challenge you to resolve and forgive one person this week. That is your homework. You will be forgiven just as you forgive. It is only by the mutual understanding of another that relations may be restored. It is important to forgive and forget; otherwise we cannot move on ourselves. So get unstuck and dissolve those roadblocks. You are on the highway of life, full speed ahead my friends!"

We participate in a calm, relaxing meditation session to the cleansing sounds of the waterfall.

Shortly thereafter, the choir sings a beautiful rendition of "Amazing Grace" and we place our offering in the collection plate as the service draws to a close.

The reverend returns to the podium as he continues to hum the choir's tune and then proclaims in question, "Did you listen to those words? What I mean is, did you *hear* those words? I once was lost, and now I'm found, was blind but now I see. Hopefully you desire to be found and clear up your vision so you can see where you're going because this stuff is truly *amazing;* can I get an amen?"

"Amen," we vocalize along with the rest of the congregation.

"Next week, I'll be discussing the soul and fate. Have you ever met someone whom you feel you've met before, someone who you're so comfortable with that it's like talking to yourself? Someone who understands and does not judge you, someone with whom you have so much spiritual karma that it's, as we say, *weird*. Well, it's not weird. They are in your life as a mutual participant in your respective life lessons. And some of you could have more than one soul mate, but you must be open to cooperation with your soul mate so that you can learn and grow through the lessons of your evolution in this journey called life. It is important to be in harmony with the awareness that all is in divine order and we are all where we are supposed to be at any given time. It is not a coincidence, there are no coincidences in life—it is fate, it is written and so it is. Now let us stand and sing 'Let There Be Peace on Earth.' "

As we leave the sanctuary Malik says, "Now that was deep. That is exactly what I was telling you last week at the office. I can't believe this. It is not a coincidence that we've met and that we came here today."

As we proceed to get into my car we see Robin and Tanya. Also, no coincidence.

"Oh, fancy meeting the two of you here . . . together," Robin nosily remarks. "We came down here with my aunt, who is a regular member here."

"That's nice," says Malik, half-listening.

"Hello," I reply to Robin's stare.

"Is your daughter here? Don't you have a teenager?" asks Tanya.

"Yes, I have three. And, no, she's not here."

Robin replies with a smirk, "Oh, I would have thought you were hooking her up with Malik or something. Malik, have you spoken to Brenda lately?"

"No, I've been busy this weekend. I'm sure I'll talk to her soon," he hurriedly replies.

"*Surely* you have been busy and *surely* you will talk to her soon. We will be *sure* to tell her you both send your best. When are you leaving?"

"I'm not," he replies as he turns toward me and motions for me to proceed. He opens the driver's door for me to get in the car. "Good-bye, ladies."

They stand in place looking dumbfounded as Malik gets in the passenger seat and we drive off.

"I cannot believe that after a positive church

service those two would be so catty. You'd think the spiritual message would at least get their negative butts through to Monday," says Malik.

"No comment. I'm too positively fired up and inspired to stoop to that level. I want you to meet my mother!"

I drive to the Marina Del Rey Convalescent Home and Malik senses that I am a bit quiet. "Are you all right?" he asks.

"I'm always like this before I go inside. I'm just reflecting."

We walk down the halls of the nursing home and I once again notice the same stale Lysol smell like something is being covered up. However, this home is better than most I've visited. Besides, the staff is helpful and they appear to be concerned.

We walk into my mom's room through the door that reads NAOMI TURNER. She likes to lie down near the sunlit window. She's sleeping on her right side toward the seeping rays of daylight peeking through the sheer powder-blue lace curtain.

"Hey, Mom," I say while gently rubbing her forehead as she opens her eyes, "it's Mariah."

My mom sort of opens her mouth and mumbles a greeting. Her eyes are always open wide in refreshed amazement when she focuses upon my face.

"This is my friend, Malik. I want you to meet him."

Malik slowly walks over to the side of her bed as I step away for him to get closer.

"Hi, Mrs. Turner. It's nice to meet you."

My mom stares into his eyes without blinking. She looks at me and then looks at him and then looks at me again.

"Malik is kinda young, huh?" Just then she lightly chuckles and covers her mouth like a shy kid.

We all laugh and she instantaneously reaches out her hand for Malik's hand. He places her beautiful, frail, time-weathered, vanilla wafer–colored hand in his and then places his other hand over her wrist as he rubs her arm. She begins to close her eyes as if his touch is soothing.

"Watch it! She likes them young too, you know!" I tease.

We turn on her cassette player so she can listen to her favorite music. She likes anything by Nancy Wilson. She taps her perfectly manicured fingers to the beat and bobs her head to the rhythm.

"She looks so much like you that it's amazing. She has your face and especially your smile," Malik tells me, examining her face as if it is very familiar.

"I'm glad you are able to meet her. She's a very good judge of people."

We visit for maybe an hour or so until she falls back to sleep. I gently place her favorite stuffed animal, a white miniature bunny rabbit, near her chest. Malik tries to take his hand away but he realizes her strong grip has him locked up. She awakens as he continues to rub her arm and I say,

"We're going to leave now, Mom. We'll see you later." She smiles and puckers her lips for a kiss. I move in for the lip lock but she pulls away from me. As she looks to Malik she puckers again. He lowers his head and kisses her on her cheek. She makes the loudest smacking sound I've ever heard.

"Wow, she really meant that! I think she likes you," I say, enjoying the sight.

Quickly she closes her eyes again and we quietly tiptoe toward the door. On the way to the parking lot, Malik rubs my back and hugs me.

"This is very difficult," I confess.

"The great thing is you have a mother to visit. A lot of people don't."

I know exactly what he means by that. "You're right," I admit.

He softly conveys, "Thank you for letting me share that part of your life. That was nice."

"How about we go to my house and I'll make breakfast?"

"And you cook too?"

"Yeah, I'll hook you up with some instant oatmeal and frozen waffles. How about that?" I tease.

"Okay, that's cool," he says as he laughs. "That's like French toast, turkey sausage and an omelet from anyone else."

"Well then, that's sort of what you'll get. French toast, turkey sausage, and some Negro fried eggs. I don't make omelets."

"You make it and I'll eat it . . ."

"Bet you won't?" I confirm.

"Uh-huh, tear it up."

"Okay, I forgot . . . you will!"

"See, you're the one with the dirty mind," he finally discovers.

14

THE AFTERNOON UNWINDS as we devour our four-course breakfast. I take off my shoes and sit back to watch Malik feast. My enjoyment is in his every bite. And the way he swirls his last piece of French toast around to absorb the final bit of syrup . . . He tantalizingly savors exact portions of each course as if to relish equal parts of the pungent experience. Yeah, he enjoys eating, all right. Oh, he also helps me finish my laundry.

"By the way, I have a confession to make," I disclose.

"You're really only twenty-eight?"

"No, seriously. It's something that really bothers me."

"Okay, what?"

"When I called you yesterday and hung up . . ."

"Yeah?"

I take a moment and then say, "I was trying to get your prefix right because I couldn't read your phone numbers on the back of your picture."

"I write kinda wild," he admits.

"No, it wasn't your writing. It was my washing."

"Your washing?" he asks as if he's perplexed.

"See, I accidentally washed your picture yesterday morning. I didn't realize it was in my pocket. I'm sorry," I say as I give my Betty Boop pout and flash my Natalie Wood eyes.

"Baby, it's cool. What made you think I'd be mad?"

"In my eyes and in my heart, that picture represented a lot. Your gesture was very special to me."

"There are more where those pictures came from. I've gotta watch you. You can be really goofy sometimes," he says, seeming to realize he's made a discovery.

"Oh, you think so?"

"Heck yeah! You let the Alizé kick your butt and then you decide to launder photographs? Maybe you should leave the laundry to me."

"Fine with me."

He reaches for some of my clothes to fold as I quickly reject his assistance.

"I'll fold those, thank you." I snatch my dryer-sheet-softened unmentionables from him.

"See what I mean by watching you? You're almost forty years old and wearing these?" He holds up my black-and-white polka-dot G-string with the black satin bow on the rear. "I'm not even gonna waste time folding these. You can just put those in the drawer and forget it. And with all that back you got? What's the point if all you get is a string up your cheeks?"

"Excuse me? Now that's my *bid-ness*, if you don't mind. A girl needs to feel free and breathe.

After all, the other ones end up creeping any-way."

"You mean to tell me you don't wear regular underwear because they creep up there any-way?" he asks in amazement.

"Yes, is that okay with you?" I declare as I snatch a pair of lime green panties from him.

"Hey, I ain't complaining. It's all right with me. You get no argument here. You know I heard they're called G-strings because they hit the ex-ternal G-spot in just the right . . . *spot*. Hey, how about letting me take a pair of these to Baltimore with me next week? I'll just put it in my gym bag and take it for a little trip."

"Oh, you are tripping big-time now. That's nasty," I say, turning up my nose and laughing.

"No, seriously. My buddy takes his girl's un-derwear with him when he travels, and he puts them on the other pillow when he sleeps so he has her next to him all night."

"I'm sorry but that is too kinky. I'll bet he wears them himself and prances around like a wanna-be girl or something," I suggest, shaking my butt from side to side as if to mimic.

"Well, I think that's sweet of him to want a token of her to remind him of her. Anyway, these are too clean. You need to put that lime green one on for a few hours and walk around and then I'll take them."

"Cut it out! No more talking about draws. Take the scent with you? You are really sick—sick! On a more serious note, I have an idea."

"I'm all ears," he says as he picks up another leopard pair with his fingertips.

"Then maybe you can give me some eyes too!" I say as I snatch the pair before he brings them to his face. "How about if we write our fathers and try to reconnect like the rev talked about? After all, how can we grow and move on if we're stuck and blocked by issues of serious abandonment from our dads?"

"I don't know, baby. My father has a new life now and I think we should leave the past in the past. I think sometimes you just need to be at peace with it without knowing why."

"But that's not the resolution. That's putting a bandage on it. I want to deal with it and heal it. Please?"

"See, you keep working those eyes, you just prepared a breakfast like that and I'm standing here surrounded by G-strings. You win. We'll do it this week. Deal?"

"Deal! For now let's just kick it."

He turns on the TV and starts to watch BET.

"Just like my kids, music videos 24-7-365."

"Heck, this is educational," he says, leaning back on the sofa with the remote in his hand.

"How do you learn anything from curse words being bleeped out and hoochie dance moves that resemble stripper routines? I grew up with the Beatles, Ozzie and Harriet, Batman and Robin, *The Brady Bunch* and *That Girl*."

"I'm not sure if we have an age difference or a color difference," he quips.

"All right, then. *Julia*, Aretha Franklin, Flip Wilson and the Jackson Five."

"That's better," he acknowledges.

"Besides, the oldies music was pure, deep and inspirational, like Stevie Wonder. Maybe the most X-rated song you'd find back then was 'Sexual Healing' by Marvin Gaye."

Malik begins to look through my old thirty-three record albums. "Oh, what about this Minnie Ripperton cut, 'Inside My Love'?"

"No, she sang, 'You can see inside me, do you wanna run inside my love.' "

"Oh bull, you know what she meant. Even Lauryn Hill remade that cut."

"Okay, I'll give you that. That's another thing. What's with this thing where the new artists remake the old music? Sampling ain't nothing but stealing."

"It's borrowing music as a tribute to the original artists. Anyway, I know every song, lyric and artist on every album you have. Test me," he dares.

"Who sang 'Smiling Faces'?"

"It's 'Smiling Faces Sometimes,' and it was the Temptations off the *Sky's the Limit* album, 1971."

"Here's one. Who sang 'Love Won't Let Me Wait'?"

"Major Harris!"

"Ahh, you *are* good. How about 'I Just Don't Wanna Be Lonely'?"

"Carl Carlton, off the *Everlasting Love* album."

"Carl Carlton? It was Cuba Gooding Sr., Mr. Oldie But Goodie!"

"Cuba Gooding had a record back then? He's not that old," he says, either joking or learning.

"See, you didn't even know there was a Cuba Gooding Sr.," I exclaim with a jokerlike grin as if I've finally got him.

"Dang, girl, calm down. I do know one thing, Miss Back in the Day. Most of the Nelson family members were on drugs and the fathers on *The Brady Bunch* and *Bewitched* were gay. Nothing has changed."

"Well, when I was growing up . . ." Malik looks at me like my kids do when I start to go back to the sixties. "Oh, forget it. Actually, believe it or not, my favorite artist is DMX."

In unison, "What y'all really want?"

"Uh-huh! I knew you liked rap. You know, he's dating Diahann Carroll. She left her husband for him. Now that's a real May-December romance!"

I cannot help but laugh, but I say, "You are not funny. Now can we please watch something to stimulate our minds, like MSNBC or CNN? After all, that is my true calling—the news business."

"So maybe you'll be covering the news in Baltimore one day?"

"You never know. But I'm almost to the point where I want to just throw in the towel. A forty-year-old reporter should be way beyond 'up-and-coming' by now. Besides, I started late." I place the last bit of folded clothes in the laundry basket.

"Don't give up. It has to be difficult in Los Angeles."

"Yes, but I want to talk about your contract, Mr.

Football. You seem so humble and nonchalant about the whole thing." I take a seat beside him.

"I suppose once I go to training camp and get suited up, it will finally hit me. And I haven't actually made the team yet. There's a chance I could get cut, you know."

"That's not going to happen. That much I know. The important question is, what number will you be wearing? I know that's a typical girl question."

"Yeah, that and what color is the uniform? I've always been number twenty-four."

"Malik, that's Donovan's number. I can't believe that," I exclaim, pushing him to the side like he needs to get out of here.

"I've had that number since I was in Pop Warner."

"What's Pop Warner?"

"That's the name of the football league and the man who created it—Mr. Warner. We call him Pop." He looks at me, waiting for my reaction.

"No, it's not."

"Is so."

"Is not," I say, holding up my hand to motion for him to stop.

"You're such a baby, Mariah."

"Me? Don't get me started on you. You really think I don't know what Pop Warner is with a son who plays football—please. I know that Pop Warner had one of the winningest coaching records. Just because you're headed to the NFL does not mean you can clown me."

He laughs. "Clown me? Stop trying to talk hip.

I'll bet you don't even know what 'clown' means. Anyway, 'clown' is out. And, don't try to act cool because if you didn't have teenagers you wouldn't know half this stuff. You'd be watching *Lawrence Welk* reruns and still using terms like 'can you dig it?'," Malik says as he tickles me across the couch and we fall to the floor. "You need some serious help," he teases.

"Get off me, little boy. Okay, you can watch BET if you've done your homework," I kid with him in return, pushing him away.

"No, Granny, come back. We can watch the news."

Oh no, he did not. "I give up, you win. We can watch videos or whatever. I'm fine with either one, really." He crawls back to the couch.

"Okay, if you don't mind," he says as he pants in exhaustion, taking the remote again to switch to BET. "Now this is DJ Quik."

"I know who that is," I say in a "duh" tone as I stand up to check my voice mail. Who the hell is DJ Quik?

"The kids called. I need to pick them up at eight tonight," I inform Malik as I dial my mother-in-law's number. "Hi, Mrs. Pijeaux, this is Mariah. How are you? All right."

I motion to Malik that she is putting them on. "Hey, baby, what's up? Ready to come home?" I ask Chloe. "That sounds like fun. I'll be there at eight. By the way, I have something to tell you both once you come home. Did Kyle call you? He did? Well, I'm glad he caught you. I miss you so much. See you in a little while."

Malik's eyes are fixed upon me as I hang up.

"Seeing you in your motherly role is such a trip. When do I get to meet them?"

"I need to talk to them first. The most important thing to me is that they're okay with our friendship. I'm not the type of mom who just says, 'Deal with it because it's my happiness and I'm doing this anyway.' I need to be careful about how I introduce you considering the, you know, the age disparity. You do understand, don't you?" I return to my place next to him.

"Yes, I totally agree. Age disparity," he mumbles.

"Besides, I'd like them to know you as a friend before anything else."

I hear the vibration of his pager going off. He ignores it. It goes off again. I say nothing about it.

"It's six-thirty already, Mariah. Can I use your phone to call for a ride home?"

Part of me wants to offer to take him home but that would be giving and mothering. I don't offer. I just let him make his own plans. "Sure, go right ahead."

Malik picks up the phone and begins to dial as he stares at my hips and scoots his butt over to squish me into the arm of the loveseat. "Yo, Brian, can you pick me up, man, like we talked about? It's 6200 Fairfax near Slauson and La Cienega. Thanks, dog. Late."

"Get off me!" I threaten as I stand up to clear the table. "And what's up with the word 'dog'? Why do you guys call each other the very name you don't want us to call you?"

"It's like Blacks calling each other the 'n' word. It's all right for us to say it, but we'd be ready to kill if another race uses it. Actually, it's like *dawg*. Get it right. It's a term of endearment. See, I can call him my dog, but you wouldn't call me a dog now, would you?"

"Oh no. Not you. You, my brother, are far from a dog," I remark under my breath. "You are more like a cat by the way you lick!"

"Okay, let's not go there. Besides, we were both buzzin' so it's probably a good thing we were saved by the ring of the phone. Kareem knew exactly what he was doing. He was able to sense an invasion upon his territory. He probably has a Lojack installed somewhere below your waist. I don't know if I should thank him or run up on him."

"Anyway, you are very talented and skilled far beyond your years," I compliment him while planting a kiss on his cheek.

"I think you're the one whose erotic nature was showing. Is it that peaking thing they talk about? We're both about there, aren't we?"

"Maybe. It's just the combination of the two of us together. We'd better not go there. I'm sure we'd hurt each other."

"You mean we can't sleep together?" he asks as if he heard me incorrectly.

"Oh, we can do that. It's just that I can't let you in until the time is right."

"In—in?"

"In! I think it's a good idea to wait until the imperfect phase and then we can see all the imperfections before we consummate our whatever-this-is. After all, friendship is the root and sex is the bloom. Making love should be between two people who love each other and then the two people can express that love through sex. I've been told that romance is between the ears, not between the legs."

"Well, whoever told you that needs a serious lesson in anatomy," he asserts.

"I am serious. If we play around without knowing the downsides of our personalities, that's just lust."

"Lust is fine with me. And from what I can tell, we'd lust ourselves right on into love."

"Malik, no 'in' until later, okay?"

"Fine. When would that be? And is there an admittance fee to get in?" he asks as he follows me back into the living room after placing the dishes in the sink.

"When we work through all of the stuff, I deal with mine, including Kareem, and you get going with your career."

"But can't I get my rewards in increments a little at a time?" he asks.

"That's possible. I didn't say we couldn't play. I just cannot let you in. You know and I know it would be an intense, orgasmic, emotional experience and I would surely bond to you. What do you think?" Feminine.

"I think you can play this waiting crap all you want. A brotha will wait you out!"

"I'm sure that's true but by then, hopefully we will have worked through the issues that indicate whether or not we're compatible and whether there's chemistry and whether or not we can communicate. The three Cs, I call them. Chemistry, compatibility and communication."

"The three Cs? Well, excuse my bluntness but how about the clit, the coochie and the cock, in that order? Those are my darn three Cs," he says while leaning back on the sofa with his arms extended like he's all that. Damn, he's a bad boy!

"That's crazy. That's another C! Don't forget we've only known each other less than one week."

"Maybe it feels like we've known each other longer because it's meant to be. Whatever, I'm all for getting to know you better. Here are a few questions for you. Do you burp, fart, snore, take long showers, squeeze toothpaste from the bottom of the tube, are you frugal, a shopaholic, do you scream in bed, are you an early riser, are you moody, late for appointments, do you have bad credit, bad feet, bad breath? These are a few of the things I want to know."

"I'd say two out of the last three are true," I respond as I blow my breath in his face.

He looks at me as he blinks rapidly and then looks down at my feet and says, "So I guess your credit is good, huh?"

We laugh as I sit beside him and we hold each other.

"Really, Malik. We must also consider the most important aspect of this possible connection, and that's my children. I want them to accept you but I mean, let's face it, you are just a tad bit older than my daughter. And honestly, they've bonded to Kareem like he's family. Donovan is very protective of me and yet very supportive, just as Kyle is. But I would definitely need to consider their feelings in this situation. If I have any doubts, it would be because of them."

He replies, "I understand that. You will not get any argument from me. After all, I don't have any kids so that's something I do not have on my plate. To make sure that I am being sensitive, I will go at a pace that makes you feel comfortable. You set the boundaries and I will not overstep those limitations. Is that cool with you?"

"That's cool with me."

He leans on top of me, laying me down on my back. "Seriously, I'm looking forward to getting to know more about you and I'm looking forward to feeling more for you. I'm looking forward to loving you, Mariah."

I feel my senses rising as he kisses my neck and moves his hand inside my blouse, feeling the fullness and softness of my left breast. I place my hands in his back pockets and pull his body closer. My insides melt down into hot butter while he kisses my lips from side to side with the tip of his tongue.

Pulling his hot tongue away, he asks, "Do you have any Hershey's syrup in the kitchen so I can lick your name off of this tittie?"

Honk, honk.

Malik reluctantly stands up and peers out the window behind the couch, taking a moment to return to normal. "Brian's outside, baby. I'm out. I'll call you tonight after you pick up the kids, okay?" He pulls me to my feet.

"I'll talk to you then," I say, retying my disheveled blouse.

He squeezes my hand, and then he walks down my stairs toward Brian's car as I hear a woman yelling.

15

"I LEFT A MESSAGE FOR YOU yesterday afternoon and told you I had something important to tell you. I haven't heard from you since! Not to mention that I've been paging you for the last three hours. I heard you were at church with that old dried-up grandma. What the hell are you doing? I thought I meant something to you and you're over here!" Just then I hear the sound of a slap. It is Brenda as she gives Malik an open hand across his face. "I'm going to go up there and talk to her," she threatens as if she took a vow.

"No, you're not going to bother her with this nonsense. Now calm down and go home," Malik shouts.

I walk down the stairs and over to where Brenda is standing. Malik's friend Brian comes over to restrain her as she gets louder. "Don't come up to me like you want some of this. You need to be sleeping with Ben Gay, Charlie Horse and Arthur-itis. Not fucking with my man," she roars rudely.

"Brenda, what do you want to say to me? Come to me like a woman," I warn with a sharp edge.

"Well, woman, don't you know Malik is my man? Why don't you let me introduce you to my uncle Leroy or some shit? Save the young ones for the tight ones," she clowns defiantly.

Malik speaks up. "Brenda, that's it! I am not your man. We never discussed anything like that."

"We didn't have to. You and I had sex just last Thursday night. You said you didn't want to leave that night because it felt so right. That meant something to me, Malik. And is this the coworker you wanted to stand me up for lunch with?" she hoots, with a deadly sneer at me.

Fast losing my patience, I unsuccessfully reach out my hand to Brenda. "You know it's obvious that you're hurting but you and I don't have to be adversaries. It sounds like you and Malik need to deal with this one-on-one." I drop my extended hand and look to Malik as I state angrily, "But would the two of you please take this crap somewhere else? This is a quiet neighborhood and I have phone calls to return. And Brenda, you need to stop watching *Jerry Springer*. All of this drama is unnecessary." I turn and walk away.

Brian says, "Damn, dog. You runnin' 'em!"

"No, Brian, he ain't runnin' me," says Brenda.

"Where you been keepin' her, dude?"

"Brian, back up! That's disrespectful."

Brenda shouts, "He's being disrespectful? What about your ass?"

"You know I'm not even going to ask you how you got here or how you found out where Mariah lives or what you're smoking. I'm just telling you to leave now!" he demands, counting to three.

"Oh, I'm leaving but you're gonna talk to me sooner or later—dog!" she idly threatens.

I peek through my window and see Brenda looking up at me as she yells, "Coocoo-ka-roo, Mrs. Robinson?" She slams the door and speeds off in her Range Rover.

Malik comes up the stairs and raises his hand to knock at my door. He changes his mind and walks to Brian's Explorer. They drive away slowly as Malik reclines the passenger seat back and slouches his long body down into the seat. His massive hands are covering his blushing, embarrassed face.

I call Violet once again and explain what happened.

"What the heck was that bull, girl?" Violet asks. "Obviously he whooped her and he doesn't feel the same. I mean he told her right in front of you that they're not together. Shit, she's fatal. Maybe that's an example of that oxytocin fix you guys told me about. Damn, he must be good for her to be tripping like that after one time. So what now, are you through with him and Kareem's looking like a keeper?"

"Honey, please. I've been through that same scene with Kareem so many times. The only difference is I'm always the one in Brenda's position, looking stupid as I bust up on him and some other woman. You know I've caught him kissing women in parking lots, begged him to make women leave his apartment and fought over him at parties. I guess that's the power of the love hormone talking. But you know what? I actually believe Malik."

"That's not like you." She's got that right.

"He has every right to sleep with whomever he wants to sleep with. Hell, I just slept with Kareem last Tuesday night. Besides, I have a boyfriend so who I am to get mad at him? And after all, I did ask him what was up with her."

"What did he say?"

"He said he was attracted to her but that he is not attached."

"Girl, men are all alike, nine or ninety-nine, age is nothing but a number. The only number that matters is how many inches."

"Vi, I'm telling you that you must come to the seminar I went to with Ariana. You could learn a thing or two yourself. You're the biggest female player I know and you won't even admit it."

"Yeah . . . yeah . . . so what did his friend who was driving look like?" she says, shifting right into player mode.

"Good-bye, Vi. I've got to go and get my kids."

"Did you screw Malik?"

"Violet, I'm hanging up."

"Hell, you'd better watch out. He might whoop your 'P' too if you're not careful."

"No, get it right. I'm the whooper, not the whoopee," I claim in denial.

"Yeah, right. That's why Kareem has had you on a string for the last seven. You'd better tell that lie to someone else. He has his name written in graffiti on your kitten, okay?"

"Okay. I've gotta go."

Actually, I'm not even mad at Malik. My experience with him so far has been positive and that's what I want to base my opinion upon. It feels good not being mad at a man for disappointing me. That's a great feeling. I believe he's a good man. He did not disrespect her outside of my apartment, he didn't allow her to disrespect me and unlike some men he didn't just pull off and leave us to cat fight with each other. He didn't even bang my door down like some men would so they could convince me that they were innocent of all wrongdoing and then deny responsibility. He simply left. He'll call.

16

As I PULL UP in front of my mother-in-law's home I see Donovan and Chloe talking to her near the front door. I roll down my window as I prepare to park and politely say, "Hello, Mrs. Pijeaux! Thanks so much for taking care of them this weekend. I really appreciate it. I . . ."

"Oh, I'm sure it gave you time alone or whatever," Mrs. Pijeaux says with an air of spitefulness.

She always makes them wait for me outside and she never asks me in. She props them at the door with their bags like orphans. The kids and I put the bags in the trunk and wave good-bye as she swiftly closes her front door. Oh, that pisses me off. Part of me says there will be no next time. But my love for Donovan Sr. tells me to allow our kids to know his family. At times I think it would be easier on me to not have her in my life at all. But I know it's more important to have her in my kids' lives for now. At least until they're old enough to decide on their own.

"Mom, Grandpa says hi. He's so funny when he does those old Creole Mardi Gras dances. He had us cracking up," Donovan explains.

"You would not believe how many family members showed up. And Daddy's old math teacher from elementary school stopped by. She told us so many cool stories about him. He was just like Donovan when it came to sports, huh?" asks Chloe.

Wow! Chloe seems good as new, just as if she's forgotten Friday ever happened. That's cool, but she's still on punishment and cannot talk on the phone for one week. I know she's sick of me.

"Yeah, your daddy was quite an athlete."

"What did you do this weekend?" asks Chloe.

"I cleaned the house, rearranged furniture around, washed clothes, went to church and visited your grandmother."

"All of your favorite things to do, right?" asks Donovan.

Donovan and Chloe give each other daps for being away from a weekend of *chore hell*.

"What did you want to talk to us about?" Chloe inquires.

"Oh, it's not important right now. We'll talk about it later."

I realize that I don't want to let them know about Malik yet. A flutter passes through my stomach and a chilly sensation runs across my shoulders. The kind of feeling I've had many times before when I am unsure and feeling unsafe.

Chloe fiddles with the radio and argues with Donovan over which station to listen to. She decides I can listen to my jazz station. And there it is, Kenny G's "Loving You." That's the song

Chloe and I chose for my brother's funeral. For years I've been unable to listen to it in its entirety because it hurts too much and I start to cry. Yet it always comes on when I'm in deep thought or like last year when I was at dinner with Kareem on my birthday. We got in the car and just as he turned the ignition, there it was. Or when I was in Sears looking for a gift for my mother for Mother's Day and it came on over the speakers in the store.

"Turn the station, Chloe," Donovan says. "It will make Mom sad."

"No, baby, I want to hear it this time."

Chloe and Donovan cautiously keep an eye on me for any sign of body jitters or the wiping of a tear from my cheek. Astonishingly, for the first time nothing happens physically. Yet emotionally and mentally I'm thanking my brother for watching over me. Even though he's invisible to the naked eye, he's my angel in spirit and I know he's comforting me once again. First my dad left us when I was five years old and then my kids' father died. And he's the one I knew would never leave me. To top it all off, my big, strong brother dies. He was my best friend. Why? What's the lesson for me in this? God's will is beginning to sound a little selfish to me and I don't want to feel that way. We ride the rest of the way home without saying a word to one another as I silently talk to my brother: *I get the message. Thank you for the visit.*

We settle in at home and before I know it they're both asleep. Chloe didn't even try to get on the phone.

I check my service just knowing Kareem will be calling to find out what's on my mind and why I need to "talk." There's only one message on my service.

"It's Malik, please call me as soon as possible. I need to talk to you. I apologize for Brenda's actions. It was tacky and it should not have been brought into your space in life. You did not deserve that. I'm sorry. Please call me after you pick up the kids. If I do not hear from you, I'll just try back later. Thanks."

I return his call immediately. "Malik, it's Mariah."

"Baby, did you get my message?" he asks with concern.

"Yes."

"Can I just tell you how sorry I am? I've straightened her out and she owes you an apology for insulting you. I am not interested in her in that way and I hope you will forgive me."

"Of course I forgive you. If I don't forgive you it will only block my blessings and we both know what that's about," I say, referring to our church message by the rev.

"Thank you. I hope it didn't ruin your Sunday."

"It didn't ruin my day. I wouldn't let it," I express with an ounce of attitude.

"I hope we can still get together this week, I need to mentor this week, and at some point I have to fly to training camp in Maryland. But I'm pretty much available any evening. Do you have an assignment this week?"

"Not yet. I'll know in the morning."

"I take it you didn't talk to them about us, right?"

"Right. But I'm sure I will."

"Are you sure you feel okay? Do you need anything?" he asks, sensing distance.

"No, I'm fine."

"You just don't sound the same, Mariah. Please tell me what I can do to make you feel better." Masculine.

"Nothing. I just want to take a hot bath and relax. I really did have a great day today. But, Malik, I want you to take care of your business," I admit.

"I get the message. I have done just that and I promise you I do not want Brenda. It was the heat of the moment and . . ."

I cut in, "You don't owe me an explanation. I don't want one."

"I know, but considering what we've discussed . . ."

I cut in again, "I have a boyfriend. How can you owe me anything?"

"Well, like I said, I'll take care of my business! I'll call you tomorrow and we'll discuss writing those letters we talked about, okay?"

"Fine, good night," I say to bring the conversation to a close.

"Good night, baby."

IF I DON'T GET SOME MONEY coming in soon I'm going to be in real trouble. These sporadic temp gigs are cool but the pay leaves much to be desired. Seems as though I cannot afford the extras that I used to enjoy before I started auditioning and freelancing as a journalist. My savings is going fast. I just might have to accept a longer assignment if one comes available. So I call the temp agency at eight on Monday morning to let them know I'm available.

"It's Mariah Pijeaux. Please put me on your list for today. You can reach me at home."

I've already taken Donovan to school and Chloe is still sleeping.

Violet calls from work. "Mariah, girl, you know who came by last night with a shower curtain and some baby oil. We were slipping and sliding all over my living room," she says as if she's trying to catch her breath from this most recent aerobic activity.

See, Violet got with this guy a while ago after he told her he was single. I don't know how he managed to be with her morning, noon and night, but he did. After four months or so, his cell phone rang at one in the morning. He tried to play it off like it was his buddy Tevin. Vi heard a woman's voice and snatched the phone. From that point on he was busted. Violet and his wife talked for over an hour and totally exposed his ass. He just sat there and shook his head like they were the ones trippin'. She even found out his wife was pregnant. He begged and made excuses but she refused to see him for a few weeks. Finally she let him come by one night, and that was it. The sex was so crazy wild that she decided to just see him when she needed to be serviced. The two rules are that he must wear a condom and he cannot ask her a damn thing about who she sees and what she does. They get together maybe every other week or so. I believe he really truly cares for her. Unfortunately, she'd already bonded to him before she found out he was Mr. Wrong. I'm sure his wife is hip to the game. She probably just wants her kid's dad around and will keep her family together at any cost. Sometimes it's cheaper to keep him. Violet is always looking to upgrade, but it seems all the men with the Little Miss at home always, always hit on her. The trip is, she wouldn't put up with Kareem for two seconds. We butt heads about who really has a right to throw stones.

"That's nice, Vi. I don't even know why he surprises you anymore. He's always been and always will be a freak."

"It takes one to know one." She returns my comment.

"I don't know what you want me to tell you after you describe an evening with someone else's man."

"I don't care about that anymore. Why are you worried about it?" she interjects with her loving flair.

"Because you deserve better. Next time I go to see Dr. Singer, I'm making you go along with me. You just think you're okay with it. I know better."

"Until you get rid of your dead weight, I'm not trying to hear it."

"I'm working on that," I admit.

My doorbell rings. I look out of the peephole and it's big, long, tall Kareem once again coming over without calling.

"Speaking of dead weight, Kareem's at the door. I've got to go."

"Good-bye. And get your butt some work today," she teases. Now that's the smartest thing she's said in a long time.

OBVIOUSLY KAREEM HAS TIME to deal with me now that all of his priorities are taken care of. I cautiously open the door in exhaustion from this game.

"I'm glad I caught you. Are you working today?"

"I don't know yet." In discontent, I walk away as he closes the door.

"What did you want to talk about?"

"If you don't mind, it can wait until I come by tonight. Moreover, Chloe is here and this is just between you and me."

"Well, tell me what it's about. That's not fair to make me wait until tonight. I've been worried all weekend," he expresses as if he actually has feelings.

"Yeah, right!"

"I have been. And I told you I need to borrow your VCR for a few days. I'll bring it back on Friday."

"I'm not comfortable loaning you things anymore," I say, standing in the middle of the living room, hoping he doesn't get too comfortable.

"Wow. Have you been talking to Violet or Ariana? They're always trying to get you to be as miserable as they are. They're just jealous because they don't have a man."

I fold my arms across my chest and tilt my

head to the side as if I've had a lightbulb moment. "Kareem, I really don't have one either."

"Oh, baby, just because we argued the other night . . ."

"Why is it that you always make time to discuss us when you're ready to talk?"

"It's not like you were around this weekend anyway," he states with a tit-for-tat childishness.

"Look, I refuse to go into this right now. If you don't want to talk tonight, we just won't talk at all." I walk toward the door.

"Oh, you are really tough today. You probably met some dude who said you were the shit and now you've got an attitude with me."

"You're going to wake up Chloe. I'll talk to you later. Good-bye," I say as I turn the doorknob and pave the way for his exit.

"I'll page you when I get home," he says, bending down to walk through the door, and then he stops in silence.

"Talk to you later," I reply with much attitude, backing away from him.

"Bye!" he says with attitude of his own as he exits, slamming the door.

"Mom, it's your agency," Chloe mumbles with sleep in her eyes as she hands me the telephone.

"This morning? Where? That's good. And what time? Eight-thirty? I'll be leaving in the next twenty minutes or so!" I hang up.

"Mom, are you okay?"

"I'm fine, I have to get ready for work. Thank God I got an assignment for today," I say, heading for my room.

"I love you!" she expresses. Be still my heart.

I stop and hug Chloe with the strength of a lion, nearly lifting her up from the ground.

"I love you too," I reply.

She knows as well as I do that I have to deal with the Kareem issue. Once again I'm setting a bad example for her to emulate. I've never quite learned to practice what I preach.

17

MY ASSIGNMENT is at a studio near my home. The day comes and goes fairly quickly even though there's not much to do except stare at silent phones and *think*. Thinking is the one thing that always gets me in trouble. If only I could turn my brain off every now and then. That would be a relief to my soul.

Later that afternoon I call home to check in and Chloe tells me Malik called.

"Who's Malik, Mom? He sounds cool. He said hello to me as if he knew me."

"Malik is a friend of mine whom I met last week while working. He's an intern and that's something I want you to learn more about. Especially as you think about work-study later this year."

"And Carlotta called. She wants you to go with her to see Dr. Singer tomorrow night."

"Wow. That's coming up again. I have to invite Violet this time. She needs to go more than I do."

"Who's Dr. Singer?"

"She's a woman who hosts relationship seminars each week at the local playhouse. Just a girlie thing I'm going to start doing."

"Are you and Kareem still together?"

"I know you're pretty close to him, Chloe, but I do intend to break up with him tonight. I'm not happy and I think you know it."

"Yes. If that's best for you, then I'll be fine. Are you looking for a man like Daddy?"

"No, even though he is a tough act to follow. First of all, I'm not looking for a man. Secondly, no one could or should compare to him."

"I know, but you get what I mean. Don't you?" she asks.

"I do, but I think I'm looking for happiness in life. It would be nice to have a man to share it with. A man who accepts me and adds to my life."

"Kind of a hero instead of a zero?"

"Yeah, kinda like that. A *man* who protects me and cares about how I feel. I'm becoming more and more old-fashioned and I don't think that's a bad thing."

"What about making sure guys respect you? That's what you always tell me."

"I know I've told you that, but I think if a man is respectable he will be man enough to put you first. He will get respect in return from cherishing you. I know it's confusing but that's my new word now—*cherish*."

"I like that word . . . cherish. I'm sorry about last Friday. I made a bad choice. I let someone have what they wanted instead of giving myself what I wanted," she maturely admits.

"What do you want, Chloe?"

"I want to be happy too. I know I shouldn't

have slept with that guy but he was so persistent. It seems like some guys say what they need to say when all they want is to use you for whatever reason. The ones I've met don't seem to care about my feelings. But I suppose if I disrespect myself by letting them have their way, I've allowed them to do the same."

"It's okay, Chloe. But you are so precious. Your self-respect is more valuable than their disrespect. We must value our bodies and our minds. It's similar to my decision to no longer make Kareem's needs a priority. The gift for you in this is that you get this lesson now and learn it at your age, as opposed to learning it later like me."

"Better late than never, right?" Uh-oh, that's my line.

"Better late than never. I have to go and get that call. I'll see you tonight. And, Chloe?"

"Yes?" she answers.

"Stay off the phone."

"All right. Good grief."

Chloe quickly hangs up as I pick up the other line. "Publicity!"

The caller asks for Cindy Thomas, Sarah's *friend* who worked for *The Opposite Sex*. I look up her extension and transfer the call. I later call Cindy myself to say hello.

"Cindy, what's up? It's Mariah. I met you the other night with Sarah. I'm temping on the lot for the day. What a small world! I didn't know you worked here on the lot."

"No shit, Sherlock—how are you?"

"Great. Can't wait until six o'clock though—it's been slow. How's Sarah?"

"Mariah, she slept all night Friday until nearly four o'clock in the afternoon the next day. She was good for nothing all weekend. We're thinking about getting a few people together next week for a card party and we want you there. I wish we could have had lunch today but I have an appointment. Will you be back tomorrow?"

"I'm not sure but I'll let you know. Sarah has my number."

"It's nice talking to you. Actually, I told Sarah you were the cutie with the big booty," she teases.

"Should I say thank you?"

"That is a compliment. You had those girls wondering who you were."

"Kinda like new meat?" I ask as a giveaway to my own private train of thought.

"All that!"

"Thanks."

"I have to go but I'll talk to you later. Be good," she encourages.

"You too. Take care, Cindy."

"Ciao," she closes.

Ciao, that's so damn Hollywood. But she's a sweetheart. I decide to make another call before I leave.

"Malik, it's me. Chloe said you called."

"She seems to be very mature. We talked for a few minutes. You have been on my mind quite a bit today. I miss you."

"I've thought a lot about you today also. I miss you too," I admit.

"Chloe said you're working at Culver Studios. What time do you get off?"

"Six o'clock, but I have to meet with Kareem tonight."

"Tonight?" he asks with concern.

"I need to handle my business too."

Protectively he asks, "Yeah, but are you sure you'll be all right? I mean, he can't be too happy because he has to know what you're about to do. Do you have to go over there?"

"Yes, I'll be fine," I assure him.

"I don't understand why you can't say this over the telephone or Dear John the dude."

"Would you want someone you've been with for seven years to Dear John you?"

"Okay. Point made. Just make sure you call me when you get back home. I'll be here," he reassures me.

"I will. It shouldn't be too late."

"Please be careful!" he warns.

"I'll call you later."

I RECEIVE A PAGE from Kareem at seven while I'm at home getting dinner ready for the kids. We decide I should come by at eight.

As I drive up, I feel at peace. I feel like I'm finally putting my needs first, which includes refusing to allow myself to be used and unloved.

Normally I use Kareem's extra garage remote to park underground behind his car. This time I don't. Even when I'd use the clicker before, I'd have to walk outside to the front door of the building and buzz him because he didn't give me an elevator key to get up to the second level. This time I park on the street.

"It's me." He buzzes me in.

As I approach his door for the last time, I feel I am not alone. I feel strong and protected.

"You look good. Come on in."

I immediately notice a tiny stuffed animal and a pale pink rose on his bar. I ignore it, knowing it's not for me. He always has some new token of affection from some admirer, some freshly opened bottle of wine (he doesn't even drink wine), some newly prepared dish still left over in the refrigerator (that nigga don't cook). Or some lipstick-stained Kleenex in the trash can and I don't think it's his shade. The worst part is that I used to count the number of condoms in his condom drawer every time I'd come over. There would be twelve the day I left and then ten the night I'd come back over. But he'd always say I was tripping or his friend borrowed them. Eventually he decided to hide them somewhere else, which still never cleared up the real problem, which is that he's fucking women other than me. Some women might say at least he's having safe sex. I say fuck that! I want to be the only one, not number one. AIDS is trickier than a rubber.

Normally we would have argued about who, what, when, where and why by now. Tonight, we won't. It doesn't matter anymore and I don't care. As usual, he walks over to turn off the ringer on his telephone. On his desk next to the telephone I notice two books he's been reading, *The Pinocchio Theory* and *In Search of Good Pussy*.

"Kareem, let's sit down."

I smell smoke, as usual. He lights up right in front of me even though I've asked him not to. He's deep into his glass of Tanqueray and 7UP.

"Tonight I bought you a bottle of that red Alizé you like and I found two of the best porno movies. One of them has this couple portraying Anita Hill and Long Dong Clarence Thomas. I thought we could do our role-playing thing. Actually, I bought five of them but these two are the best. But since my VCR is broken and you wouldn't let me borrow yours, we can't watch them."

"I won't be here long enough for that, Kareem. Please sit down," I insist.

"I don't want to sit down. What is this about? Is it about when Carlotta saw me at the club on Saturday night? I was just with my cousins and that girl was my second cousin Sheridan. I knew she would start some shit when I saw her," he says suspiciously.

"Kareem, Carlotta didn't tell me anything."

"I know she called you," he says as if he's fishing.

"She called but I didn't get to talk to her."

"If this is about the run-in-your-stocking comment, see, you made me think . . ."

"No, I didn't make you think anything. You see, Kareem, you think what you want to think. I am not responsible for your insecurities and jealousy."

"What shrink have you been talking to?" he remarks.

I take a deep breath, plant my feet and brace myself as I answer his question. "None. I just know that it is perfectly all right for you to discard people when it's convenient for you, not commit to people because you're not ready, use people for sex and money, run the streets, date lots of women, travel by yourself, party all the time and talk to people like they're shit. You have every right to do that. However, I am not comfortable with it and I will no longer be in a relationship with you as of this very second. I choose to be treated the way I deserve to be treated and I can no longer tolerate your behavior, period!"

I swallow my saliva so hard I can feel it slowly creeping down my throat as it gets stuck in my chest. . . . He just stares at me in frozen mode for what seems like fifteen minutes. I start breathing harder.

"Yeah, you're tripping, all right. These are not your words and I wanna know who put this shit in your head," he demands, elevating his voice.

"No one. Contrary to what you believe, I just love myself more than you," I reply while trying to remain calm.

"You just suddenly decide to do this after nearly eight years. I don't buy this 'love yourself' bullshit. So what we argue, you accuse me, I accuse you, I always break up with you, but you know I always come back."

I raise my voice to him as if my cup runneth over. "Listen to you. That's exactly what I'm talking about. That's not normal or acceptable. I'm not abiding by your rules, your time frame, when you're ready, your freeway headed to your destination, which reads *nowhere*. Your destination with me after all this time should read *marriage* or something other than this rubber band you've had me tied to. No, make that the rubber band that I let you tie me to. You keep pulling away as far as you can and then you snap back. Well, it's now at a point of no return because the band is worn and torn. It isn't strong enough to handle the strain. Seven years is six years too long for you to know if I'm Miss Right or not. So therefore I'm setting you free. Go find her and leave me the hell alone."

Out of instinct, I jump in reaction to his hand on my shoulder. "Calm down. You are Miss Right. You know that."

"Are you ready to marry anyone and make anyone an honest woman?" I roll my eyes.

He pauses in thought. "Not right now. I have things I need to do in my life first."

I back away from him. "That's an excuse. There is no Miss Right in your lifetime. You're forty-five years old and all you want to do is drink, smoke, party, screw and meet new women. You're the one who needs to talk to a shrink. You have issues."

He laughs at me in anger. "Yeah, issues, huh? Well, if this is what you want I can't say anything. So you don't want me to call you anymore?"

There's that question he always asks me when I'm having second thoughts. He knows I look forward to hearing from him. He knows his phone call means he desires me, especially physically, something my horny ass craves. What a familiar question. I pause. He stares at me and moves toward me with that "I've got her now" look. I picture him looking at so many other women the same way and yet again I imagine that massive penis no longer pleasing me.

"Well, do you?" he inquires with raised eyebrows as if he's reading my mind.

Again, I swallow as the saliva moves from my chest to the pit of my stomach. I clear my throat and back away even further.

"*No*, Kareem. I don't ever want you to call me for the rest of your fucking life. Is that clear enough for you?" I exhale.

Suddenly he takes his glass of Tanqueray and throws it against the wall behind me. I delicately jump for a second, yet I look him dead in the eye. I can no longer comfort this little boy by giving him his way like I'm his mother.

"If you do this, you'll be sorry," he threatens with a roar.

"I'd be sorry if I didn't do it. Good-bye!"

As I cautiously turn to walk toward the door and grab the door handle, Kareem quickly walks toward me. He tries to block the door but I force it open and begin to run down the hall. Kareem runs after me, grabs my arms, turns me toward him and shakes me violently.

"Have you met someone else?"

"No, now let go of me!" I scream.

He snatches my keys and picks me up like a rag doll. He hurriedly carries me back to his apartment as I kick and scream in protest. He raises me above his head with both arms and shoots me onto his leather sofa as if he is shooting a free throw. I slam onto my back and my legs slide from the sofa as I bounce off the couch and my butt violently bangs to the floor. He runs to lock the door and continues to rant.

"Now, I want to know who the fuck he is," he demands as if his eyes are about to pop out of his head.

I jump to my feet and lean into his face to reiterate my newfound lack of fear.

"The only person I've met is me. I want Mariah to be happy first. Can't you understand that?" I ask in exhausted defiance.

"Fine, lie if you want to. But I know there's some tired-ass brother putting this shit in your head. Love you first? If that ain't some bullshit," he says as he gets ready to step away.

"Forget you, Kareem!" I retort with ominous conviction.

Just then he balls up his hand and pulls his right arm back with enough force to propel his fist right into my face. I quickly run toward his fireplace and pick up the brass poker. In my head I can hear the song "Respect" clear as day. This is not a time to demand cherishing.

"I want my damn keys now! I'm not playing with you. I will use this!" I threaten.

Just then I recall painful slow-motioned flashbacks of my mother running down the street with the fireplace poker in her hand while my father chases behind her. It's as if someone has just popped a thirty-five-year-old tape into the VCR of my mind. I am my mom and he is my dad. My hands begin to shake uncontrollably in protest of repeating a cycle in time. I stare at him and freeze in place as he throws my keys at my feet.

"Fine. Get the hell out of here. You'll regret this shit one day. You will see soon enough."

I slowly pick up my keys from the floor while keeping one eye on him and walk toward the door still grasping the poker. I drop it at the threshold and walk away. Kareem comes to the door yelling at me as though I'm fifty miles away.

"I never broke up with you when you were down and out. You come over here after seven and a half years when I'm having money problems and stressed out. Here you are just kicking me straight in my ass. Get to steppin' with all your self-love bullshit. I don't give a shit about a fucking relationship. I have more important things to deal with. The only reason you ever accused me anyway is because of your guilty conscience. You were the unfaithful one, not me. Acting like you're going to use a fucking poker on me. Shit, bitch, I'm six-nine. I can take you out right now! But you're not worth it. You're dismissed. I give you the green light to go ahead and fuck whomever, whenever, wherever, however without guilt. Have a nice life. I've got plenty of women who would love to portray Anita Hill. And the only way you could play Anita Hill would be if I bought you some fucking lips, with your no-dick-sucking yellow ass."

As he slams the door I listen carefully for the sound of footsteps rushing toward me like he has done so many times in the past once his second thoughts kick in. But not this time. I take each stair down to the lobby one at a time, expecting the familiar feeling of turning back. Deep inside, part of me knows he's relieved to have his freedom back. What's more important is that I'm on the road to being one hundred percent me. I'll miss . . . I'll miss . . . the sex. That's it, the sex. Dr. Singer was right, I've bonded to a penis attached to the wrong man.

18

I DRIVE HOME the same route I've taken from his house so many times. This time I cannot recall any specific traffic lights or corners. I just arrive. I'm proud of myself yet I feel the all-too-familiar fear of not being wanted, just like when I was five years old after my dad left us. Here I am doing the leaving so as not to be left first. As I walk in the house I hear Chloe answering the telephone.

"Oh, she just walked in. Who's calling? Mom, it's Malik. Dang, he's cool."

"Thanks, baby." She looks me over as I take the phone. My blouse is ripped just behind my underarm.

"Hey, I'm sorry to call before you could get back in the house and settled in. Do you want to call me back?" Malik asks.

"No, I'm fine," I say while heading straight for my room.

"Everything went okay, right?"

"Yeah."

His tone is filled with concern. "Uh-oh, you're not in the mood to talk about it, huh? I can tell."

"You're right, I've used more words in one

night than I've used all week. I'm drained." I remove my blouse and put on a short cotton robe, switching the phone from ear to ear.

"Mariah, did he hurt you?"

"I allowed him to hurt me emotionally for years. Tonight I'm fine."

"Well, I'm proud of you and I understand. If you want to get together tomorrow rather than tonight, that's fine."

"That would be better. I just don't want to go from one and seemingly run to you; I really need to be alone. Thanks for understanding," I say in appreciation.

"We can talk about it when you're ready. And if it's not too deep or too soon, I want to hopefully meet the kids and write those letters."

"What letters?"

"The ones we talked about after church, to our dads."

"I'll see if I'm up to that, baby, but I'm tired. I'll talk to you about it tomorrow," I say in exhaustion.

"I am proud of you. You did the right thing. Just make sure you're the only person you did it for."

"Yes, I did it for me," I reassure him.

"Good, then it's something that needed to be done no matter what happens between us."

"I agree."

"Go run that bathwater, get those candles, and I'll call you tomorrow. If you need me tonight let me know," he tenders.

"Thanks." Slowly, I hang up the phone and walk into the living room in deep thought.

"Mom, you did break up with Kareem tonight, didn't you?" Chloe asks while logging onto the laptop.

"Why?"

"Because he called about five minutes ago yet I know you went to see him. He was very quiet and distant. What happened?" she asks with an air of worry.

"Yes, I did, Chloe. Just know that I'm happier without him."

Donovan walks in; obviously he overheard our conversation. "Mom, what happened?"

"Donovan, I broke up with Kareem tonight."

"Why?" he asks as if he's surprised.

"Because I do not believe that Kareem and I are compatible. He is a good man for someone, but not for me. It has taken me a long time to come to terms with this, but I've been learning about how important it is to honor my wants and needs, and I have to expect the man in my life to honor my feelings on my terms. I've been honoring his thinking for far too long. I want both of you to be okay with this."

"Honoring his thinking?" Donovan asks like I'm speaking Spanish.

Oh shoot, I sound like Dr. Singer. "What I mean is, I've been staying with him all these years because I've put him first," I explain.

"I know it's hard dating, but I thought he was going to be our stepfather one day," Donovan reminds me.

"That's not something Kareem is ready for," I say.

"But he sat up here and told me that one day he actually prayed to God and thanked Him and Daddy for all of us. Why wouldn't he want us?" Donovan asks.

"It's not about what he doesn't want. I believe he wants us in his life, but I think he wants us within his time frame and without growth. Some people aren't financially ready or mature enough to take the step on the responsibility for a woman and her children. It's difficult for some single men without children to even fathom that. But I apologize for any feeling of loss that you might be having."

Donovan pauses in thought and then continues, "I guess it's okay if you don't want to see him anymore. But you have done this before, and he always ends up calling me."

"He can't do that this time. Trust me, he does care about you, but it's too awkward right now for him to do that," I say in an attempt to soothe his fears.

"Mom, I'm fine with it. I never really saw him as a fatherly image anyway. He felt more like a friend than anything. If you're happy, I'm happy," Chloe conveys.

"I am happy, and I'm not the type of mother who just tells you 'This is my life and like it or not I'm going to do what pleases me in spite of your feelings.' You have both been through such intense losses with your father and your uncle. I do not want you to see this as Kareem abandoning you. It was my choice."

Donovan looks at Chloe and then looks at me

and says, "I agree with Chloe. As long as you're happy, I'm fine."

"Thanks for your support," I say with reassuring smiles for both.

Before long, Donovan, Chloe and I fall asleep on the sofa. I wake up and tuck them in. I pray they are really okay with not having Kareem in their lives. I must be more careful next time.

For the first time I actually fall asleep in the bathtub. I awake to zero bubbles, the candles have burned down to the quick and the barely lukewarm water has half-drained from my Roman tub. It's just me, my radio and En Vogue singing "Give It Up, Turn It Loose."

19

"OKAY, LADIES, hold up your right hand and repeat after me," Dr. Singer exclaims. I have returned to the relationship seminar. This time I'm with Violet and Carlotta. Ariana refused to come back. *"I promise to serve my own womanhood by guiding the man in my life toward a higher level of spirituality, by requiring him to love me before he makes loves to me, to serve my feelings before he asks me to serve his thinking and to allow me to set the spiritual standards of our sexual affairs for the benefit of us both."*

"Oh, she's a trip. What does that mean?" asks Violet, squinting her eyes as she stares at Dr. Singer with caution. "Didn't anyone ever tell you that most psychotherapists are psycho?"

"Shush," Carlotta says to Violet as she stands and inquires, "Does that mean it's not a good idea to have sex until he loves you?"

Dr. Singer explains, "No, you can have all the sex you want if you're not seeking a husband. You'll get a sexual partner who treats you like a freebie, and you can treat him like one. Love is mind, body and soul. Take the body out of the equation and see what you have left. I'm talking about making love. How can you make love unless there is love? Hopefully, he'll be making love to you because he loves you more than you love him, but either way you must set the tone."

"So how do you set the spiritual standards in a relationship?" another woman asks.

"You can say 'I'm not comfortable having casual sex with you because I would surely bond to you,' meaning his magic wand. 'I'd prefer getting to know you above the waist first and discuss the possibility of a long-term, monogamous, committed relationship,' if that's what you both want. He'll either tell you yes, that's what he wants, and sometimes he'll say that just to get you into bed—better to find out sooner than later—or he'll say no, that's not what he's looking for. And if he says no, you'd better believe he means no."

"And then what?" asks Carlotta.

"And then you decide that his *no* really means *no*, and he doesn't want a wife. He wants to play. Or you say, 'Okay fine, let's just screw our brains out until I meet someone else.' Now that's a bad move, ladies. It won't work! You'll be doing drive-bys and checking his pager within six weeks, guaranteed. Would anyone like to come up and share?"

I say, "I will." The audience claps as I approach the stage.

"Well, last night I broke up with my boyfriend of seven and a half years."

"I remember you from our last session. Did you do the breaking up or did he?"

"I did the breaking up."

"Is that what *you* really wanted?" she asks.

I pause to think and then answer, totally assured, "Yes."

"Good. Did you tell him he had every right?"

"Yes, I told him he had every right to act, think, et cetera, however, I was no longer comfortable and I wished him a nice life."

"Very good. What did he say?"

"He was angry."

"Most little boys are when they lose their toy," she informs us.

"He keeps calling."

"We don't care about him, we care about you. How are you?"

"I'm happy. But this is so unlike me, it's scary," I admit.

"And he knows it. He's hoping you will cave in and allow him sex without commitment for another seven years. You have done a great thing here. I told you seven years is six years too long. You fell into bondage and I'm sure when the two of you first started dating, you didn't signal him before sex that you were moving toward marriage. You didn't set the standards. That usually means hurt feelings and time wasted. It's not your fault, but don't make the same mistake again. He'll find his next victim. Just be glad it's not you."

"But the thought of him making love to someone else really hurts," I confess.

"So don't think about it. He had sex with you for free, that's not making love. Like I said, just be glad it's not you. And when you get to the point where you feel sorry for that person he's laying with, you'll be over him. The pain will subside, but your next step is the hardest."

"What's that?" I ask with reserved curiosity.

"You must get ready to de-tox, and it's no different from kicking a cigarette or alcohol habit. It's called de-bonding. The sex part of your relationship has been the thread that held the two of you together. In that way it's an addiction. His next move is for him to call you and ask to just be *friends*. Just say no. Once you say yes, he will know he has a shot if he can just insert his cigar into your ashtray one more time. Don't do it! This will be difficult, but you can do it. When you get a craving, call your girlfriend, or call me, take a walk or just start writing. Your vagina still thinks it belongs to him, but your mind is stronger and it belongs to you. Focus on controlling your thoughts and keep coming back here; it will get easier. Aren't we proud of her, people?" Everyone cheers and claps. "Next."

I cannot believe it. Violet goes up onstage. "Yes, my dear, how can we help you?"

"My name is Violet and I'm bonded to a married man." The audience aahhs.

"You make it sound like an AA meeting. Lighten up." The crowd laughs. "No, I'm just kidding. But married-man bonding is very common. What do you want to do? Do you want him to leave her?"

"Oh heck no! He's got money problems, cannot keep a job and he's a dog. I want to break it off," Violet tells her.

"If he's so bad, then why are you with him? I know, the sex is good, right?"

"Oh hell yes, he can rock it." The ladies chortle.

"Is it that he can rock it or is it that you feel safe from commitment from a man who's already committed, therefore you allow yourself to lose control and enjoy? Or, is it the thrill of getting caught with a forbidden love?"

"Oh no, I'm not in love with him, he just turns me on. And we already got caught," Violet acknowledges.

"Okay. Violet, right? Do you want to get married or chase guys and be a sexual conqueror like you're the masculine?"

"What?" Vi replies as if she's perplexed.

"Do you want to be respected or cherished?"

"Both. No, okay . . . cherished."

"Is he cherishing you?"

"No," Vi avows.

"Then stop acting like you have a penis and make yourself available to an available penis who can cherish you and your vagina." The volume of my snickering leads the way to humored audience reaction.

"Dr. Singer, you are so vulgar," Violet replies loudly with a sudden burst of shy anger.

"Well, if you enjoy the sex and don't mind playing second fiddle to a wife, keep going on like you are. But I don't think you're happy. That's why you're here. You said you wanted to break it off, correct?"

"Yes."

"Then tell him he has every right to fool

around on his wife and seek a mistress or two, whatever he chooses. It's been fun, but you're no longer comfortable. See ya!"

"Then what?" Vi questions.

"Then date up a storm—*duty date*. Meet as many men as you can, stay busy, date all week or weekend, say four or five guys. You too, Mariah. Listen up. No sex! Just take the time to listen to everything these men have to say on your dates and shut up. Don't talk. Think—all ears. Stop gabbing. Too many women run their mouths on a date, giving away their own power and virtue and telling all their business, giving away their hand before he gets a chance to give a shit. Just listen and within two weeks of hearing all of their baggage, you'll drop them easily because you're not in love. Soon, you'll narrow it down to one, and maybe you'll want to start thinking about setting the parameters for whether or not he's looking for a temporary sex partner or a committed relationship. If that doesn't work out, date some more and on and on. You'll be too damn busy to think about Mr. Married throw-down-in-bed. And he will call. Married men are greedy that way. Got it?"

Violet pauses and then admits, "Actually, I do. But I beg to differ on the no-sex portion of your theory. But more importantly, where do I meet all of these *duty-dating* men?"

"Come back next week. I'll show you how. Everybody give a hand to Violet."

Several women approach me and Violet after the seminar is over. They share similar stories. A few of them congratulate me for being able to do what their vaginas won't let them do.

Violet and Carlotta decide to go to dinner. I am doing nothing other than going home to talk to the kids before Malik comes over at nine.

DONOVAN IS IN HIS ROOM playing video games and Chloe is in her room painting her toes.

"Donovan, come in Chloe's room for a minute, please."

"Now?" he asks, obviously hoping to avoid the need to press Pause.

"Now, please."

"What's up?" Donovan asks, running into the room.

"A friend of mine is coming over tonight. I worked a temp assignment with him and we're going to do some writing, okay?"

"Is this Malik?" Chloe recalls.

"Yes, it's Malik. He's from New York and he's interning in town for the summer. He plays football, Donovan."

"Professionally?" Donovan asks.

"Right now he plays college ball."

"College ball? How old is he?" Chloe inquires.

"He's twenty-one," I say, expecting to be committed for insanity.

"Mom!" Donovan exclaims, like I should think twice.

Chloe remarks, "Wow, he's just a few years older than I am."

"Yes, he is. I told you he was in college."

"But that's pretty much all you did tell me. What else?" asks Chloe, sounding suspicious.

"What are the two of you writing?" asks Donovan.

"We're writing a couple of letters," I explain briefly.

"And what else do you two have in common?" Chloe asks.

"Okay, now listen to me carefully. I will be totally honest with you. I have gone out on a date with him already and we have a lot in common actually. I have more in common with this man than most men my age, even some men who are older. He is nice to me, he is a gentleman and he is very mature. I would like him to meet the two of you and you can see for yourself."

"What does he want with you?" asks Donovan.

"Donovan! What does that mean?" I ask, nearly offended.

"I mean is he after you for some other reason?" Donovan asks out of protection.

"As in, does he have an ulterior motive? Well, I'm not rolling in the dough, so I don't think it's money he's after. I think we both just connected and we're seeing what happens, okay?"

"Mom, he's almost two decades younger than you," Chloe reminds me as if I need a reality check.

"I know that, Chloe. I'm concerned about the age difference. That has been my reservation too. But you also know I wouldn't bring him around you if I didn't think he was a good man and if I thought he was just fooling around and looking to play. You've only really met maybe three or four men I've dated since your daddy."

"I know," Chloe admits.

"Your dad is a high standard to live up to. I wasn't mature enough to really know what I had. But I know now. He was a good man."

"Mom, can I go back and finish playing?" Donovan asks.

"If you've said all you'd like to say, yes."

"I'm fine, Mom," Donovan says, walking away at a slower pace than when he entered the room.

"Chloe, he is very nice. If you would rather not meet him tonight, I will cancel."

"I know he's nice. I knew that when I talked to him on the phone. But just be careful. Please," she admonishes as if she's the mom.

"I will, Chloe. Thanks for being concerned." She continues applying a second coat of polish to her toenails and looks up at me as I stand deep in thought.

"Mom?"

"Yes," I reply.

She winks at me just as I walk out of her room.

20

"MOM, MALIK IS AT THE DOOR," Chloe yells. As I walk by her she whispers, "He's cute!"

I hurry to the door and invitingly grab his hand. "Come on in, Malik. I'm on the phone with Kyle's dad. It will only take a second."

Malik takes a seat on the living room sofa across from Chloe who is watching videos on BET.

I continue my phone conversation. "No, I want to see him every weekend, every week, every day. Okay, so what are you asking me? No, I want him here this Saturday at ten in the morning as agreed. The only time I get to see him adds up to less than four damn days every month; there is no room for rearranging. I have had it. I don't even remember how this happened, but Kyle is coming back home to live with me one way or another. No, it's not all of a sudden. I have been gradually accommodating you so much that you've just left me with every other weekend, and now you want to negotiate that. What? Oh, shoot, I forgot this weekend is Father's Day weekend. Then fine, I'll have him home two weekends in a row then, until . . . yes until. Oh heck, I'm not even gonna argue with you, action speaks louder, right? Let me talk to Kyle."

Kyle takes the phone. "Hey, how's everything? I miss you too. I called your science teacher and she said you pulled your grade up to an A. Wow! That was quick, huh? Yes, they're here. All right, hold on."

I hand Chloe the phone. "It's your brother!"

As Chloe talks to Kyle, I notice Donovan is now sitting on the sofa next to Malik. They are discussing, what else, sports.

"So I heard you're number twenty-four also," Malik says.

"Yeah, that was my dad's number in high school so it means a lot to me. Your number is twenty-four?"

"Yes, my mother was that age, twenty-four, when she had me and that number meant a lot to her. I just started requesting it when I'd play and it stuck with me. And I see you have trophies for both basketball and football," he says, looking at the glass trophy case. "I was good at both sports too but because I received more attention for football, I decided to put more energy into that."

"Oh, so you've met, huh? Donovan, Malik is going to training camp next week to play for the Baltimore Ravens," I add.

"That's cool. You've been drafted?" Donovan asks as if he's impressed.

"Yeah, I was the last pick, number two hundred forty-one."

Suddenly a light goes off in my head as I remark, "Think about that number, number twenty-four and number one! Number twenty-four-one!"

"I've never thought of it in that way. That's positive!" Malik says as if to humor me.

"My mom is always coming up with goofy stuff like that. Wait, I remember hearing about you on ESPN—are you from Harlem?"

"Yes, I am."

"He's obviously quite talented," I interject.

"I didn't know Donovan received a call from a coach already. They're not supposed to call until he's a senior."

"I didn't talk to him though. My mom told me not to do anything to blow the recruiting thing. Eventually I want to get paid like you."

Malik adds, "But more importantly, you want an education, and sports can give you that. A full ride is the greatest compliment to your academic and athletic ability. But it takes both."

"Did you go to high school in Los Angeles?" Donovan asks.

"Donovan, telephone," Chloe says.

"No, I grew up in New York City," Malik replies.

"Oh, that's right!" Donovan recalls.

I say, "Donovan, go get the phone, it's Kyle."

"He's handsome and funny," Malik replies as Donovan goes into the kitchen to talk to his brother.

"I know one thing. If these fast girls keep calling him and passing his number around, I'm going to lose it. Especially one White girl named

Becky! It's okay though because he'd just as soon tell a girl he's playing Sega than talk on the phone."

"Unlike me, huh, Mommy," asks Chloe.

Chloe walks in, handing Malik a tall chilled glass of Kool-Aid.

"Here's your red Kool-Aid," says Chloe.

"Oh, that's right. Blacks request Kool-Aid by color, not flavor. I heard that one," jokes Malik.

Chloe says, "Mom, he doesn't really look early twenties, more like mid-twenties."

"Oh, big difference!" I reply.

"I guess I should say thanks," says Malik.

"No, it's more in the way you act than look, really. I don't know. You're cool," Chloe states.

"And so are you. Your mom tells me you like Prince, or The Artist."

"Oh my God! I will marry him one day, once he gets rid of that tired wife of his."

"Chloe, that's not nice. She's just kidding," I tell Malik.

"No, I'm not. She can't even hang with me," she says with confidence.

"Oh, I guess you're the bomb-diggy?" I teasingly ask.

"Mommy, it's the bomb. Anyway, that's old!"

Chloe and Malik laugh at my tired sense of hip.

"You should hear my mom try to say things like, 'you're molded,' " Chloe tells him.

"Mariah, it's 'moded,' not 'molded,' " says Malik.

"I know now. I've been corrected many a day by these two."

"She still says 'fresh,' and worst of all, she says 'groovy.' "

"Chloe, now you know the only reason I say 'groovy' is to get a laugh."

"I bet it does!" jokes Malik

"What's so funny?" asks Donovan, returning to the living room. "Mom, Kyle wants to say good-bye."

"Mom's talking old school again," Chloe says as I take the phone and walk to the kitchen.

"Kyle, I talked to your dad and you'll come home next weekend because of Father's Day, cool? Two weekends in a row like we did when you went to Florida. Keep up the good work and I'll talk to you this weekend. Bye, baby!"

"Mom, we're going to watch the movie *Friday*, okay?" Donovan yells to me as I return to the living room.

"It's late, and it won't be over until almost eleven. Don't you have one more final tomorrow, Donovan?"

"I did study! It's just a grammar test in English."

"Go ahead and watch it," I say with reservation.

"Anyway, this is the movie with Miss Parker," Donovan says with a testosterone grin.

"Donovan has a crush on Miss Parker," says Chloe.

"Yeah, shoot. Miss Parker is fine," Donovan tells Malik.

"I ain't mad at you," Malik interjects.

"You need to be studying your grammar too, talking like that," I say to Malik in jest.

"Mom, you got the big head!" says Chloe.

I correct Chloe on the spot. "I *have* a big head? Seems to me you *got* to be in that room brushing up on your grammar too, girlie. Put the movie on before I change my mind."

I decide to make buttered popcorn and more of that red Kool-Aid. The three of them are laughing and having a great time. The telephone rings.

"Hello, hold on. Mommy, it's Walter, Kareem's friend," says Chloe. I'm checking out Malik's reaction but he doesn't even notice, I think.

"Hey, what's up? I didn't do anything to anybody. With all due respect, Walter, it's none of your business. I don't expect you to understand my position. He's your best friend. You know what, I can't talk. We're watching a movie and I have to go. I know he's hardheaded and can't express how he really feels, that's not my problem any longer. No, no more break up to make up games; it's over, Walter. Now I'd like to consider the possibility of being your friend eventually, but I really think it's too soon. You'd only be his source of information. I have to go. Thanks for calling." Call waiting clicks in. "I'm sure he'll be just fine, Walter, now good night." I click over. "Violet? I'm through with you."

"Is that fine-ass Mandingo warrior over there taking five hundred years of slavery out on your punanny yet?"

"Get your mind out of the stinking trash for once."

"My mind used to have a running buddy in that gutter. Your mind was leading the way," she reminds me.

"Well, not now. I'm going to forward my phone. What a night."

"What happened?" she asks as if hoping for a scoop.

"First Kyle's dad, and then Walter."

"Walter, what's he talking about?"

"I'll tell you tomorrow. Right now, Malik, the kids and I are all watching a movie and I'm missing most of it."

"Excuse me, sorry to interrupt the Huxtables bond night," she kids around.

"I love you, Vi. Now bye."

"Fuck you, hoe! You got yourself a young-ass boy toy and now . . ."

I hang up and shake my head in amazement.

"Here's the part, Mom," says Donovan.

"Hello, Miss Parker," Chloe and Donovan say in unison.

Chloe asks, "She is kind of cute to be older, huh, Malik?" I'm going to get her for that.

"Yeah, she's a beautiful woman just like your mom." Good answer.

"Oh, I bet your mom's pretty too," says Chloe.

"Yes, she was. My mom died when I was very young."

"Sorry," says Chloe.

Silence.

"Chloe, you're always being nosy and running your mouth," says Donovan.

"No, I think what she said was very sweet. My mom was pretty," Malik says to relieve the tension.

"You know our daddy died, right?" asks Chloe.

"Yes, your mom told me. I'm sorry also."

"Can I show you a picture of him?" she asks.

"Sure," Makik says.

"He doesn't want to see pictures right now, do you?" asks Donovan.

"I'd love to see him if you want to share." Chloe hands Malik an eight-by-ten framed family portrait from the end table. "He looks just like you, Donovan," exclaims Malik.

Donovan frowns and continues to watch the movie. Two seconds later his frown turns to a smile. "Here's that part where the Janet Jackson look-alike rolls up and . . ."

". . . he says she's more like Freddie Jackson?" Malik finishes his sentence.

They lean into each other for a high five. Chloe places the picture back on the end table next to Malik. I go into the hallway to forward the telephone to ensure no more interruptions.

"Good night, Donovan, you have to lift weights early in the morning, don't you?" I ask as he stands from the couch.

"Not during finals." Donovan yawns.

"So I expect you in the shower at seven. And I want to hear that you got an A on that 'just grammar' final. See you in the morning."

Malik says, "Donovan. It was nice meeting you." He extends his hand and pulls Donovan to him for a hug.

"You too. Good night, twenty-four," Donovan replies.

"Good night, twenty-four," Malik says, smiling.

Chloe is in her room on the telephone. Once again I let her slide.

"Mariah, we don't have to write these letters tonight if you're not up to it," Malik says as we sit on my sofa with the laptop on the coffee table.

I reply, "No, actually, I heard someone on the radio today talking about creating good relationships and making amends, saying you're sorry and doing it in prayer also. It's like cleaning out closets so you can move forward. I'm proud of both of us."

"I got my father's address today from my grandfather. I can't believe I finally brought up that whole issue. What a trip," Malik proclaims.

"We're blessed to have fathers to write to, Malik. I know it's hard. Let's do it."

MY LETTER:

Dear Dad,

I'm writing you this letter to clear up some issues in my life which have caused me grief and stagnation. This letter is written in an attempt to help me move beyond all of that.

This letter is not written to blame you or make you feel bad. As Father's Day approaches, I feel it's a great time to open up and discuss our past so that we can move forward toward a positive and improved future.

My memories of being five years old are very vivid. I can recall good times, but for the most part I remember you and Mom fighting and screaming. One thing I knew for sure was that I was Daddy's little girl. One day you and I were on our way to get manicures. I was sitting right next to you on the middle seat of our nineteen fifty-nine Cadillac convertible, feeling proud and cherished with my arm around my protector, driving down Santa Barbara Boulevard with my braids blowing in the wind. The next day, you were gone. That was thirty-five years ago.

In my opinion, as a little girl, I took on a subconscious message that I wasn't good enough. I internalized the belief that I wasn't worth your time, your parenting or your love.

That issue has followed me into my adult relationships with men. I'm sure you are unaware of this but . . . I admit that I was an awful wife to Donovan. The entire time I was married, the need for answers to many questions of abandonment were slowly rising to the surface. I chased charming men, like my dad, and chased unavailable men who would eventually leave, like my dad. I've learned to expect to not be worthy of the love. I've expected to be abandoned and I've learned to accept the blame for being unlovable.

This is a brief summary of my experience from my point of view. It is a summary reached without your input. That's not fair to you. I'd like your input and I'd like to know what happened.

Why did you leave? Was Mom so intolerable to live with, was she insanely jealous, was she unfaithful, was she boring? You had a reason and I want to accept that reason. I want to love you for your choice. You dealt with the situation based upon your own level of awareness at that time in your life. I understand that without blame and judgment.

Please find it in your heart to call me and talk to me when you feel comfortable. If not, I suppose writing this letter will have to do.

Forever Love—Your Little Girl,
Mariah

MALIK'S LETTER:

Dear Father,

It's taken me a long time to get to the point where I can actually sit down and unscramble my thoughts and feelings about an issue that has had such an impact on my life. But now is the time for me to be a man and speak on it.

I'll never forget the day you left. The memory is embedded in my mind like a regretted tattoo. As a nine-year-old kid, I felt you were my life. You were my dad. You were my mentor. You were everything I wanted to be, personified. You were my partner. You know, I used to look at all of the other kids at school who didn't have fathers and I wondered why. Every kid was supposed to have a daddy, right?

Well, I guess I was wrong. Because despite where I am in my I life now and where you are in yours, the fact still remains that you were not there for me.

Three years before you left, Mom died. And

then I found myself without a father and a mother. Did you ever think about how that could make a child feel? Did you ever want to reach out to me and hug me and tell me, "It's okay, son. I love you." That would have brightened my whole world. But instead I was reaching out to you like a child whose balloon floated up to the ceiling and no matter how hard he strained to balance on the tip of his toes, his middle finger barely grazed it. You were not within my reach. But thank God Grandpa was.

The purpose of this letter is not to point fingers or blame you, although it may sound like that's what I'm doing. I just want to let you know how I feel. That's all. It was hard, Dad. I know everyone makes mistakes. I'm the first person to attest to that. And after all of the tears are swept away and all of the layers of anger, frustration and confusion are peeled away, there is a time when you realize that you are who you are at this point in time because of everything that's happened to you up until this point. There is a reason why our lives turned out the way they did. I am a good man, Dad. I am responsible, hardworking, loyal and honest. I want you to know that I do not hold anything against you. You did what you thought was best at the time you did it and I cannot argue with you about that. But I can say that I will not forget the extra scrapes and bruises that I had to gain climbing up that mountain of life because I didn't have your hand to boost me up. If I ever get in trouble, or even get married, <u>will you be there when I need you?</u>

Now that I'm entering the NFL, I want you to be a part of my life. I will not shut you out and I will not exclude you as you excluded me; it's never too late. Life is too short to not let go and move on. And this is just a letter to say that <u>I'm willing to start from here; I'm willing to be a man.</u>

Malik

As we address and seal the envelopes with sentimental tears, I kiss him gently and tenderly. Malik takes his time down the stairway and in to his grandfather's car and pulls off.

21

IT'S NINE O'CLOCK on a gloomy Wednesday morning. My children are off starting their day, the telephone is quiet and no one has called to offer work for the day. I remember to run errands, pay overdue bills, and file an unemployment claim over the telephone. I stop to page Malik with a code of "510," my height, followed by "24," which means just thinking of you. I smile. The day must include a trip to the post office to mail the bills, overdue yet right on time.

He calls upon receiving my page.

I'm sure he can hear the glee in my voice as I tell him, "Hey, baby, I didn't mean for you to call me, I just wanted to let you know the thought of you made me smile this morning."

"That's sweet, but it gave me an excuse to call you anyway. How's your morning?" Malik asks.

"Quiet, kind of a much-needed lull. Is it supposed to rain or what?"

"Not that I know of, but it looks ugly. Mariah, I need to talk to you. I got a call from my coach this morning. I'm leaving on Tuesday of next week to go to training camp in Baltimore for a while. The first thing I thought about was you, missing you. This has been the best time this past week. It's been very deep."

"Don't be sad, baby, you'll be back. And in the meantime I thought it would be nice to have a picnic here for you, kind of a going-away party, NFL celebration, real-man barbecue. What do you think?"

"I hadn't thought about it but that's a great idea, very sweet of you. When?"

"This weekend, the Saturday before Father's Day. I wish Kyle could be here so you could meet him before you go. But you will meet him when you get back."

"Yeah, you'll have him two weekends in a row, right?" Malik remembers.

"Yes, we will."

"Baby, I wanted to tell you, my uncle is an attorney and I can hook you up with him if you want to get some feedback about getting custody. I can have him call you while I'm gone," he offers.

"Would you? Is he expensive? You know, I've been putting it off for no reason other than money. That's tired. There should be no price too high to pay for losing out on the very years we can relate to."

"That's why I think you should get on it. If you want to, of course."

"I want to," I say in agreement.

"Fine, then I'll call him today."

"I don't know what to say to you, you are so sweet and generous and you're like my best friend already."

"So, best friend, don't forget to mail those letters today, unless you've changed your mind."

"Oh no, not me. Have you?" I ask.

"No, not me, have you?"

"No, Malik, have you?" I ask again as if I could not possibly be the one to have second thoughts.

"We've come too far to back out. Shoot, I ain't scared. I'll come over there and send them overnight mail, let's get on it," he says with confidence.

"I got it. They're as good as gone. What are you doing today?"

"I have to do that mentor thing at Culver High School or at some youth center. I'm not sure which one, probably for the next few weekdays."

"I forgot about that. I'm proud of you," I profess.

"Well, thank you. Anyway, I'm gone. I miss you already, baby."

"So do I."

"And if you want to do something later, let me know, I'm down. And what time should I tell my buddies to come by this Saturday?"

"Let's say one o'clock, and invite your grandparents too."

"I will. Let me know what you need me to bring," he offers.

"I will. Have a blessed day."

WEDNESDAY NIGHT, Malik and I take the kids bowling before we eat barbecue at Smokey's. Malik and Donovan battle in their own testosterone macho way as Chloe and I struggle to break one hundred.

By Thursday morning I find myself home again looking through newspapers for new agencies. I decide to make a few calls to invite my friends to the party.

"Violet, it's at one this Saturday. It's a going-away party for Malik."

"Is he leaving you already?" Violet toys with me as usual.

"No, he's going to training camp. I'll call you later; now be there or be square, I love you!" I then call Ariana.

"Make sure you tell the twins, China and Trina. Don't forget, and come early so you can help a girl out." I make more calls.

"Carlotta, what's up?"

Carlotta says, as if she's dishing the dirt, "Girl, I saw Kareem last night at the Leimert Club. The boy was wasted and he tried to pull me aside and bend my ear with his side of the story about the two of you breaking up."

I attempt to change the subject. "Well, anyway, can you come by Friday and help out? Thanks!" I make another call.

"Sarah, I spoke to Cindy and she told me about the card party. I forgot. This one you must attend. We know how to get our card game on too! Bring Cindy or whomever. It's gonna be nice. It's a going-away party for Malik. He's going to the NFL. In Baltimore."

"He's going where?" she replies in disbelief.

"To play for the Ravens."

"And the two of you are what, friends? I knew something was up with you two. What are you going to do while he's in the NFL? Knit and play bingo?"

"I don't know, Sarah. See, you're trying to be funny and I've really been thinking about that. Even if we end up being more than friends, lovers or whatever, how am I going to handle that? Once he makes the team, how could I even begin to expect him to be satisfied with a forty-year-old woman with all of those young groupies and cheerleaders around?"

"Yes, you've lost your mind all right," Sarah says.

"Oh, don't remind me. I say I'm going to just enjoy it while it lasts."

"In the meantime, just take great delight in kicking it with that young stud because you seem to be the type who needs a baby boy to pull your hair and spank you from the back anyway."

"Hopefully it will remain a little deeper than that. Besides, I don't have any hair to be pullin' on. I don't play that mess. Maybe a little spanking, though, you know."

"When and where? We'll be there. I mean when and where is the barbecue?" Sarah jokes with her usual borderline humor.

"I know what you meant. This Saturday, around one. I'm the upstairs duplex on the corner of Sixty-second and Fairfax, 6200 Fairfax, and bring a little freak juice for yourself."

"Just say BYOB," she suggests.

"That could mean bring your own bitch to you," I tease with a jab of my own.

"See, I can't believe I let you assist me for a few

days. That's before I knew you were a child mo-lester. That boy's still experiencing puberty."

"Okay now, wear your ass-kicking pad. Bye," I say as I hang up snickering.

That woman is a great person. Sometimes you meet people and have no idea what they're really like until you give them a chance to be in your life. She's a good one.

The telephone rings as soon as I hang up. It's for Chloe.

After her conversation, Chloe comes running into my bedroom excited and screaming, "Mommy, I just got a call from my friend Chanette," she says, busily flailing her hands about.

"Chanette?"

"Yes, she works in the mall."

"And?"

"I talked to her last week and told her I need a summer job and she said she'd talk to her boss. Well, today one of the girls quit and they need to replace her immediately so her boss told her that if I could be there from three until eleven today, I could have the job until school starts. Mommy, it pays twelve dollars per hour."

"Congratulations, baby, what are you going to be doing?"

"I'm going to be working at the yo-yo cart."

"The yo-yo cart?" I ask. I need her verification that I heard her correctly.

"Yes, it's one of those carts you see in the mall that sells stuff, only we sell yo-yos."

"Yo-yos are back?" I ask with surprise.

"Yes. Duncan yo-yos, all kinds."

"And the yo-yo cart makes enough money to pay you twelve an hour?"

"Are you being funny? Some of them cost up to twenty-eight dollars each. They glow in the dark and some of them are like boomerangs. They're hot," she explains.

"I am happy for you, I really am. Make sure you take your driver's license and Social Security card just in case you fill out a W-4 or an application."

"I have it already," she says, one step ahead of me.

I told her she needed to get a job, and she did. That's my girl. That's so sweet. Yo-yos.

I receive a phone call from Donovan. He needs to be picked up from school. It's his last day. Of course he's starving because he didn't remember to ask me for lunch money this morning and he never makes his own lunch.

He's getting too old to not look out for himself and I refuse to make lunch for someone who's taller than I am. Last year I just stopped asking when he would get out of the car, "Do you need lunch money?" And you surely don't give him, like, a twenty for the week. It would only last a couple of days. That's why I buy more than enough food for lunches. But maybe bringing your lunch isn't cool nowadays. I mean he is a jock and all. Perhaps if he were to brown-bag it, he would, as they say, get clowned. I drive up to his school as he approaches the car working his cool walk.

"Hey, handsome, you want to have lunch with your mother today?"

"I was going to ask you if I could go to my friend's house to watch tapes."

"Tapes of what?" There's no telling nowadays.

"Of the plays we ran in practice; you know we have an alumni game this weekend and we need to get ready."

"Okay, you mean with Justin, the quarterback?"

"Yeah, please?"

"When?"

"Now. Can you drop me off?" he begs.

"All right, but aren't you hungry?" Stupid question.

We drive through McDonald's. He orders three Big Macs and super-size drinks and fries, as usual. We also get something for Justin.

"Donovan, Chloe got a job today . . . in the mall at the yo-yo cart."

"Cool. She gets all the fun stuff to do. I want her to hook me up. Yo-yos are the thing now, Mom."

"Okay, you say so!"

I drop him off and stop at the magazine stand for the latest *Broadcasting & Cable*. They post all of the current job openings in journalism. As I pull into my driveway, Kareem is waiting for me, sitting on my patio chair at my back door, puffing on his cancer sticks.

"Mariah, I've left tons of messages and you keep ignoring me like I don't exist. It's time for us to talk seriously."

"Kareem, you have to call first. You don't just show up at people's houses."

"Like I said, you haven't returned my calls. For all you know, something could have happened to my mom or whatever."

"Come on, I'm sure your mom is fine," I say as if I'm no longer playing along.

He walks over to me close enough to smell his nicotine-laced breath and leans his towering six-nine frame over me. He backs me up to the wall and reaches his right arm high enough over my head so that his forearm rests on the top of the stairwell.

"It's time to get serious," he says, with a serious face to match.

"What do you mean?" I ask, playing dumb.

"I mean I want you with me. I want you to cut off everyone else. It has to be just the two of us, you and me. When I travel, I want you with me; when I play basketball, I want you in the stands; when I give pool parties with Walter, I want you there. I don't want to lose you."

"You put your hands on me for the last time. You act like it's no big deal."

"I didn't hit you. I was trying to stop you from walking out of my life," he says with his usual sense of denial.

Silence.

"It's a little bit late for all of this. It seems to me you're saying you want me for another seven or eight years of being your girlfriend until the next time you need your space. You're not saying you want me to be your wife, right?" I already know the answer.

"I still have so many things I need to do. I cannot say I'm ready for that. Let's just take it a day at a time."

"Kareem, a day at a time is why I was thirty-two when I met you and now I'm almost forty. How long in dog years do you need?"

"I really wish you would stop insulting me, Mariah!"

I reiterate, "I've been your girlfriend long enough. I can no longer be in your life. You refuse to remove me from your 'good-for-now woman' list. To you, I am not wife material and that's fine. But as I told you, no more freebies and no more break up to make up games. We have to move on. You know I'm not Miss Right."

After a second of deep thought he answers, "You might be." As if he'd have to guess about something like that? I'm not asking him his shoe size in centimeters.

I use his words, "Might be? If I were, you would know it by now. I'm your Miss Right Now as opposed to your Miss Right!"

"Baby, you're my best friend. We have been through so much together. We have the greatest sex life."

"Then why do you constantly screw around on me?"

"I only did it that one time."

"Oh, sometimes you sound like Eddie Murphy in the *Raw* comedy video: I fucked her, baby, but

I make love to you. You try to make me feel as if I'm special because I'm number one; I have to be the only one. And I don't believe you could ever be satisfied with just one, Kareem. I know you better than that," I say, taking long strides to make my way to the back door.

"That's your problem, you only know what people tell you. People who don't know me, they only think they know me because I used to play ball. People are always coming up to you starting shit and you run with it. If I'm seen with a woman, people think I'm fuckin' her, when she could be my damn cousin," he says in a tone that would have done the trick three years ago.

"I don't have time to hear your victim stories again. When are you going to be responsible for your own actions? I used to trust you until Miss Thang came up to me at the gas station talking about how she just left your house that morning, kinda like *if that's your boyfriend he wasn't last night*. You had to admit that shit because I saw her car parked behind yours so many times."

"Well, if you hadn't been doing drive-bys so damn much," he accuses me, exacting my steps with his toes to my heels.

I stop at the door. "See, there you go again—it's always my fault. The days of insecure Mariah driving by anyone's house are over. I deserve better. Get it through your head, that's exactly why we're not together. I get a damn headache rehashing this shit. Please leave," I request as if I'm serious, attempting to open the lock of my door, only to suddenly find that every key looks alike. "Dammit!"

"Mariah, I'm going to get you back," he says, and I can smell the warm nicotine of his breath meet the top of my head.

Speaking of breath. "Don't hold your breath, Kareem."

I open my door and slam it behind me, crying as I run to throw myself on top of my bed, re-playing scenes of infidelity again and again in my head. I suppose I need to remind myself of the bad so I don't open that door and pull him into my bedroom to lick him up and down like I used to. It would be so easy to do, just let him do me one more time and, as he knows, I'd be addicted again. Gloedene and Barry, watching X-rated tapes, letting him call me his hoe in bed and play-ing out his fantasies as I did before. We'd be back together and everything would be just as it was. But getting back together is easy; the hard part is letting go. I'm going to get up and change my clothes to go running. Mariah is first from now on. Mariah needs to clear her head.

22

LATER THAT EVENING, Donovan walks through the door. Justin's dad dropped him off. I throw together his favorite fried chicken dinner and we sit down to eat together. Chloe is still at work. Her first day at the yo-yo cart.

After dinner I decide to call Kyle to say hello.

"He can't talk right now because I'm on the other line," says his new White stepmother. "I'll have him call you back."

He never calls me back when I leave a message with her. I always end up calling again and again. I just want to cuss her butt out so damn bad, but I can't. It would only reflect negatively on Kyle because she would take it out on him. I know I won't hear from him tonight. I want to buy him a pager just so I can reach him, or buy him his own cell phone so I can call. But his dad isn't having either one. I want to scream, but I say, "Okay, that would be fine, thank you. Good-bye."

An hour or so later the phone rings. I'm hoping it's Kyle but it's my actor friend again. I remember the day I would have wanted to get together

with him once Kareem and I broke up. But now I
cannot.

"So, is everything straight, you need anything?" he asks.

"Yes, everything is fine."

I know he must think I'm still happy in my relationship. If he only knew.

"I have some stuff for Donovan, just some Hilfiger and some PlayStation games, you know, my
boy hooked me up."

"Donovan doesn't need that, but thanks for offering, and please don't tell him you have it," I insist.

"No, I wouldn't do that. It's cool though, if you
don't want me to give it to him, I understand," he
says, like it's no big deal.

"You always do understand, that's why we've
been friends for so long, but to be honest with
you, I can't see you anymore like this. I have to be
true to myself and you deserve more than just
being someone I turn to when my man pisses me
off."

"No, it's cool, baby. I was just checking on you
as I do from time to time, just looking out for
you."

Funny, he'll never say he just wants to come
over and get some. He never verbalizes what this
is really about. It's always to see if I'm straight,
when in reality, he's getting more than anything
he could ever give me. He's getting my body and
my self-respect. It's no longer for sale.

"Really, I can't do this anymore. You are such a
giving and sweet man. But I know you have a

wife, or at least a woman. It's not fair to her or to me. I can no longer accept your calls. Please do not call anymore."

"I thought we were friends. Aren't we?" he asks, sounding confused.

"No, we're not. The only friend I've been to you is your booty-call buddy. I know nothing about you, and you know nothing about me. After all these years, we should know something. Now I have to go."

He just hangs up. And I'm cool with that. A part of me doesn't want him to be mad, but a bigger part of me doesn't want to disappoint myself any longer.

Malik leaves a message on my voice mail that he's invited maybe ten or twelve people, and wants to go shopping tonight. He'll be over in about an hour.

He comes over around seven-thirty and we go to Smart and Final to buy a gang of alcohol, ribs, chicken, potatoes, desserts, and he won't let me pay, even though I'm giving this party for him. He brings the groceries in from the car and leaves to help his grandfather clean out the garage. What a man, what a man, what a man, what a mighty good man!

FRIDAY MORNING, I receive a call from the studio that hired me to work for Sarah. They need me to come back for the day to work in the home video department again. That's where Brenda, Robin and Tanya work. The thought of it makes me ill. I tell them to call my agency directly. A while later my agency calls. I turn the job down.

I spend the day as if I'm a millionaire's house-wife, planning a refined dinner for fifty of our closest Hollywood friends. It's not like I've got money in the bank and a maid in the kitchen. What I've got is nerve.

Thank goodness Carlotta shows up to help out. "I hope you're taking heed to Dr. Singer's rules, girl. You might need a special rule to handle that boy," she jokes.

"Dr. Singer says all men are men, no matter what the age. It's just that the older ones lose some of their testosterone when they hit fifty and then they calm down a bit."

"Well, Malik ain't nowhere near there. How old is he, anyway?" she asks.

"Old enough to be my friend, Carlotta, old enough to deal with this thirty-nine-year-old baggage-filled woman."

"Have you guys . . . ?" I suppose the curiosity is just killing her.

"Don't ask!" I warn her.

"Okay. Anyway, I told you about Kareem try-ing to defend himself the other night at the club. He was bending the hell out of my ear. I didn't even listen to him. That brotha is in constant de-nial," she says, frying sausage links for the baked beans.

"That's Kareem for you."

"Girl, can you believe he had the nerve to try and hit on me?" she asks as if she's amazed. I'm not.

"Yes. New subject. So what the heck is up with you? Why is it you and Ariana never tell me any of your drama? You two are always in my business," I tell her as I place a dish of macaroni and cheese in the oven.

"My boring-ass life. I'm hoping to get hooked up tomorrow with some young buck like you have. What are Malik's friends like?"

"Carlotta, aren't you supposed to be duty dating ever since you broke off the engagement with Mr. Wrong?"

"Violet needs that shit, not me. Anyway, we've gotta wait until Dr. Singer tells us how. Ain't nobody breaking my door down to get with me right now. I'm doing my duty with my dildo," she admits with a perverted stare, pointing a fork at me.

"I suppose sex with a dildo is nonbonding and safe. But you're not going to meet marriage-material available men at the sex shop. Besides, the majority of those men are probably married anyway. You have to get yourself out there and be available to meet them. I know you cannot possibly have that problem. You're the one who's a big old guy magnet." Just then my phone rings. I pick it up as we are laughing.

"Hey, Daddy? How are you?" My laughter instantly dies and my smile turns to a face ridden with amazement and shock.

"Not so good, Mariah, I received your letter," he says, sounding down.

I excuse myself from the kitchen and go into my bedroom for privacy.

"What's wrong?" I anxiously inquire while closing the door.

"What I want to know is, what talk show have you been watching?"

"Excuse me?" I respond with disbelief.

"This is so trendy, using words like 'dysfunctional' and 'abandoned,'" he answers haughtily.

"Daddy, as I said, the letter is not to blame you, it was only written for me." My voice is sundering from his comment. It feels like I am being scolded as if I'm once again five years old.

"Then you should have mailed it to yourself, not to me," he says with a furious edge. My legs collapse as I fall back onto my bed.

"Why are you reacting like this?" I inquire with fury and caution.

"How did you expect me to react? After more than three decades you're still blaming me for your relationships with men? Get over it and move on," he says rigidly in a deep, raised voice.

"Wow, I guess you never really know how someone feels until you bring it up. I didn't mean to make you mad, I just wanted a dad." The tone of my voice is elevating with every rapid beat of my broken heart.

"The only father you need is God. You need the Heavenly Father in your life, that's your problem," he interjects with an admonishing growl.

"What did you say?" I ask as I feel my jaw tightening with each word. "Like a little girl can look to the Heavenly Father to tuck her in at night and teach her to ride a bike. I'm sorry you don't get it."

"I'm sorry you can't get over it. What a shame that is!" he says with condescending disdain.

"Forget it, Dad. I was just reaching out and trying to bring closure," I say, no longer yelling. I can now taste the hurt as it travels from my heart up to my tongue. I can barely speak from the sour, salty, bitter flavor of his baleful reaction.

"I reject your trying. The only trying you're into is blaming me. I'm not taking the blame. I was recently baptized and forgiven for my sins. I suggest you do the same."

"To be born again doesn't wipe away your heart and your memories, does it?" I stiffly remark, prepared to end the conversation.

"You try it and let me know."

I slam the phone down and once again begin to cry . . . over a man.

Carlotta comes into my room and fretfully asks, "What was that all about?"

"Girl, my dad received this letter I wrote him asking him why he left me and my brothers, not even why he left, just what happened. But once again he rejected me. I guess I'm no different from my mother, always asking why he left. He actually told me the only father I need is God."

"Oh, that is so fucked up. I'm sorry."

Carlotta sits on my bed next to me and rocks this wounded and disappointed five-year-old. We rock and rock and rock until I am dizzy. Why is all of this happening to me? Why are my relationships with women so much better than my relationships with men? Why have I lost my husband and my brother? They were two of the best men in my life and they're dead. At times I even feel a loss for my Kyle, battling to make it right. My younger brother and I have never been close. Even my stepfather has never really shown the strength of a father to me. Am I too busy blaming others to simply get over it? When will I? I'm exhausted. I dare not call him back.

23

IT'S EARLY SATURDAY AFTERNOON, a bright, sunny day, nearly ninety-two degrees already. But to me, it's a dismal day filled with resignation and dolor.

However, I do look good today in my soft pale-pink knee-length tube dress. Not to mention my hair. I highlighted my twists with a soft cognac shade early this morning because I couldn't sleep. My toes look decent in my tannish brown sandals. I used Chloe's nail polish again; some color called Chiclets—sort of a pale lavender thing. I hope my friends mingle and get along with Malik's friends, or should I say I hope they don't devour the poor boys. Carlotta and I made a truckload of food last night. How I found the energy, I'll never know.

The backyard is mainly concrete, just a small amount of grass in the corner where Malik is setting up the barbecue pit. Maybe six or seven small round tables with four antique wrought-iron chairs each. And of course we had to set up the folding table for all of the dominoes- and card-playing, trash-talking brothers and sisters.

Malik is in the backyard getting things ready. His grandparents couldn't make it today but his grandmother sent over an enormous pot of mustard greens. The soulful kind with the ham pieces. She also made a huge dish of apple cobbler that I've been tasting all morning. Grandma Simpson can cook!

Malik is wearing some jammin' jean shorts, some well-known label, I'm sure. Of course not the shorts men used to wear back in the day when shorts were actually short. Damn, I wish they were today so I could see those black marble-cut quads and hamstrings. But those calves are flashing a mighty powerful view, very shapely and tight. No doubt he can run that ball right on into the pros. That's my boo!

He's also wearing his Ravens hat the team sent him. He brought one for Donovan too. Donovan and Chloe are in charge of the music this afternoon. And of course Donovan will be shooting hoops most of the day. He'll probably start a pickup game if he can get enough guys, or girls.

Ariana and Violet arrive first. My girl Vi is always complaining she needs to lose weight even though she says her greatest fears are the gym and celibacy. But we both know the guys like us sisters thick, so we don't want to hear it. Besides, she can get away with it.

Girlfriend looks good to me. She's thirty-seven with beautiful mahogany skin and deep-set dimples. Her raisin-colored, healthy, shoulder-length hair consistently looks like she just stepped out of Shameka's Hair Nook, always freshly trimmed and bouncin' like she had a press and curl to the root. She's wearing a long, white, tight knit dress, showing her major silhouette, front and back. That's pretty risqué for her. She never wears form-fitting clothes. Her waist is small and her hips are representing her heritage, curvy and wide. And those breast-tis-ses. She puts Pam Grier to shame. Makes the guys go, "Please, baby, baby, please!"

Let's not mention baby girl's fingernails. Her favorite shade is that tangerine candy thing. Vi prides herself in grooming and it shows. She looks like she spends hours at the Perfect Body salon on Slauson getting hooked up with massages, waxes, mud baths and pedicures. She whisks her citrus fragrant body past me after she leans her nosy ass out of the backdoor to check out Malik and sticks her tangerine thumb into her Riviera red lipstick-lined mouth with an X-rated sucking motion.

Ariana, on the other hand, could stand to gain a few pounds; she's one of those women who could have been a model back in the day. She's a tall glass of water, damn near six feet in her stocking feet, but she's never grown to be very comfortable with her height. She probably has a thirty-six-inch inseam so it's hard for her to find any pants long enough other than jeans or else she has them made. After all, she is a designer for Nordstrom, so she can afford it and can surely create it. Today she has on a short red, white and blue cotton dress, sort of a gingham print, with a sexy pair of red sandals, red toes, red nails, red lips. You go, girl!

"Hey, girls, bring it on in," I call from the kitchen, where I'm arranging some more ice in the cooler.

"What's up? And who's that young Black studmuffin back there hooking up the barbecue?" asks Violet.

"You know that's Malik, don't even try it," I say as if she needs to quit.

Vi still remarks, "Damn, he's just as fine as he is young, Mariah."

"Thanks, I think," I say while keeping one eye on her keeping an eye on him.

"Where's Carlotta?" asks Ariana.

"She was here all night helping me cook, bless her heart. She's probably sleeping."

"With whom?" asks Vi.

"Violet, why do you think Carlotta is such a hoochie? She's maturing and very supportive. I see her as a good friend. She's on my good side for the moment."

"Yeah, after all, she's the one who hipped us to Dr. Singer," says Violet.

"Oh, we owe her one, all right," threatens Ariana.

Suddenly I hear a voice in the backyard, subtle at first and then louder.

"Don't worry, Malik. I didn't come here to start anything with you."

I know that voice. Not today. Please, dear Lord. It's the same high-pitched, annoying, insecure, the boy is mine, young voice that I heard outside my apartment that day who was so-called claiming Malik. She cannot possibly believe I will allow her fan-tod behavior to ruin my party. It is the Brenda from hell.

Malik says with wrath, "Brenda, leave now!"

Violet looks at me, shakes her head in derision and says, "This is gonna be a jiggy day," as she spins around and samples some of my potato salad.

I proceed outside to bellow in disgust, "Brenda, what are you doing here?"

"I heard you were having a little get-together, and I wanted to talk to you for a minute before everyone gets here."

Malik asks in a mocking tone, "You heard she was having a little . . . Girl, you are really gone."

"Malik, you made me promise I'd apologize, so I'm here to do that. You haven't given me a minute."

"What, Brenda?" I inquire without patience as I walk back into the kitchen while Brenda follows behind.

"Mariah, just let me talk, girl. I know we didn't meet on the best of terms but I want to let you know how bad I feel about coming over the other day. I don't want us to be enemies over no man. You seem like an intelligent woman and I disrespected you by calling you dried up and causing a scene."

Violet laughs as I instruct, "Go! Good-bye, Violet, and you too Ariana."

Chloe quickly rushes into the kitchen.

"What's going on, Mommy?"

"Chloe, take everyone outside and introduce them, please," I tell her as I toss the kitchen towel onto the tile counter.

"Okay," Chloe replies as she smirks and walks out the back door. Violet bumps into the service porch wall, too busy trying to keep an eye on what's going on behind her, as if she has eyes in the back of her big old head. She blushes crimson-rosebud red yet still tries to play it off.

I take Brenda into my bedroom and I hear Violet say, "Someone had their oxytocin shake for breakfast." I close the door, breaking a direct stare at Vi. Brenda and I sit on my bed.

"Anyway, Brenda, do you really think I've never been where you are when it comes to men? I'm nearly twice your age—I understand how it feels to be hurt. But take it from me, you only hurt yourself when you confront people and make a scene. You end up stroking his ego and disrespecting yourself. Do you understand what I'm saying?"

"Well, believe it or not, I'm normally not like this. I've just had some bad experiences with men in the past and I get so frustrated sometimes when I catch one slippin'."

"Slippin', believe it or not, not all of them slip . . . but a hell of a lot of them do. Maybe because of the notion that there are too many women and too little time," I inform her.

"Whatever it is, I'm tired of it. I'm ready to be celibate and forget it. But I really liked Malik. He appeared to be different," she says with what I think is sincerity.

"I believe he is. You know what? You're a pretty woman, you've got a lot going for yourself at work, you're very intelligent and I'm sure you have no trouble meeting men. Just know that sometimes what sex means to us is different from what it means to them. To us, organs are internal; when they enter us, we take them into our hearts as well as our bodies, most times. Their organs are external, and some of them are more into the physical than wanting to hug and talk and cuddle afterward. Even though I met one who did and then I was the one trying to force myself to stay awake because all he wanted to do was run his mouth. We have to know what we won't put up with and set the tone. And take it from me, you can always tell if a man likes you by whether or not he wants you to hang around afterward."

"Shoot, sometimes they just want you around so they can get some more in the morning," she says as if from experience.

"True. See you already have this game peeped, right?"

"Right!" she agrees as if she knows no naivete.

"I believe you are sincere in coming over here. You didn't have to come apologize. But you could have called first," I say as if to admonish.

"Malik said if I didn't apologize, he was going to have someone jack my Rover. I couldn't have that. That's why we requested you back as a temp, but you weren't available."

I'm still semireluctant, but I suppose I must respect the girl for being woman enough to apologize. She may be a little bold, but she's all right. I believe we women have more in common than we think. We've all been hurt and jealous because of what we believe is an action caused by or involving another woman.

"Brenda, I understand, okay? I don't hold any grudges against you. I'm too old for high school shit. Just promise me you'll stop running around starting mess over a man you barely know. But know this, I'm with Malik, okay? Whatever happened between the two of you is over," I inform her to reinforce what Malik has told her.

"I'm cool with that. No more drama, I promise," she says. She looks like an eight-year-old child being scolded. "I'm sorry."

I stand up and say, "All righty then, are you gonna help me with this food or what? Because you're staying! Let's get cracking before all these Negroes show up. And one more thing . . ."

"Yes?" she answers, rising from the bed.

"I'm far from dried up, girl! I don't know who you've been talking to," I state as I open the bedroom door and we enter the kitchen.

We laugh as Malik walks in the kitchen and stops on a dime. "Oh my God!" he says, shaking his head. He stares for a moment and turns right around to walk out.

We head for the backyard holding two bowls of potato salad and baked beans so big they look like they could feed a football team. And from the look of Malik's friends who have arrived, a football team is just what we have. Big, fine brothas, big, fine, *young* brothas. What am I doing?

Brenda looks at me and says, "I'm glad I

stopped by," as she proceeds to set the bowl of baked beans on the food table. She sashays on out to mingle, grabbing a Seagram's Ice along the way. That's the last bit of help I'll probably get from her.

24

I PEEP THE SCENE. Look at Violet, my best friend, always talking smack. Over there flirting with Brian, Malik's friend who looks maybe twenty and probably still breast-fed, or would like to be sucking on those forty double Ds staring him in the face. Look at her getting her groove on. Homegirl needs to get with that young boy, anything to get her mind off of that lowlife, poor excuse for a human being married man she's dating. Please, don't get me started. Vi looks like she's at least amused by whatever Brian is saying to her. I suppose she's practicing her feminine charms.

And look, Carlotta is here already. Sometimes I'm not sure if what people say about her is true. Despite popular belief, I don't believe she'd steal a crouton off my plate if I turned my head. I really try to trust her when it comes to men because I love this child. She's barely twenty-seven, my youngest girlfriend. Carlotta is half Hispanic and half Black. She calls herself "Blaxican."

She's another tall glass of water, maybe five-ten like me. With her light skin and short hair, people think we're sisters. That kills her because I'm so much older. And she makes sure she tells people that she was in grammar school when I graduated from high school. I just laugh and consider it a compliment. She thinks she's too young to kick it with my generation, and too good to kick it with the younger generation. But she is pretty mature, so I guess she can hang.

She keeps in touch with Kareem, probably just to get some good gossip, or maybe more—I wouldn't be surprised. I've seen him checking her out through the years ever since she was Chloe's age. He even brought her name up in bed and asked me if I'd like her to join us, obviously his fantasy and not mine. She works as a weight trainer at the gym in the Marina. And is she ever compulsive about working out? She has nightmares about tiny cellulite fat cells chasing her through a dark haunted house like a swarm of bees.

She's wearing the daisiest of blue jean dukes, kinda like hot pants back in the day. She's trying to show off all that hard work. Oh, no she didn't. That heifer is too much. No, she did not just bend her big behind over in front of Malik and his friends with her three-inch denim-colored hoochie-mama ankle-strap heels. Please. Look at Malik. He's shaking his head. Tramp, who invited her anyway? Oh shit, I did. I can't believe that's the same woman who comforted me last night when I needed her. It's like she has an evil twin who showed up for the day. Let me go back in the kitchen and get me some Alizé before I hurt somebody. I'm already pissed off. Next thing she'll be shaking her butt in front of Donovan, then I'll have to pull a Brenda on her.

Malik's friend Tony Brown walks in with his massive self. He's even bigger and taller than Malik. Tony has been playing in the NFL for about five years, from what Malik tells me. He kinda looks like O. J. Simpson did when he was young and innocent. And . . . he brought a White woman. I see Violet and Ariana gathering with the twins, China and Trina. They're having a sister gathering to discuss what the wind just blew in. He is fine though, I ain't mad at her. Malik introduces Donovan to Tony. Donovan's mouth hangs open in amazement, both at Tony and at his White escort. My jungle fever-ridden son has it bad, about one hundred and ten degrees!

"Tony, be on the lookout for this young man. He's next. He's bad and he has no idea what's about to happen to him. Colleges are sending letters and calling already," Malik explains. Tony shakes hands with Donovan.

Sarah and Cindy stroll in looking ever so casual with their jeans and T-shirts. So I guess there's more than one White person at this shindig. I greet them both and Malik comes over to get his hugs.

Malik has another friend who walks in with a girl. She's definitely a girl, maybe eighteen. She's wearing at least six-inch gold curved nails, a gold streak in her hair, which is laid by the way, gold sandals, gold lipstick, a gold G-string showing under her sheer white lace shorts and a gold sequin tube top. Oh, a nose ring, a belly button ring surrounded by a sunburst tattoo and gold toe rings on every toe.

"Why do all these young brothers bring sand to the beach?" Ariana asks in frustration.

"I don't know," Violet replies in agreement.

"Shit. He's still fair game. What does she have that I don't have?" Ariana asks.

"A man!" Violet replies with her rude self.

Malik walks up to introduce his other friend to Violet, Ariana and me.

"Baby, this is Troy. I grew up with him in New York and now he lives out here. He's the director of operations over at 7UP." Troy hands Malik a case of soda.

"Nice to meet you, Troy. That's quite a position," I comment.

"Well, it's nothing like the NFL, but it's a job. And this is Chardonnay."

"How you doin'?" Chardonnay asks.

Oh no, please tell me she does not have a gold tooth. And she also has her tongue pierced with a round gold stud. Don't let Sarah and Cindy get ahold of her.

"Fine, nice to meet you. Chardonnay, did he say?" I inquire, just to confirm.

"Yes, Chardonnay. You can call me Char."

"Okay, Char, this is Violet."

"How you doin'?" Char asks Vi.

"Fine, thanks, nice to meet you. Mingle and have fun. Bye," Violet says at a fast pace as she grabs my hand and turns to run for the kitchen. "Mariah, I need you."

I lean into Malik and say, "See what you're missing out on?"

"I'm gonna get you one of those tongue studs, baby," Malik says as he slaps my butt as I pass by.

I know what Vi wants to say.

"Mariah, what is a corporate brotha like that doing with her, ghetto queen Char? Her mom named her after a fucking wine. Chardonnay, okay? She probably works over there at Ebony and Ivory's Strip Club on Main. Or maybe she works at a place called Goldie's."

"Maybe that's just evidence of a generation gap. Shoot, if I still had that muscle tone and was eighteen again, I'd probably dress like that and pierce something too. She's young and has the body to pull it off."

"I'd like to pull that gold streak right off of her damn head. I'm not ready," she says in exhaustion, peaking out of the backdoor.

"Vi, be nice, she's a cute girl."

"Is that all that matters, being cute? What about class and a diploma?"

"I think we have a generation gap here, that's all. It's a new day. Now, show some class today and behave. Just take a deep breath because I'm going back out there. I'm not gossiping today."

"Okay, Miss Dried Up. Are you letting *her* stay here?" Vi asks, just to irritate me further.

"Yes, Brenda stays. Now come on."

I grab her hand and she grabs a beer and asks, "Do people really get acrylics on their toes?"

I find myself laughing out loud but I'm still constantly reminded of the conversation with my dad. Who does he think he is anyway? A voice breaks my train of thought.

Violet bellows out to me as she's once again rubbing up on Brian, "Mariah, who's in charge of this music? All I hear is booty this and booty that, gangsta this and gangsta that. I'm all rapped out. Where's the Al Green, Isleys and Teddy P.?" Damn, she can talk a mile a minute and is always complaining. She thinks she's cute now because Brian tried to get with her.

"Girrrrl, please, talk to the hand," I answer as if I do not want to be bothered. "Anyway, Chloe and Donovan are in charge of that. Plus, Malik's friends are groovin'." The twins China and Trina are doing that new hoochie dance with Troy; those girls have just taken him away from his date. It sounds like a cut by Lil' Kim.

"Oh, I'll show them how to groove, I'm going to my car to get my oldies CD." Vi walks out front with Brian.

I think I need a nap.

"It's all because men are triflin'," Ariana says as she sets her cold bottle of lite beer down on my peach-colored tablecloth.

Fem Cindy pushes her Gucci sunglasses down the bridge to the tip of her nose with her perfectly manicured index finger and replies, "Girl, it's not all men, it's just the boys. If you get a real man he'll respect you, be faithful to you and will provide for you. And if you believe that, I've got some tickets to a George Michael concert I'd like to sell you."

Brenda says, "Hey, don't playa hate all men

now. If you say there aren't any good men left, you're blocking your goodness and claiming your fate." Look who's talking.

"But men are dogs, Brenda. Trust me," claims Sarah.

Ariana gives Brenda a look and says, "I'm thirty-four years old and I'm telling you, I haven't found one decent man yet. They have no sensitivity. I want to be held and caressed and cuddled. Is that too much to ask? My opinion is men just don't do that. They don't have the same nurturing manner that women have. If I want understanding, I call my girlfriends."

Sarah's ears perk up as she asks, "Ariana, did you ever play basketball in school? You're so tall and you're in great shape."

"Yes, I did. But there was no WNBA back then. I even thought about playing volleyball in Brazil, but I wanted to be a designer instead."

"You look like you could still do it," Sarah comments as she checks out Ariana's long legs like a term paper cheat sheet. And she actually has the nerve to tickle her finger along Ariana's thigh on the side. "Do you shave? Your legs are so smooth," Sarah asks with enthusiasm.

Ariana must be that blind if she doesn't think she's getting hit on.

"No, I'm lucky that way. I'm just not very hairy."

"Hmmm, that's a blessing," purrs Sarah.

Carlotta walks up and asks, "Have y'all seen Mariah's oldest son lately? Girl, better keep an eye on him. He's a man now." She walks away, obviously feeling those four strawberry-kiwi wine coolers.

Ariana strolls over to the cooler to get some more beer and wine spritzers to cool her from the blazing sun and the heat Sarah is giving off.

"God bless America," says Xavier, Malik's wild friend who lives across the street from Malik's grandparents. "Red, white and blue never looked so good."

"Thanks," replies Ariana while returning to Sarah's web.

"No, baby, thank you for representing your country so well," Xavier proclaims as he turns toward Malik, who is working that barbecue pit. My baby looks good! He's wearing his number twenty-four Ravens jersey, just like Donovan. His chocolate bald head glistens in the sun as he pours more charcoal on the grill. Xavier walks over to him. "Hey, man, honey over there in the pink is fine, dog. You see all that wagon she's draggin'?"

"Man, that's Mariah. Don't hate."

"You hitting that, man? Damn? You get props for that one." Xavier tries to high-five Malik, but he's left hangin'.

"Look, Xavier. Kill that, man," says Malik.

"My bad, dog. No disrespect."

"None taken."

"What about Miss Cutie over there in the black shorts?" He points to Chloe, who is showing Donovan and Tony how to work that dang rainbow yo-yo.

"Man, that's Mariah's daughter, Chloe. She's

off limits too. Too young for your old dirty Uncle Chester the Molester tactics."

"So what about Miss America the Beautiful?"

"That's Ariana, she's cool," Malik says.

"That's a big girl, talk about climbing a tree," Xavier jokes.

"She don't like no short dogs, chill," Malik jokes back.

Xavier's gigantic ego responds as he is all of five foot nine. "Why are you blocking a brother today? What's up?"

"I'm not about to get in the way of a dog and his bone. You're on your own. But Mariah is taken, that's all I know. I've got plans for her."

"Cool, I'm with it. But what I'd really be with is a game of bid whist." Xavier yells out in a deep, life of the party tone, "You all card-playing niggas or what?"

Before you know it, Brenda, Xavier, Cindy and Chardonnay are grabbing chairs for a game or two.

Ariana asks, "Anybody down for a pick-up game? Donovan and I will choose our teams."

"Oh man, she's talking trash," Donovan says to Chloe.

Donovan, Tony and Carlotta team up against Ariana, Sarah and Chloe.

"Oh, it's on now," says Tony, handing his girl-friend his Tanqueray and Seven. While checking out Tony's date, Donovan bumps into Chloe as he picks up the basketball.

"You could see where you're going if you keep your eyes in front of you and not on that girl.

We've gotta get you to come back to the Africa!" Chloe teases.

Donovan just stares at Chloe as if his game will speak louder than her words.

"We've got sports, card playing and booty shakin'. All you had better work up an appetite because the chef is almost done," belts Malik. "Hey, girl, what's your name?" he playfully inquires.

"Kiss my saxophone, mister," I say with seduction.

"When and where?" Malik says as he pinches my thigh. "I'll meet you in the bathroom in ten!"

Just then, Malik hears a voice behind him with an attitude, "Hey, man, what's up with that, chill. That's my woman!"

Malik quickly turns around. It's Paris. Paris is one of his closest friends. They were football rivals in high school. He's a pilot for United Airlines. Makes a grip, and he's single.

"Hey, big man, you been hitting them weights or what?" asks Malik.

Paris playfully smiles and punches Malik in the chest. He replies, "I hear you doing big things nowadays."

"Yeah, I'm doing the league thing. Finally. I can't believe it."

"Malik, we always knew you were going to the top. You were always glued to a damn football. Just don't forget a brotha when you makin' them Gs," Paris advises.

"Paris, you are a true homie. You know if I go to the top, I'm taking care of you, bro. Forever love, brother, forever love."

They give each other daps and Malik calls me over to meet him.

"Baby, now this is my boy, this is Paris. We go way back."

"Nice to meet you. So you know a lot about him, huh? All of his real secrets?" I ask.

"All of them, and I'll sell you a few stories for a beer and a rib."

"No problem," I say, taking my man by his hand.

"Shoot, I'm a whore for ratting on my boys if you feed me," Paris says, pulling me by the arm toward the food.

Paris and I walk away and converse.

Everyone piles their plates high with ribs, links, chicken, greens, potato salad, string beans, rice casserole, baked beans and monkey bread.

After a while, Paris asks everyone to fill their glasses and raise them high for a toast. I asked him to keep it clean in respect of the teenagers.

"All right now, all of you listen up. Yes, you too, over there in the corner getting your mack on"—referring to Brian and Vi—"My name is Paris. I grew up with Malik. His woman, the lovely Mariah, has asked me to say a few words. Let me just say that I always knew this brother had it in him. It's called heart. Some people have it and some people don't. Along with that heart you need an energy, a spark, an aura, a personality, charisma, charm, wit, a look and a walk. For now, he'll do fine with just the heart. But really, when he was nine years old, we knew he was destined for greatness. The boy always had a football or basketball or baseball in his hands, he always had some sort of ball he was trying to play with, and from what I hear, he still does."

Malik says, "Man, do you want to get on with it?"

"See, he's always been a funny man too, but he can't take a joke too well, kinda sensitive. Malik is a good brother and he deserves to be in the league getting paid! Just don't forget us common folk when you get to the top. We might need you to send us some change every now and then to help us pay our cable bill so we can watch your moves on Fox Sports West or ESPN. Break a brother off something is what I'm talking about."

He continues, "Now, Tony, I see your pro-league veteran butt over there looking all legendary and stuff. I ask you one thing. Please keep an eye on this rookie brother or else we're coming after you. You might be able to tackle with your big self, but I heard you can't run too fast so just remember what I'm saying. All kidding aside, I love you, Malik. I'm proud of you, and your lady is fine, dog, so hurry back because I'm going to be looking after her. Now get your buzz on and I got next at the card table, you tired Black people, and White folk too. I see ya!"

Brenda is eyeing Paris like she is about to hook her bait and go fishing.

Violet blurts out, "Okay, now let's get this party started right." She hands Donovan a few CDs and continues, "Now, can we get our groove on or what? It's time to go back, way back to the days when you'd bring your own record albums to a party and they wouldn't end up missing!" Vi says with a comedic flair.

Donovan plays "In Between the Sheets," and Vi starts to do the Texas hop with Brian. It looks more like she's teaching him than following him. Before I know it, Brenda asks Paris to dance and Chardonnay is dancing with Troy. And then, oh my God, Carlotta and Xavier start doing the bump to "Fire" by the Ohio Players. Even China and Trina start bumpin' with each other. It's a generation gap coming together like I've never seen before.

The next cut is "Outstanding," and dance instructor Vi begins to do the electric slide. That's when damn near everyone starts to join in, including Ariana, Cindy and Sarah.

Later, as the oldies jams mellow out, Malik and I slow dance to "Betcha by Golly Wow" by the Stylistics, and Chloe walks by and whispers, "Mom, all of these guys are on my jock! I'm going in the house to use the phone."

Malik laughs and says, "That probably would be the safest place for her with all of these Dobermans out here."

Malik and I sneak into my bathroom for a little heavy petting, hot, wet kisses and slow grinding. As we exit, I notice Chloe eyeing me with the cordless phone to her ear while walking to the kitchen. My disheveled demeanor of guilt garners a like-mother, like-daughter smirk. Malik decides to give himself a minute to deflate.

IT'S ALREADY ELEVEN O'CLOCK and the crowd is thinning out. Brenda hugs me and Malik good-bye as Paris walks her to her car and then returns to talk to Malik. Violet has already left hand in hand with Brian. Ariana exited at the same time as Cindy and Sarah. I think Carlotta slipped out with Xavier. I'm cleaning up the kitchen as I watch Paris and Malik from the window over the sink. They're standing outside talking. I can barely make out their muffled, minimized-volume conversation.

"So what's up with Brenda, man?" Paris curiously asks.

"She's a cool, nice person."

"She told me what happened. I just want you to know I'm going to call her. Is that okay with you?"

"No problem, you have my blessings. I've got work to do with Mariah. Man, I think this could be it," Malik informs Paris.

I pull the window shut in slow motion as if I've heard something I shouldn't have, but I'm smiling like I'm glad I did. I go into the backyard to say good-bye to the last few guests.

Chloe is making take-home plates for everyone. Donovan is starting on his fourth plate of food.

I CAN'T BELIEVE I've gotten through this day. Malik helped out so much. He got along so well with my friends. I'm sure all of his friends asked him what it's like to be with an older woman. Even though no one made me feel older, I know it came up. I don't even want to think about him leaving. Speaking of leaving, I just can't get over

Violet leaving with Brian. I can't wait to hear her story about what happened. It had better be good. Sometimes I need to watch that girl. And Ariana with Cindy and Sarah? Sarah looked like a hawk eyein' her prey. Lord, have mercy. What in the world was that all about? I don't even want to know. Yes, I do. The weather was beautiful, the food was delicious and I made a new friend, Brenda. Who would have thought? I guess that's all part of this forgiveness thing. Let me go check on Malik before I think myself to death.

Malik is stretched out across the living room sofa. He kisses my forehead and I sit on the floor with my head leaning on his arm.

"My dad called last night."

"Last night? What happened? What did he say?" Malik asks as he rubs his eyes and sits up.

We spend the next couple of hours talking about the conversation with my dad. Eventually, Malik and I both fall asleep on the couch with my sepia-colored chenille throw over our feet. I guess this is Dr. Singer's version of sleeping together. He cops a few early-morning feels for a second and then we arise to greet the day. I realize it's Father's Day.

25

"MARIAH, CALL YOUR DAD TODAY," Malik says as he stands up to stretch his legs and forces his feet into his untied Nikes.

"How can you say that after the conversation we had?" I reply with vexation.

"Because, it's your turn to reach out. At least he called," he says as though he took his wisdom pill this morning.

I continue to lay on the couch. "He never reached out to me and my brothers. When my brother called him more than eight years ago to ask him why he left, he gave him the same crock-of-shit answer. Yet when my brother died, he tried to show up and put in his two cents about the funeral plans. He didn't want my brother cremated. Since when did he have a say-so into my brother's requests? My brother wanted to be cremated and that was that."

"Have you imagined how hard that must have been on him?"

"At that time, it was all about my brother. He was like a father to me, he's all that mattered," I share with Malik while sprawled out flat on my back.

"And now, Mariah, since we've both agreed to face these issues, I think we should begin to put ourselves in their places. I mean think about it: if your dad waited until the eleventh hour to be baptized, he was facing some serious demons that he wanted to be forgiven for. He's just having a hard time admitting it." He hovers over me as if checking to see if I get it.

"That's just too bad. I appreciate what you're trying to do, but I have a hangover and I cannot handle this conversation today." My stomach rumbles in agreement and I turn onto my side.

"How about church? I thought the rev was going to talk about the seven spiritual laws," he offers.

"I don't think I'm going to make it to church today. Even though I'm sure my dad says that's where I need to be spending all my time. I'm going to take my kids to the cemetery to visit their dad's grave, visit my brother's grave and then go and see my mother."

"I guess I'll just go home and hang out with my grandparents. You know what? I'd give anything to receive a phone call."

"Even one with that type of response?" I peer up at him.

"Even the one you got, baby. Be careful what you ask for. By the way, you did a great job yesterday. Thank you for everything. I love you." He leans over to give me a soft peck on the lips. Oh hell, did he just say what I think he said? Ignore it, danger ahead, red alert.

"I'll see you later tonight, or maybe tomorrow?" Malik says as if he's hoping I say later tonight.

"For sure, tonight would be nice."

"I would go with you guys today but I'll let you be alone with the kids for a while," he says, seemingly out of respect.

"Thanks. And, Malik?"

"Yes," he responds, preparing to exit.

I think to myself, don't say it. "Tell your grandfather I said happy Father's Day."

THE ENTIRE DAY comes and goes and I never even begin to pick up the phone, I never have an urge to call. The negativity of the conversation is all I can think about. It consumes and overrides my every desire to reach out, so I don't. It's like that phone call carries the weight of the world. The weight of my hurt and my victimness.

Today I have two commercial auditions. Now that's what I'm talking about. Let's get some real money coming in here. A national commercial for Crest and one for Oreo cookies. I play a wife and mom in both. Before the day is over, I receive a call back for the Oreo cookie commercial for the next day. *Okay?*

Malik comes by and throws down with a shrimp pasta dinner for us. It is delicious, his mom's recipe. He leaves early to go shopping for his trip this week. He'll be leaving in a few days.

Tuesday morning while I am at the audition, my pager goes off with an unfamiliar number. I decide to call before I go in to demonstrate my acting abilities. I play the part of a reporter warning the world of an impending shortage of milk. Right up my alley. Again my pager goes off with the same number, but followed by 911. I immediately run to a pay phone.

"Uncle Riley, what's up? Yeah, I know that. What?" I exclaim as my voice cracks with a clamorous intensity.

"When? This morning at breakfast? A heart attack? No, please tell me you're lying. Please tell me you're lying, Uncle Riley." I fall to the floor screaming, "No, God, no!" Suddenly I begin to hyperventilate and I cannot catch my breath. My heart races and I feel as though I'm going to pass out from anxiety. My mind reels in thought and denial and pain. I run to my car and bang on the steering wheel, hoping if I hit it hard enough, I will awaken from this sinister nightmare. If only I could go back to Sunday morning when Malik told me to call. The biggest *if* of my life. My daddy is dead.

26

I HEAD STRAIGHT HOME, breaking every speed limit and running stop signs. I just want to go to bed, hide under the covers and curl up in an embryonic position clutching my stomach until someone awakens me from this horror. Chloe and Donovan cry with me most of the afternoon. I find myself telling them stories of happy times about my father. Suddenly the brief five years of memories seem like forty years of memories. There are more stories to tell than I imagined.

My concerns also include my children, who have been through more than any children should have to bear. And through it all, Donovan tells me he's glad Grandpa lived such a long life. Chloe says, "Now we have something in common, Mommy. Now we've both experienced the death of our fathers."

At that moment, Kyle calls and we tell him. He didn't know his grandpa, but he does remember one special visit to my grandmother's house last summer when my dad showed up out of the blue. Kyle says, "Mom, you're just like your dad. You both have a wild sense of humor and you're always teasing. I'll always remember that about my grandpa."

Kyle's dad gets on the phone to offer his condolences. In the background I hear his wife offers hers as well.

Later that afternoon, Malik, Uncle Riley, my brother Craig, Donovan, Chloe and I all go to the hospital to sign a release to have my dad's body sent to the mortuary. He had already handled all of his own arrangements. His wish was to be buried next to his mother who had just died last August, and his father who died nearly twenty years ago. They were buried at Forest Lawn in Glendale, California. He was a veteran of World War II and will receive full honors.

Little did my brother and I realize all this time, but because my father was not married when he died, the hospital and mortuary will not make a move unless the surviving children sign a release stating no other next of kin could claim him. What a trip! After all of those years of not knowing my dad, who would have thought my brother and I would be the only family members authorized to bury him. Burying someone you don't even know.

AT THE HOSPITAL, the administrators ask us to sign several documents. They also turn over his belongings to us. We are all in a small, cold, stale, sterile, barren, holding-cell type room with dingy white walls. My kids appear apprehensive about their decision to come with me, and even I'm wondering if it was such a good idea.

The charge nurse brings us a small manila envelope labeled *C. Malone* and empties the contents onto a steel folding table. Inside is my dad's tarnished silver wristwatch, which the nurse hands my uncle, his money clip and wallet, a total of twenty-seven dollars, which my brother takes. In his wallet, which I accept, I find the other half of our heart necklace he's had for more than thirty-five years. He'd been keeping it in his pocket wherever he went. My heart fills with tears of pain for myself and for him. I place the heart in the palm of my hand and my arm begins to wobble, unbalanced. I quickly close my hand and my eyes. I take myself back to the night he placed my half under my pillow.

Not once in thirty-five years had I ever given a moment of thought as to what the other half meant to him or if there even was another half. Suddenly it represents a symbol that I was someone who mattered. Someone who mattered enough to carry around my memory with him daily, everywhere he went, just as I did.

Also, there are two small gold angel pins. I'm sure one is for me and one is for my brother.

We all quietly walk outside as the nurse tells us that his body will be sent to the funeral home later that evening.

In the street outside of the hospital, I hug my uncle good-bye. As he walks away, I notice Donovan breaking down crying as he leans against my car. His body is jerking like he is having a convulsion. Chloe cries, I cry and Malik embraces the three of us. I'm not sure if my big strong son is crying for me or from the weight on his young shoulders. Perhaps they are tears shed from the memories of his own father. The weight of it all is just too intense.

Tonight I'm sleeping with the complete heart, both halves around my neck, together at last. I sleep like a baby. For some reason I feel at peace, at least for the moment.

The next day includes the task of going to my dad's apartment to gather his belongings and look for insurance papers or other documents he may have left. My uncle tells us we can have whatever we want from his apartment.

His apartment! I never thought that my dad actually had one. I mean, I never thought about where he lived and what it looked like. Now I'm actually walking through the doors of my dad's apartment, someone I don't even know. It is small, dirty and unkempt. You can barely find a place to step in the living room that isn't cluttered with junk. Old furniture, old everything. How did he live like this? It is obvious to me that he was sleeping on the brown faded living room sofa. There's a tiny, flat, dirty beige pillow and a dingy plaid-fringed blanket on the couch. On the coffee table there are books pertaining to congestive heart failure, heart disease, impotency and general health, as well as a Bible. There are three or four bottles of prescription medication and a half-empty glass of water previously invaded by a now dead fly.

The kitchen is tiny, no refrigerator, but tons of dirty dishes, unopened mail and various papers stacked upon the sink. There are boxes on the floor, still unpacked from many years. And all along the hallway he has calendars taped to the wall marking his health on a daily basis. It is clear that on one particular night the week before he died, he didn't believe he was going to make it through to the next morning: *hard to breathe, congested, blood in my stool and numbness in my left arm.* Oh my God!

His bathroom toilet is like one in a neglected public rest room, too filthy to imagine sitting upon. His tub is backed up and clogged with the stench of mildew. His bedroom has too much junk to fully enter the room. The disarray of clothes and boxes hide the full-size mattress.

As I exhale from the shock and sadness of the clutter, I step back into the living room. My brother lifts the pillow on the sofa and uncovers a gun, a revolver, obviously for protection. Craig quickly takes the bullets out and puts the gun in a pillowcase so my kids won't see it once Malik brings them over later.

And in the corner next to the sofa, shining brightly and proudly, is my dad's treasure, his saxophone. My brother approaches it like an eight-year-old eyeing a new bike. He carefully slides his index finger up and down the shapely brass cold body.

My dad kept his baby in good condition, unlike the rest of the things in his apartment. It is shiny and gleaming yet appears abandoned and orphaned as if it too is in mourning. It seems to have been propped up by careful, loving hands on its stand. Surely he wasn't able to muster enough wind to bring it to life. Even the reed looks virgin new and untouched.

Craig picks it up and generates a deep, forceful blow. In response the sax gives off a melodic tone of captivation to rewind us back in time to 1961. My brother is just as spellbound as I by the beauty of this sexy, yet powerful instrument. He is in love.

Among the wonder and curiosity of all of this clutter is the amazement that on each and every wall are pictures of my brothers and me. It is like a shrine and a tribute in our memory. We are frozen in time, ages five, seven and eleven. Every inch of the walls in the living room is filled with childhood pictures of his greatest treasures, his children. We just never knew it, until now.

When I was five years old, my teacher had all of the students make individual shadow profiles of our faces that were cut out in black cardboard paper. Here I am looking at that very picture from decades ago, mounted in a wooden frame and hung just above the sofa. He has an enlarged picture I'd given my grandmother of my brothers and me a few years ago. It is hung smack dab in the middle of the wall in the dining room. The room is absent of a dining room table and chairs, only more boxes.

As I kneel to look in one box, I see thirty-five years of greeting cards taped together. These are cards I'd sent my dad by way of my grandmother— Father's Day, Christmas and his birthday. Even my high school graduation invitation as well as the birth announcement for Chloe and birthday invites. All of which he never used. I am too stunned to cry.

And buried at the bottom of one particular box I find a letter. *The* letter. The letter that holds the answer to "why." The letter my brother would have given his left arm to receive. The letter that answers all the "what happened" questions I'd asked less than one week ago. It is dated June 12, 1965, and it is addressed to my eldest brother:

Charles III,

I hope one day you'll understand why you woke up one morning and I was gone. I pray you'll forgive me and be man enough to do as I say, not as I've done. I am where I want to be. I am in love. I am no longer in love with your mother. This was all about two adults who had problems with each other, not with you. It is not your fault, your brother's fault or your sister's fault. Don't blame yourself.

I pray that one day you follow your heart as I have, be it wrong or right, I could no longer live a lie.

I'm writing to you because you're the oldest. Take care of your baby brother and especially your baby sister. She'll always be my little girl, please let her know that.

Love,
Your Dad
6/12/65

Why was this letter never mailed? Surely we would have understood the core of his efforts and at least we would have appreciated his honesty. I immediately turn to show it to my brother. The first words we've spoken since we walked in.

"Craig, here it is! The answer to years of mystery and rejection," I vociferate with excitement.

As I begin to read out loud, I can tell Craig is uninterested, he's only exploring his affection for the priceless saxophone he's been reunited with. As I stop reading he says with calm, "That's nice."

I now know this isn't his issue. He doesn't need to know like Charles and I needed to know. And that's fine because in spirit, my eldest brother now has the answer he's always wanted. He too is in this apartment. After all, he is the one who led me to the letter in the first place. Maybe he had a meeting with my dad in heaven and already knew. Or maybe in heaven, none of this matters. One thing is for sure, he knew I needed to know. Thank you!

27

AFTER NEARLY TWO DAYS of checking for more documents and rummaging through what to throw out and what to keep, there is still no sight of any insurance papers. I remember my dad asking my brother and me for our Social Security numbers years ago because he had a small amount put away for us.

He'd worked at a rental car company for twenty years after his musician days were over. But he retired last year and we were told he didn't elect Cobra benefits and unless he bought a plan on his own, he would not be covered. He also took a lump sum distribution on his 401(k) and bought a car. His bank account balances are minimal, not quite enough to pay a utility bill, let alone extra burial costs. He lived on Social Security retirement benefits that would come in the mail soon, only to be returned to sender.

THE MOVERS HAVE COME NOW and Malik is at my house with Donovan and Chloe. Tonight is just my uncle and me. My uncle Riley has chosen a midnight blue suit with a canary yellow tie from the closet as my dad's last outfit. He says it's the suit my dad was baptized in.

The bedroom is cleared out enough to get near the closet. Oddly enough, the closet is well organized, unlike the rest of the apartment. In the closet I see an antique-looking natural wheat-colored wicker chair; strange again, I'm thinking. Why would a chair be in the closet?

It is a beautiful chair. I cannot take my eyes off of it. I plan to place it in his living room so I can remember to take it home with me. It will go well with the decor in my dining room. The back of the chair is shaped like a curvaceous heart. It has tiny, rose-colored flowers and an inlay of pale green leaves around the border. It is exquisite. To my surprise as I lift the chair, I spy an envelope. *Mariah* it reads. My heart rages with the velocity of a race-car driver approaching a turn so difficult and winding that he must downshift and take extra hold of the wheel before flooring it to handle the curve ahead.

I take a deep breath and open the envelope with much trepidation and I am amazed at the sight of a stack of hundreds and more hundreds and more one-hundred-dollar bills simply placed in the envelope. I close my eyes as if I'd just found something I should return to the lost and found, something a stranger has surely lost. Inside the envelope has to be nearly five thousand dollars in cash.

I imagine what he was thinking when he put the envelope under the chair. How did he know I would find it and when did he leave it? Maybe he meant for me to have it before that regretted conversation last week, yet I also know this too was no accident. I am meant to find it because he knew I'd be the one to handle his funeral arrangements. Perhaps it is also an attempt to amend his actions and reconcile from what now seems so very insignificant. If I only had the opportunity to continue on with an estranged relationship with a father who's alive, I would give any amount of money for the opportunity to mend it in person. To have a dead father and five thousand in cash is the worst-case scenario I can imagine. However, now that he's no longer in pain, I trust he's at peace with himself and he has completed his journey. Now the question is—what am I going to do to "get over it" and move on? As I tuck the envelope into my bra, I whisper, "Thanks, Daddy!"

Suddenly I hear a knock at the door. A soft-spoken woman with a cracking German accent is standing in the doorway crying. Her nose is red, her eyes are bloodshot and she is cradling a worn and tattered photo album in her arms.

"My name is Margaret. I was with your dad when he died. I live next door."

My God, Margaret is the woman my dad left my mother for. This woman's name has haunted me for years. She is the villain, she is *the* White woman who took my dad from us. This tiny, frail woman with her strong accent, in the pink-flowered sundress and matching pink slippers, is the villain. This woman knows him better than I do. She was with him for more than three decades. She knows the whole story. It shouldn't matter that she is White, or the enemy or a home wrecker. I grab her like she's a puppy about to run into the street and hug her tightly. We cry together as if we've met before.

She takes me into her spotless, neat apartment with shelves full of framed photos of their lives together.

"Mariah, your daddy loved you," she informs me as though she feels the need to erase all doubt.

"I didn't even call him on Father's Day!" I say as I weep uncontrollably.

"I know, and that bothered him. But he doesn't want you to feel bad. He was a good man, Mariah, a good man. Everyone loved him. He was my lover, my friend, my everything." I should want to slap the fuck out of her for taking my daddy from his family. For some reason, I feel only sorrow for both of our losses.

"But what happened the morning he died?" I ask as she offers me a hand-embroidered handkerchief.

"He couldn't sleep the night before. I heard him on the other side of the wall suffering through a deep, dry coughing spell. I called him, but he said he was fine. He coughed all night. See, we tried living together but it just never worked out. A few years ago, I moved out and rented this apartment next door just to be close to him and keep an eye on him. This way I'm sure he felt he could also keep an eye on me, because he was very jealous. I suppose deep down he didn't want to remarry out of guilt for leaving the four of you.

"Anyway, I called him that morning and invited him to breakfast at his favorite coffee shop around the corner. I drove him there in his car and we ate and talked, as we would always do. He was worried about my daughter and me. We too were having problems like you and your dad. It's so like him to always worry about someone else and put his problems aside. Suddenly he grabbed his chest, looked at me from across the table, tried to reach one hand out toward me and fell over with his head on the table as still as if he was sleeping. I screamed and the manager came over and tried to awaken him or whatever. I touched his wrist to check his pulse. Mariah, there was nothing. I screamed and yelled, and within what seemed like seconds, the ambulance came and took him away. I called your uncle and I drove your dad's car home. It was like a dream. I dared not go to the hospital because I've been afraid of how you would react toward me."

I am numb as she continues. "But I knew I had to meet you face-to-face one day. You look so much like your dad. So you are Charles's daughter, Mariah? The one and only. He loved you like he loved no one ever before. He always told me you would always be his little girl."

"I'm so sorry you had to go through that. You are very strong," I say, taking her tiny hand in mine.

"Your daddy knew he had congestive heart failure for a long time. He was in and out of the hospital but he never wanted you to know. He was trying to reach out to you in his later years but it just seemed to him that he couldn't do it the way it would have taken for you to respond and forgive. He suffered with guilt for most of his life. That's the main reason he was baptized recently. But it's over now, Mariah. It's over," she admits as if she's dreaded this day.

We start looking through her photo albums for what seems like hours. They shared the love of photographs. She even has his old albums from when he performed with Sammy Davis Jr. I ask to take a few pictures to share with my children and she gracefully gives me the entire album.

"Margaret, please ride in the limousine tomorrow, you and your daughter. You are family. My dad really loved you, and I cannot help but love you too. Please?"

"I will, Mariah, bless you for asking! Come outside with me. I want to show you something."

28

MARGARET GUIDES ME by the hand to the back of the apartment building toward a parking space in the corner. She removes a cover from a car and unveils the same fifty-nine Cadillac Coupe de Ville I used to proudly ride in with my daddy nearly four decades ago. I gasp for air and cover my heart to soothe the intense pounding of a five-year-old girl. I tremble with childlike delight as I walk around to the passenger side and see the same clean butterscotch tan leather upholstery that used to stick to my almond skin on hot summer days.

The middle seat that pulls down, originally created as an elbow rest, was my throne. The ebony convertible top is in first-rate condition. And that ivory tusk steering wheel that my dad would direct with one hand while the other hand was around my shoulder suddenly doesn't look so big. The carbon black paint job is as if it is less than one year old. The whitewall tires are whited out like someone brushed them, inch by inch, with Liquid Paper.

"Margaret, oh my God! Did he still drive this?" I ask in extemporaneous wonder.

"Every day. This is the car we got around in. To him, it held memories of all of his kids. There's no way he could have parted with it. Even though many offered to buy it from him."

"Is this the car you drove home from the restaurant the morning he died?"

"Yes, he trusted me with it so much that I had my own key. He called this his 'angel with wings.' But now it is yours," she declares as she hands me his key ring.

And wings it does have. This model has the huge fins and twin bullet-type tail lamps. And it has plenty of chrome.

I take the key ring with the faded silver cross that reads *paid in full*. Glancing at my daddy's Caddy and then catching a glimpse of the love in her eyes, I ask, "Where is your car?"

"I don't get around much. I sold my car over five years ago."

"Then you must keep this treasure in memory of my dad. I know he'd want that. He knows you'd never sell it and you obviously have taken the time to take great care of it."

"No way, Mariah. This is part of your inheritance from him. I wouldn't think of it," she states in rejection.

"Believe me, I'm just as stubborn as my dad. It's yours." I hand the keys back to her, closing my hands around hers.

"Mariah . . ."

"Thanks for sharing it with me. But I don't think I could handle seeing it every day," I say, shaking my head.

Margaret's eyes start to well up with tears and her soft, accented voice begins to crack "Well, at least ask your brother and uncle."

"My brother has the sax. I'll tell him you are keeping it. It's the least we can do. It looks like he didn't leave a will. So it is yours, period. It is your winged angel now."

Margaret walks to the driver side of her beloved's car with caution, as if the weight of her loss is too heavy for her frail shoulders to bear. She nervously fumbles around in an attempt to sit in the abandoned driver seat while looking up at me through the front window as if her passenger is missing. After a moment of reflection, she gets out, locks the door and reaches for the car cover. We place the cover on his baby and then embrace with a hug, walking side by side and hand in hand to her apartment door.

We say our good-byes as she closes the door. I wonder how she is going to live here now, how sad. Her life companion is gone. She's going to need a lot of support. I must find a way to be there for her. I stand there for a moment staring at her door, and then his door and then I walk away with one hand to my forehead, soothing the signs of an impending migraine. My other hand clutches the base of the rattan chair. I place it in the back seat of my car and pull off, turning back to eyeball the silhouette of that Caddy. Angels' wings? I drive home to my children and Malik.

Later that evening, I realize I have one thing to do before I can move on. I must view my dad's body.

* * *

I WALK DOWN THE HALL of the stark, monastic funeral home with Malik at my side. It's a trip I've made for my husband, brother and grandmother before. I should be used to it by now. But this is indeed the hardest thing I've ever had to do in my life. My mysterious, elusive dad is in there, in that room at the end of the hall.

I walk strong and proud with Malik holding my hand and hugging me. As I stand at the door to viewing room number four, I see him! My dad's face in a silver, satin-lined coffin. What is this? This cannot be.

I howl in lamented regret, "We're not finished, I was going to call you, I have to talk to you!" and then I lose it. I cannot proceed. My legs won't cooperate. I remain at the doorway, praying that if I just stand here for a moment I will remember that I am an actor in a television show and the director will yell "cut" as if this would be a great time to take a break. I pray I can just pick up the phone and call him, just one last time. This is the worst sight of my life. The biggest issue of my life now seems so insignificant, so trivial and so meaningless. Why did I place so much weight on the existence of this man? When it's all said and done, it doesn't matter. He was forgiven by the Father, yet I never forgave him. How un-Godlike is that?

Malik holds me up as I approach the coffin with regret. I cry so many tears that I cannot focus on his face. I attempt to imagine what he was living with and to know him for who he really was. As I turn to take myself away from my own selfishness, I notice Malik too is crying. Crying for me and for his father, just as Donovan did the other day. There's a lesson for both of us. And he is the very one who encouraged me to call. He is the one who apologized to me for my dad.

I've always remembered the feeling of touching my husband's face for the first time when he died. It was so cold . . . but it finalized the fact that it was real. His spirit had really vacated this shell we call a body, and he'd moved on. I did the same with my brother also. This time, I have to touch my father one last time in order for me to fully understand the reality of this transition my pastor talks about. He hadn't died. He's made his transition. He's gone home like a shooting star.

I release one hand from Malik's and then raise the other. Both of my hands move toward my dad's face with reserve and a kind of excitement for completion. Six inches then turns into one inch and then . . . the all too familiar coldness connects with my fingertips and I know it was true, he is no longer part of this body, this body that suffered so long and so painfully. I touch that nose that looks like mine, that forehead that is responsible for my "Sade" nickname, those ears I used to whisper into when he hugged me good night, those lips I used to kiss good-bye when he'd drop me off at school. And so I do. I begin to kiss those lips that seem suddenly familiar. His face is less than a millimeter of an inch in front of me, and I smile and say, "I love you, Daddy, and I forgive you. I'm sorry and I already know you forgive me."

Malik hugs me from behind and then he leaves the room to give us privacy. My hands are suddenly led to his hands. The big strong hands that used to get manicures every week while I'd sit next to him and get my nails painted pink—never red, he said little girls wear pink. I rarely wear nail polish, but today I notice my pink fingernails are shaped like his. Someone placed a brown macrame necklace with a silver cross on his hands already. He looks so peaceful, so okay with his eleventh-hour decision to make peace with himself and with God. I remove the picture of the two of us from my wallet and place it in the casket. I kiss him good-bye one final time and I begin to walk away. I turn as I walk through the doorway and I look back again just to make sure it is true, and so it is. Malik is waiting at the end of the hallway. I walk to him and smile and we walk away, hand in hand.

29

As we exit the limousine and enter the church the next morning, the sun is shining in full effect with all of its hotter-than-July glory again. It is a scorcher, but kind of sticky-muggy as if we are in Florida. I'm wearing the same red dress I wore to my brother's funeral. He loved me in this dress—so damn it, I wore it in spite of the age-old notion that anything other than black is inappropriate. I never believed in wearing black. It's too depressing. I'm wearing a big, wide straw hat with a red sash in the back, the ribbon of the red bow draping down my back. Chloe is wearing the soft powder blue pantsuit my grandmother bought her a few years ago. She's grown into it now. We sit next to each other as I clutch her right hand to my left hand. In my right hand is my dad's Bible, highlighted and worn. In my daughter's left hand is a rosary she's had since she received her first Holy Communion in Catholic school years ago. Malik and the boys sit together to my right. They're all suited up in their Sunday best. Malik has tied three ties this morning.

The church is full of people. I do not know

many of the mourners with the exception of a few distant family members. My stepfather is sitting behind me as he places his hand on my shoulder to let me know he is here for support. I tap his hand and turn with a smile. Everyone from my dad's work is here and when the remarks section of the program is announced, many of them proceed to the altar to share their stories about him, as do his closest friends, mainly golf buddies. My dad actually played golf. I never knew that. But today I'm learning a lot of wonderful things about my dad. It's as if I'm a friend of the family hearing about his inside track for the first time. It's all news to me. Not one of the admirers hesitates to speak of how wonderful, caring and giving he was.

The most difficult part of the service occurs when my brother Craig, who decided it was important to give a tribute to his daddy, stands at the altar with my dad's guardian angel pinned to his jacket lapel. He brings our dad's saxophone to his lips and plays "Unforgettable" by Nat King Cole. First of all, I never knew he could play and he is tearing it up too. Not a dry eye anywhere. It's the most beautiful rendition I've ever heard. Now there are two songs that will forever represent intense emotion and continue to affect me for the rest of my life, "Unforgettable" and "Loving You" by Kenny G.

Bless Chloe's heart, she gets up and reads the obituary she helped me write yesterday. As she finishes, the pastor comes to the altar.

"Today, my brothers and sisters, we are here to

celebrate the life of Brother Charles Malone Jr., a man who followed the words of Psalm Thirty-seven, verses eight and nine, *Give up your anger and forsake wrath, be not vexed, it will only harm you. For evildoers shall be cut off but those who wait for the Lord shall possess the land.* Brother Malone stood here not long ago during his baptism and recited Psalm Fifty-one, verse nine, *cleanse me of sin that I may be purified, wash me and I shall be whiter than snow.* Yes, a clean heart and a steadfast spirit renews us and gives us back our joy of His salvation as our willing spirit sustains us. Brother Malone had a willing spirit and through that salvation he found the Lord. Brother Malone is with the Lord, ladies and gentlemen, and he had a clean heart in the eleventh hour. Will you? I ask you to look around at the love Chuck Malone has, how many lives he's touched, all of his beautiful family, friends, grandchildren, and loving son and daughter and girlfriend. This is the result of a child of God who is now with his Father. The ultimate Father of all Fathers who gave his life for us. What greater love can there be? Let us pray . . ."

As I watch the procession of people lining up to view his body, I see my closest friends, Violet, Ariana and Carlotta, coming up to pay their respects. I see Sarah and Cindy, Malik's grandparents, Betty and Al Simpson, and Malik's friend Brian. I see my children's friends, I see Kyle's dad with tears in his eyes as he winks at me, I see his wife and I see Kareem. I feel a lump in my throat the size of an apple. I even see my in-laws, Mr. Pijeaux, his wife and my sister-in-law. They are all lined up to view his body. Once again I cry and shed my emotions like a cocoon. Thank God for friends. When it all comes down to it, true friends are there, no matter what.

The family is the last to view the body. My children now have a chance for the first time. Chloe and Donovan were too young to view their dad's body, and Kyle has never seen a dead person before. It is a choice I've left up to them. I let them go first, and then Malik and me, my stepfather, my brother and my uncle Riley and aunt Connie, a few cousins and of course Margaret, my dad's other half, and her daughter. The sound of Margaret's cries is like that of a wounded dove. She can barely walk unassisted. The ushers fan her agony to a quiet murmur. Chloe and Donovan cry as they stand tall and take their time unrushed to view Mommy's daddy. Chloe places her childhood macramé rosary on his chest. She looks to me and blinks quickly enough to release one big tear from her left eye. I wipe it for her and offer a hug. Kyle is strong too. He is wearing the other guardian angel pin my dad had in his pocket. He stops and looks, and then he grabs my hand and stands aside for me to say good-bye. My little man. I smile and give one final glance to that face in the casket. Malik gives him a look of respect and together we give the sign of the cross. I blow my dad a kiss and turn to proceed out of the church.

We are escorted to the limousine while a few people greet us before we depart for the cemetery.

Kareem comes over to hug me and I impart, "I love you," in his ear and he too returns the expression. He whispers, "This really hurts to see you with him. What are you doing? He's too young for you, he'll leave you for a twenty-something in a minute." Malik steps up and introduces himself, more man than I ever thought he could be. Kareem extends his hand and they pat each other on the back. They both know this is neither the time nor the place.

To see a casket placed in the earth is the most final act one can imagine. Another place to visit on Sundays, holidays or Father's Day, yet I know my dad won't be here. His spirit is just another angel guiding me through life. It is a place to visit out of respect, yet he will always be in my heart wherever I go. Charles Jr. and Charles III, together again, in heaven, looking down on me. But dear Lord, no more angels, please!

30

MALIK HAS ALREADY POSTPONED his trip once. Now it's time for him to go. He still hasn't heard from his father. I know he would have told me if he did, so I don't mention it. After we pull up to the curb, he gets out to check his luggage and hops back in the car so I can park and walk to the gate with him. Malik is very quiet.

"I'm going to miss you, baby," I confess, pulling out into the long lines of cars to search for the United Airlines parking lot.

"Me too," he says with reserve. "It should only be for a week though."

"What's on your mind? You're so quiet. Are you nervous? I know we've been consumed by what I've been going through and we haven't really talked about your new career. This is a very exciting time, so I understand if you're a little jittery."

"No, that's not it and I hope you don't mind my bringing this up," he warns as he pauses.

"What?"

"I overheard you tell Kareem you love him."

"Yeah, Malik, I will always love him, not that I'm in love with him," I say in an attempt to clarify.

"Is that all it meant?" he asks with obvious doubt.

"Now wait, are you jealous? Because you don't appear to be the jealous type."

"I just think he's one lucky brotha if he gets to hear those words come out of your mouth, damn lucky."

"I said it out of my awareness of everyone's mortality at that time and I wouldn't want anything to happen to anyone I love. Especially if the last conversation I had with them is negative, like with my dad. I know you understand that."

"It's not about whether or not you love him, I just . . ."

"You just what?" I ask in an effort to pinpoint his real concern.

"I just love you, that's all." There he goes, he said it again.

"You are not getting on any plane without the two of us being one hundred percent fine with each other, no doubts or bad feelings."

"I agree."

I threaten with volume, "I'll turn this airport out!"

"I have a feeling you would do just that," he says while I pull into a great parking space just outside of the terminal.

Malik gets out first and opens my door as he offers his hand to escort me from my car. He then goes to the trunk to get his carry-on bags and we walk toward the crowded terminal.

"Are you afraid your love is unrequited?" I ask, trying to pick up where we left off.

"Yes, that's scary for me too. You know men have fears also," he says as if I could not possibly know that.

"No doubt! Well, seriously, that's one thing you don't have to worry about with me. I believe in you because you have proven that you are there for me, and I do feel for you, baby. Maybe even more than you feel for me, I don't know. But one thing is for sure; the love I'll always have for Kareem and what I feel for you are two totally different feelings that cannot be compared. What I feel for you makes me want to move forward, lay it on the line, strap on my seat belt and go for it. The love I feel for him makes me want to run, get off the ride, back up and never look back. Do you feel me?"

"Just make sure you mean that because there's a lot we need to talk about when I get back."

"Speaking of when you get back, I have something for you."

I reach in my jacket pocket and pull out a small box as we approach the gate.

"What is this, baby?" he asks.

"Just open it. Why would I put it in a box if I'm gonna tell you?" I ask him, being silly.

He slowly opens the box and laughs.

"My pair of lime green Gs," he says in X-rated amazement.

"No, this is my pair, slightly worn, I might add."

He sniffs them, trying to be incognito, and teases, "Hey, now this is what I call a going-away present."

"Good then, now you can put them away, people are watching you," I reply, looking around to see if he's been discovered.

"They're tucked away." He looks around too and stuffs them in his pants pocket.

"See, I'll be with you on that pillow watching your every move. Don't think that's it, look under the cotton square."

Malik peers under the small cotton square and pulls out a package of Sweet 'n Low.

"You are such a tramp!" he states as if he's complaining.

"Well, you didn't get to finish so we have to take up where we left off when you get back . . . and notice I'm the one who's giving you some this time."

"That's it, I'm not going, I can catch the red-eye later on. There's a Marriott right next door. Especially if it's time to get *in!*" he says, attempting to walk back to the car.

"Malik, you have been so good about waiting. I just want you to know I'm ready and I'll be waiting for you this time," I reassure him, pointing him in the departure direction.

"Dang, well, okay. Here, I forgot that I have something for you."

Malik reaches in his back pocket and hands me another picture, signed the exact same way: *You've Got a Friend. Forever, Malik,* with three telephone numbers.

"Thanks. This one is getting framed and placed beside my bed." I clutch it to my breast and kiss his cheek.

"Maybe I should have brought you some draws to put on your pillow," he suggests.

"No thanks, this will do," I answer, passing on the offer.

As we approach the gate he says, "I was just wondering why I suddenly get my way once I'm on my way out of town. Do I have to stay on the road to get spoiled by you?"

"Oh, I can spoil you whether you're on the road or not, it's just that it's time. See, now I think I can handle your downsides. Basically I haven't seen any."

"Damn, just make sure you are standing right here next week when I get off this plane!" he instructs.

"I'll be here. I'm missing you already, baby."

We stand in line hand in hand and hug each other good-bye as he prepares to board. He traces the outline of my lips with his fingertip and whispers, "Remember, it's these lips that I want to feel giving me pleasure when I get back."

I lick my upper lip from left to right and then flick my tongue rapidly in and out of my mouth. He grabs his crotch and says, "Calm down, boy," as he walks away like a pimp whose hoe just gave up the green and boards the plane.

A tear rolls down my cheek as I force myself to turn away. I pray that he is not just my imagination.

A woman approaches me and says, "I know how you feel, I just said good-bye to my son too. Where is he going?"

Oh, no she didn't.

"Ma'am, excuse me, but that was not my son!"

She replies as if she's sorry, "Oh, I didn't mean to imply that was your son. I meant your friend."

"And he's not my friend, he's my man," I say with conviction.

I've gotta get rid of this robbing the cradle guilt. Did I just say my man?

31

As I PULL UP to my apartment, Kyle is getting out of his dad's car and *she's* in the car. They both wave to Kyle as they pull off, leaving him at the curb with his overnight bag.

I tell Kyle, "I don't know why they have you pack a bag like you're visiting a friend; you have a room here, with clothes, a toothbrush and everything."

"Mama, I just brought my Super-Nintendo and some new shoes."

"Let me see, yeah, and underwear, pants, two T-shirts, Kyle! You even brought toothpaste and deodorant."

"Okay, I won't do it anymore," he surrenders.

"I'm sorry, pumpkin. You've gotten taller again," I say, reaching up on my tiptoes to pat him on the top of his head.

We continue to talk as we walk into the house.

"Mom, what's up with Malik?"

"Kyle, Malik is your mom's new . . . boyfriend, okay?"

"I knew that already. I just wanted to hear you say it," he says as if he wants me to lighten up.

*   *   *

TODAY IS A SPECIAL DAY spent with All My Children. We go to Speed Tracks and race cars, that's Kyle's favorite place on earth, and then pig out at Shakey's pizza, jammin' chicken and mojo potatoes while the boys play video games again, as if Speed Tracks didn't have enough of them.

We all visit my mother for over an hour. My stepfather is visiting also. I hug him for a good five minutes and for the first time, I sit on his lap. He looks so proud. After all, he's the one who has been around all these years while I've been ignoring his efforts because I've been too busy living in the past, wasting time asking why. The time will come when I will be able to call him dad; until then, I just want to enjoy each and every day that he's alive.

We look at my mom in unison and she giggles with pride like she's in on the emotion. She knows, even after everything this family has been through, he's been there for her and nothing else matters. He's seventeen years her junior, yet he came along and gave up his bachelorhood to take on a woman and her three children. I can only hope to be so lucky as to have a man like him, or maybe I already do.

CHLOE WALKS DOWN the freshly mopped, linoleum-lined hallway to the vending machine to get a soda for my stepfather.

"Can I come with you?" I ask.

"Sure, Mom. He has always been crazy about Mountain Dew, huh?" she says, enjoying the fact that we know him so well.

"He has at that. How are you doing?"

"I'm fine. I'm just glad that Grandma is still alive. I don't know what I'd do if she died. I'm hoping we never have to attend another funeral."

"We have definitely had our share," I admit, hugging her along the way.

"My sadness over this funeral has made me realize something I'd been unwilling to admit to myself because it hurts so much."

"What's that?" I say as she stops in place.

"I really miss Daddy," she admits as her voice trembles in a high pitch. Looking straight forward and without shedding a tear, she reaches behind me to join my hug and we continue walking.

"I know you do, Chloe. I miss him all the time too. But it's so wonderful that you can look back on your life with him and know that you were indeed Daddy's little girl. He showed you that in everything he did. You had a great relationship with your father. And that definitely makes the death even more tragic. But he loved you so much and you know that."

"And so what does it feel like for you to know that your dad loved you so much too?" she asks as if to dispel a falsehood at the same time.

"It is a shame that I found out the way I did, but at least I know. Better late than never. Sometimes things are not as they seem. Even in anger, a person could be expressing love but just not know how to show it."

"I'd say we're both Daddy's little girls after all," she summates.

There's a statement if I ever heard one. Daddy's little girls after all. Who would have thought that deep down inside, we're both just two little girls who grew up without the dads who loved them so much. Two only girls, with two brothers, who are now coming to terms with their similarities as opposed to their differences. "You hit on something real special there, Chloe."

She says, "You are so strong, Mom. I'm really seeing that now. And I do support you with Malik. He seems to be a good man and he really cares for you. That has been very obvious through Grandpa's death. He has shown so much support for you. Donovan mentioned it also. We respect him for that."

"Thanks, sweetheart," I say as she stops to put the coins in the vending machine. "So what about you now? What do you want to do after the summer?"

"I just want to focus on school and continue working, hopefully at the Berkeley Mall up north."

"And have your friends given you the low-down on the boys up there?"

"I heard there are a lot of guys, especially Black guys, up there. I thought there would be a bunch of geeks and nerds. But they still might be, who knows? Believe it or not, I'm in no hurry to have a boyfriend or make you a mother-in-law and grandmother."

"Well, thank goodness for that," I say with a sigh of relief.

She pauses as the can of Mountain Dew rolls

down, slamming against the side of the machine. "Boys are no longer a priority, Mom. They used to be." She reaches down, placing the can under her arm. "Wow, this is cold."

"I'll take it." She hands it to me, sorting through her wallet for more change.

She continues, "But I do not want to waste time seeking love from the outside. I know it sounds corny but I want to spend time loving myself. I can see what a waste of time it can be to always try to substitute the love of a father with attention from guys who give us a false sense of worth."

"Listen to you. I'm still learning to get that right. I see your grandfather's death has taught you a lot."

"No, Mom. You have," she voices with admiration.

Wow. I feel that lump starting to grow in my throat. "Do you want a soda too?" I ask, reaching into my purse.

"No, this one is on me," she says while racking up four cans altogether. "You know Kyle and Donovan have to have one too."

"I know that."

We walk back down the long hall chatting like girlfriends. Daddy's little girl is becoming a woman.

32

LATER THAT EVENING it's ladies' night out. Carlotta, Ariana, Violet and I all decide to hook up at the Leimert Club. It's our regular familiar place to meet, with great southern-style food, cheap drinks, dim lights, a big old oval Cheers-type bar, chipped linoleum, a cozy dance floor, reggae music and on some nights, down-home comedy. Most of the men are old. But we're here to female bond anyway, not to catch. We pick a bar table in the corner by the TV next to the cigarette machine. Before we know it, the waitress sets down a combo platter of shrimp, catfish, chicken strips and fried oysters sent over by that fine-ass Mr. White, the owner. All at once, the four of us each grab a piece and look around at other empty tables to see if we can find some more hot sauce and napkins. If Malik could see my unwomanly manners now.

"Can you bring some more fries, please?" asks Violet, feeling like she got gypped in the deal. "You can't get good help around here. A few measly fries for a party of four, is she crazy?" she says, shaking down the Tabasco.

"Get your mind off of the platter and give us the scoop. What happened with young sexy-ass Brian, girl?" Ariana asks Violet.

"Yes, he is young and sexy, but damn . . ." Violet says while sucking on an oyster.

"What did you do to that boy?" asks Carlotta.

"What did he do to *me*? He stuck red bows on my nipples and my pubic area and then asked me to lay on his bed like I was a birthday present. Shit, by the time I was ready to take off those bows, they were so damn stuck to my nipples I started crying. And boyfriend wanted to yank them right off of my jugs. I tried to hurt him! The worst part was peeling it off my coochie hair. He had to cut it off so we just shaved it bare after that. It looks like a raw sliced chicken breast," she says, waving her hand as if we should not even bother to go try it out.

"Only you could experience that, Vi. I'm sure the mood was killed by then," I say as I chuckle and flag down the waitress. "That actually sounds like one of Kareem's numbers."

"Don't get me wrong now. Hell, the mood was on and kicking! He had a hard-on the entire time; that young boy is freaky!" Vi says for clarification.

Carlotta starts laughing hysterically at Violet's experience but Vi quickly checks her. "You and Mariah are not the only ones who can catch young men. This older-woman, younger-man thing is *in* just like dark-skinned men are in too. I'm just not sure if I'm with it or not."

The early twenties waitress without a smile walks up. "The gentleman over there in the blue hat would like to buy a round of drinks for all four of you," she says, looking down at her receipt book.

She's referring to the veteran-looking gentleman with the royal blue brim hat, the gut and the wedding ring at the end of the bar. We look over and wave, nodding in appreciation. He mouths his "You're welcome" with a wink and waves back in excitement.

"Oh, hold on now, Grandpa. No fivesome for you," Vi mumbles, exposing a fake grin through her clinched teeth.

"How about apple martinis, ladies," Ariana suggests. "They make the best on earth."

"Apple martinis it is," I say to the waitress just to make it easy. She simply walks away.

My pager goes off. It's Malik. I can tell by the area code that he's arrived in Baltimore.

"Here, use my cellular," offers Ariana.

"Won't it cost?" I ask.

"Free weekends, go ahead."

"You sound like a commercial." I dial him up. "Hey, baby. It's me. Did you have a nice flight?"

"See, old niggas wouldn't call your ass until maybe three or four days later. They'd have gone straight from the airport to the tittie bar," says Violet.

"By the way, Violet, speaking of old niggas, how's your married friend?" Carlotta jokingly inquires.

Vi reacts, "Kiss my kitty, Carlotta. What, you want his number? You'd steal your mama's new man if he bought you a Happy Meal. Hell, don't tell Carlotta how well your man throws down, she'll keep that information for her own benefit so she can straddle his face while you're not lookin'. I saw you bending over in front of Malik last weekend. You know you tried to hit on that brother in Mariah's own backyard."

"Oh, I was just checking to see if he strays easily," Carlotta admits.

"Yeah, and if he'd taken the bite, you'd have been on it," says Ariana.

"I would not," Carlotta says, trying to downplay their suspicions.

"Oh please, he could have seen the North Pole up in there you were bent over so far," Vi reiterates.

"But like I said, the question is, did he look? I was just looking out for Mariah."

"What man wouldn't look? That doesn't mean they want to lay you. The question is, did you think he'd be more attracted to you because you're younger than Mariah? What kind of friend are you?" asks Violet.

I motion for her to be quiet. "No, Malik, it's just the girls. We're at the Leimert Club having a drink. So what's up with you tonight? No, we're behaving. Oh, so tomorrow night is boys' night out. Okay. Well, try to call me tomorrow if you get a chance. I want to hear all about your deal and don't leave out a detail. All right, bye, boo!"

" 'Bye, boo!' Oh my goodness, that's tired. And I still can't believe you haven't even given him any. You expect me to believe your nympho ass hasn't tried to rape that boy?" Violet rudely asks.

"Just because you've already raped Brian," I

respond as I hand Ariana her phone. "Thanks, girl."

"And so what?" replies Violet.

I run it down while dipping my salty fries into some major ketchup, "See, you say you want a relationship and you want to get married, but you don't. You keep setting yourself up to be alone. You touch them before you talk to them because you think you can screw the available ones into submission and the married ones into leaving their wives."

"Oh, we did a lot more than touch! And I'm proud of it. I say get all you can!" Vi exclaims.

"Well," says Carlotta, "a friend once told me to go ahead and screw a man early. But just make sure you do him real good, then he'll come back for more. Hell, keeping it from them for a long time doesn't matter. They'll just wait and wait and then . . . that shit had better be worth waiting for or they're gone right after they hit it." The mute waitress brings the apple martinis.

"Who told you that, a guy?" asks Ariana.

"Yeah," says Carlotta.

"No, duh? But, Mariah, really, think about it, what if he's no good in bed?" inquires Ariana.

"Oh, I have a feeling he's good, just a feeling."

"Did he go muff diving or something? That doesn't mean anything," says Violet.

I reply, "No comment. Anyway, good sex and making love are two different things. When you're in love, even bad sex is the hit. It's the feeling involved in caring for that person, not the stroke. Speaking of stroke, how was Brian's actual stroke anyway?"

"See, you wanna know all my juicy tidbits, but you're not telling yours," Violet says.

"There's nothing to tell. Nothing happened. We're getting to know each other first. Remember, friendship is the root, sex is the bloom," I remind Violet.

"Well then, I guess Brian was a blooming Mandingo-ass buck. That boy actually turned my nappy dug . . . out," she says, raising her martini glass to her magenta lips.

"What?" says Carlotta.

"Oh Lord, here's Carlotta getting ready for the steal," claims Ariana.

"See, I was the one bragging to him about how I'm a big girl and I don't have time for no skinny-ass games. I told him to bring it on. He brought it on all right, on and on and on, and his thing is huge. How do young guys have things that big already?" Vi asks as if she's been sheltered.

"It's not like it grows more after they're twenty-five, stupid," says Carlotta.

"Well, at one point when I was on my stomach, I looked down and I swear the tip was poking through the front of my belly. I thought it was an exorcism."

"That's more information than we needed," I comment with disgust. "What next?"

"Wait now, I thought every young man's fantasy was to have an older woman teach him something," asks Ariana.

"Believe me, there was nothing my old butt could have taught him. I was out of breath and sweating like a pig. When we were finished, he had to blow my body down like he was blowing up a balloon. I was breathing like I'd just run the marathon. Now he's calling every day wanting some more. Girl, you can have those young-ass brothers. My ego needs more stroking than my body. At least an old man will give you your props when you try to work it like a dancer for a few minutes. Brian just begged for more and more. My ass was tired."

"I know I asked but I've heard enough," I reply, taking the cherry from my glass and biting it in half.

"I'm serious. I'm at that age where quick is not the sign of premature ejaculation. It's a sign that I'm still a bad-mamma-jamma," she says as if she's proud.

I say, "Violet, we've heard enough from you, thanks very much."

"Ariana, what's up with you and the girls anyway? I'm not letting you get away with that. You never mention the guys you date," asks Violet. "After all, don't most bisexual women end up experimenting because some brother dogged them out? Bisexual women are the first to claim that men are insensitive, right?"

"Why are you asking me?" asks Ariana.

Carlotta quickly states, "Well hell, I'm never

gonna get that fed up with men. When a woman approaches me I tell her my name is Tracy."

"Tracy?" asks Ariana.

"Yeah . . . Dick Tracy. Hell, I'm strictly dickly as they say." Carlotta high-fives Violet.

Ariana admits, "I've dealt with gay women and men, especially in sports and stuff. People are people and I don't buy into all that homophobic shit you're talking."

"Well, Ariana, just because Dr. Singer said you and Mariah should go get a nice feminine vagina, didn't mean you really had to do it!" says Violet.

"Fuck all of you, anyway. Speaking of dickly, isn't that Brian over there walking this way?" asks Ariana.

Vi banters on, "You know you'd like to fuck all three of us. Hey, Brian, how are you doing?"

"Hey everybody. Hey, Violet, I've been calling you all day. Where have you been? Mariah, has Malik left yet?" Brian asks as if he's nervous.

"Yes, he just paged me," I respond.

"Damn, he didn't waste any time. That boy is crazy about you. I've never seen him like this. Seriously," admits Brian, "I think he's whooped." Brian stares Vi up and down.

"And so am I," I reply, possibly without being heard.

"Come on, Violet, let's dance. You like reggae, right?" Brian asks, snapping his fingers.

"Yeah, mon!" Violet says as they bounce away to the dance floor.

"I'm glad you're feeling better, Mariah. I love you, girl!" says Ariana.

"I love you too. Thanks to both of you for coming to the funeral."

"So Malik has really been drafted to the NFL? Do you know what that means?" asks Carlotta.

"Yeah, that's what I'm afraid of."

33

AFTER AN ENTIRE WEEKEND of missing Malik, unable to imagine how my life was before we met, I decide to get up early and make breakfast for the kids. Kyle's dad agreed to let him stay another day since there's no school tomorrow.

Donovan approaches me and hands me the phone. "Mom, telephone. It's Grandma Pijeaux."

"Ms. Pijeaux?"

"Mariah, it's Mom! I just want to tell you how sorry I am about your dad. I know it's hard, but I'm here if you need me. I just want you to know that," she declares.

"That's very nice of you, Mom!" I say as I struggle to refer to her in that way. "I appreciate your call."

"No problem, now take care."

"I will, you too, bye?" I say with a question mark, anticipating her closing.

Click! Oh well, that would be too much to ask for. Maybe she doesn't say good-bye to anyone.

Before I can walk away from the phone, the dang thing rings again. "Hey, Sarah, how are you?"

"Fine, what about you? Are you better now, sweetie? I was really worried about you last week. Your dad was a well-loved man. A good Christian man."

"I know. I'm much better, but to what do I owe the pleasure of this call?" I ask with an upbeat nature.

"It's about work," she informs me.

"I need to temp tomorrow. Where do you want me?"

"Well, you're gonna have to hold your broke butt off another couple of weeks before you work with me because I'm calling to offer you a full-time gig."

"Full-time, doing what?"

"Cindy and I are working on the new UCW show *Entertainment Headlines*."

"What are you two going to be doing?"

"Cindy is the supervising producer and I'm the executive fucking producer. Do you want the job or not?" she asks with elevated excitement.

I think I heard her but I ask again to confirm. "Sarah, you're kidding me, right? Please don't screw with me like this."

"I'm not kidding. We want you to be our co-host with Brice Goode. He just left CNN to come over and work with us."

"Oh my God!" I shriek as though I'm hooked up to a battery charger. "Sarah, I can't believe this. I have been hitting the damn pavement for so long, I was just about to give up. You haven't even seen my tape, you don't even . . ."

"I don't have to. I know you and you are what

we're looking for. Your personality, your fresh and funky look and your sincerity are all perfect for this gig. Now, are you going to stop blocking your blessings and say yes? You asked for a knock at the door, now open the door and allow your blessings to come in," my new boss advises as if I should wake up and smell the coffee.

"*Yes! Yes! Two weeks from now, where?*"

"Don't you wanna know how much you'll make?"

"Oh yes, how much?" I ask, taking a seat at my kitchen table.

"Ninety-five thousand to start on a one-year contract." I stand up again, jumping in place, holding in my screams so as not to sound like she could have had me for less. "And we will not renew that puppy unless you give us the numbers, so go and brush up on your voice-overs, writing, news gathering and all that 'cause it's on. You can read, can't you?"

"Yes! Thanks so much. Oh my God, what a way to start my week, what a way to start my life, I just cannot tell you how much I appreciate it, Sarah. I love you. Where's Cindy? I have to thank her."

"She's at the studio going over some production stuff. You can call her later. Congratulations."

"Sarah, thank you, thank you. Just let me know where I need to be," I scream as I hang up. Yes!

"Mommy, what was that about? Where are you going to be working?" asks Kyle as the kids all form a circle around me.

"Your mom is going to co-host a national entertainment magazine show starting in mid-August. Your mom is going to be on TV for real now. I have to call my agency and tell them I'm not available. I have to ask Sarah if I have a wardrobe allowance. I'd better. I don't even know what the terms are after the first year. Oh yeah, she said there won't be a second year if I screw up. But then the salary has to graduate to at least one-seventy-five! I'm so blessed!"

Donovan, Chloe, Kyle and I wail and dance around the living room.

I CALL MALIK in Baltimore. He's not in his room so I leave a message.

"Malik, call me, I have the best news. Call me please, right away."

That evening I glide my body out of the bathtub and call Malik again. He still hasn't picked up his messages. I lay my head down in refined excitement. Malik will surely call before the night is over. I fall asleep with the cordless on the bed next to me.

THE NEXT DAY, Sarah calls again right after I leave another message for Malik.

"Mariah, sit down," she says in a firm yet nervous tone.

"What? Don't tell me the offer is canceled. Are you reneging?"

"No, Mariah, it just came over the wire. Malik has been arrested for rape. He's in jail pending a bond hearing in Baltimore."

34

I TRY TO catch my breath as I swallow. "What? No way! No fucking way!" I struggle to breathe, let alone compose my next thought. "Sarah, there's got to be some kind of mistake. That's not like Malik. He wouldn't do that."

"Mariah, I think you need to call his family and find some way to get more information on what happened. Maybe you can fly out there," she suggests.

Just then, Donovan calls me into the living room with a frantic wail. The story is on ESPN.

"Newly drafted rookie Malik Tolliver, who was the last overall draft pick selected to sign with the Baltimore Ravens, has been arrested for suspicion of raping an eighteen-year-old girl. The incident is alleged to have occurred at the residence of fellow Raven Tony Brown, in the exclusive area of Larchmont. The victim's parents had this comment . . ."

One glance at her parents and I think to myself, oh my God, she's White! She's a White girl and she's eighteen. My eyes well up with tears as I force myself to continue listening in agony.

"My daughter was victimized after a night out with

*her friends. No one deserves to be forced to participate
in sex or any other activity against their will. Obviously this person used his celebrity and her naivete to
take advantage of my baby. We will pursue this to the
full extent of the law and make him pay,"* says her
father.

"Sarah, I have to go, I'm calling his grandfather," I excuse myself, clicking over and dialing.

"Mr. Simpson, what happened?"

"All I know is Malik called us last night and
we've sent an attorney out on the first flight this
morning. We were hoping to call you before you
heard about it yourself," he says with a slow, concerned voice.

"You know he wouldn't do this, right?" I ask
out of shock.

"Come on. I've known Malik his whole life.
This is a setup, pure and simple. His mama didn't
raise him to do things like this. And we know
how he feels about you, we've talked about that.
He wants a future with you and we have no problem with it. He went out there to take care of business. That's the only reason. He's not into
nonsense like that. They'll set bail and he'll call us
today, just sit tight and get to praying. We're
gonna need it." My call-waiting clicks in. "Get
that, it might be him. We'll call you back later."

It's Paris checking to see if I need anything. I
decline and again the call-waiting clicks in.
"Hello? Malik, what is going on?" I ask in concern
as I take the phone in my room and close the door.

"Just one thing. Please tell me you believe me,
please say you believe me," he pleads.

"Yes, Malik. You know I believe you. I know you wouldn't do that. Tell me what happened. How did it lead to this?" I inquire, almost sounding like I'm begging for an answer.

"Mariah, my buddy and I were set up. These two girls followed us home from this club called Platinum last night. Next thing I knew, they were at the front door. I should have gone back to my room, that's what I should have done," he says, sounding like he blames himself.

"Malik, were you talking to White girls?"

"Yes, Mariah. We talked to them."

Suddenly that issue of the White prize that makes a man leave his family begins to rise to the surface pure and strong. I find myself becoming very angry. Angry with Malik for coming into my life just as he's about to go off to the NFL. Angry with the girl for being attracted to him. Angry with myself for trusting in him.

"What do you want me to do?" I ask as if I'm not clear. My bare feet pound the pile carpet as I repeatedly pace the length of the room, back and forth.

"I want you to come to me, baby. I have a hearing set for tomorrow and I need you here," he requests in a panic.

He was there for me when I needed him, but my situation was out of my control. How much did he really contribute to this situation? Is this a sign for me to run for the hills?

"Malik, you know I don't fly! Everything will be fine and it'll all work out and be cleared up. I just can't up and leave here. Kyle is home. And besides, you'll be back here by the end of the week, contract and all. I just know it," I attempt to reassure him.

"Do you expect this to just go away and be forgotten like it never happened? My reputation is ruined. I spell trouble for any team now, Mariah. What are you thinking?" he asks as if I'm in a fog.

"What were you thinking? An eighteen-year-old White girl? Malik, please!"

"That statement sounds like you're doubting me more than giving me the benefit of the doubt. I thought you'd be there for me when I needed you. At least that's where I thought we were headed," he admits with disappointment.

"You make it sound like we took a vow or something. I'm not the one being accused here so don't try to make me feel as if I've done something wrong. I'm trying to be positive and you're wallowing in the negative. You must take responsibility for your actions and your contributions in all of this," I preach.

"I already said I should have gone to my hotel room. You know what? Just forget it. I don't need this right now. What I need is an open mind and a loving heart, and I'm sorry I called you," he says, resigning himself to my refusal.

"Malik, I'm not your mother!" I say abruptly, stopping in my place, waving my hand as if he is in the room too.

"What? I'm not looking to you to replace my mother," he replies in amazement.

"Well, maybe if I'd fucked you before you left, you wouldn't have been so damn horny!"

"How can you say that? I thought I knew you! That's not fair. Why are you so hard on me?"

"Because I fell in love with you and I gave you the benefit of the doubt to not be like all the other men in my life. Just what I thought, chasing White women as soon as you're away from me. One way or another I knew you'd leave me. After all, you're in the NFL," I profess as I begin to cry like I've just been stabbed in the heart.

Malik says calmly, "I'm not leaving you. I'm here. This is just one of those down times we discussed. I need you to come to me. I'm not going to hurt you. I'm not going to break your heart. I need you to be here for me," he entreats.

"I have to go now. I need to go for a walk. I cannot talk right now. Where are you?" I ask, rambling.

"I'm in the hotel and I'm not leaving. My attorney is on his way."

"I'll call you later," I say stubbornly.

"Mariah, please come to me now. Please?"

"I'll call you back." I hang up.

Why am I so mean to him? How could I turn his misfortune into a symbol of my past and me?

35

I RUN OUTSIDE, barefoot and all, and I walk and walk and walk. I sit on a curb and cry harder and harder and pray for an answer. None. I consider running all the way to my mom's bedside to just lay at her feet and cry. She would know the answer. She would know just the right thing to say. I cannot think straight. All I can hear is music blasting in my head as usual, songs are playing, scenes are rewinding and voices are ringing. I run home like I'm being chased by a demon. I start thinking about Kareem and how he was there for me through all the years when my brother died, how we'd laugh together and take walks on the pier, we'd make turkey burgers and have card parties, he would wash my hair and I'd shave his head, we would spoon together in bed and sleep all day, we'd play Scrabble, watch Def Jam comedy, get our drink on and of course, screw all night long.

"Hi, Kareem, it's Mariah. What are you doing?"

"Oh, I'm just sitting here with a friend making dinner," says Kareem with a reserved bit of scoffing.

I hear a female voice in the background interject with an edge, "Friend?" The voice is familiar,
but I cannot pinpoint exactly who it is, or if I even
care. I apologize for the interruption and hang
up.

My legs give way as I slowly slope down into
a chair in my dining room. It is the rattan chair
from my dad's apartment. My legs are stretched
in front of me. My shoes seem to plop off all by
themselves. My head gives way to listlessness as
the nape of my neck lowers into the V formation
of the heart-shaped chair back. I lay back and in-
hale for a moment just to simply close my eyes
and release. Suddenly I feel a slight, soft tap on
my back. I turn around, and no one is there. It
must be my imagination. I then hear the sound of
something daintily shattering and breaking in my
bathroom. The first thing that comes to mind is
that it's one of the kids. I jump up and dash to the
bathroom to investigate. I turn on the light to re-
veal that my tiniest, most fragile and cherished
Black angel with the rose-colored wings has
fallen to the bathroom floor and fragmented into
many pieces. It's the one my mother gave me
when I got married. As I carefully pick up the
broken ceramic chips from the bathroom tile
floor, I look around to see what could have happened. I notice the window is closed so it couldn't
have been a soft breeze. In puzzlement, I walk to
the kitchen for a broom and dustpan. Astonished
by what greets my eyes, I jump in place and put
my hand over my wide-opened mouth as I look
toward the dining room chair to the right of me. I

see a faint silhouette of a vision, and next to that chair another vision and next to that chair yet another vision. I wipe my eyes and shake my head in confusion, but still the vision is persistent and real. The ghostly background silhouettes resemble my husband's face, especially his blue eyes; my brother, a massive figure looking at me as if I've done something wrong; and my dad, a vision more faint than the other two. It's a Redd Foxx-looking gentleman with a cigar between his teeth—yes, it is him. I rub my eyes again and gingerly fall back into the wicker chair, too spellbound to run for the door, too frightened to yell for my children just in case they see it also. I cannot feel my tongue. I'm sure my eyes are as large as ice cubes, yet dry as the desert. I feel like weeping but no tears are shed. I just freeze in place at this enigma, anticipating the next moment. Yet at the same time, dreading my next breath.

"My little girl, let go of us and be happy. Trust me," imparts my daddy.

"Go to him, we give you permission," yields my brother.

"He's good for you, I approve," concedes my husband.

And in a split second, they are gone. Gone just as quickly as they appeared. Yet I smell the faint aroma of a burning cigar lingering in the air just subtle enough to let me know I wasn't imagining this sight. It is true. My father smoked cigars when I was a little girl. The aroma comforts me. I do not cry. I do not ask why. I have no doubt that I've just witnessed a miracle.

Perhaps God did not buy my earlier conversation with Chloe so he had to reinforce the message with a vision and a visit.

I tiptoe to the telephone to call my dad's girlfriend. "Margaret, it's Mariah. I have an emergency! Will you do me a big favor and keep an eye on the kids for a couple of days?" I'm using the rest of the money my dad left me to go to Baltimore. I explain my journey to my children, and I am off.

I PAY CASH for my ticket and board the plane. My red-eye flight takes off just after midnight; I should arrive at eight in the morning. Not in enough time to get to the hotel before Malik leaves, but enough time to get to the courthouse. The flight itself doesn't bother me for some reason, even though this is the first time I've ever flown alone. I barely think about it. I caress Malik's picture in my hand and caress the cherished vision in my mind. The vision of my angels is the most beautiful sight of my life next to the birth of my children. My three wise men, together, giving me the permission I need to trust and move on. This time I'm the one who is being born. If ever there were such a thing as having been born again, this is it. This is the ultimate. As I doze off, I put on the stereo headphones and I'll be damned if the song following the Barry Manilow medley isn't "Loving You" by Kenny G. I feel as if I'm floating on a cloud, being loved and loving myself.

36

As I walk into the courtroom, the media is everywhere. A weeping eighteen-year-old girl is on the stand wiping her eyes with her hand. The judge hands her a small box of designer tissues. She femininely takes one and thanks him, and proceeds to wipe her nose as she sniffles. She is pretty and petite. Her skin is tanned and firm and youthful looking. She wears little or no makeup—no need to wear mascara with those long eyelashes and big crystal blue eyes. Her shimmering lips look as if they are adorned with that new colorless lip gloss that's popular nowadays. Her shoulder-length, permed hair is a mousy brown shade with dirty-blond highlights that frame her post puberty-ridden face.

Her hands are clasped in front of her, the tear-stained tissue between her fingers. She's obviously shaking from the pressure of testifying. Her fingernails are a polished grape color and she's wearing a pure virgin white blouse with a large gold cross hanging from her neck. Her blouse is unbuttoned just low enough to see that her bra size is far beyond her years, probably double.

She is answering questions from one of Malik's attorneys, and then she stops and turns to the judge. Her name is Amber.

"I don't know what came over me. We were playing charades and my girlfriend and I just started to remove our clothes and we began to strip. You see, we were trying to act out one of the words which was 'nude.' Next thing I knew, both of us were kissing Tony Brown. My friend had been with him before and they had talked about a threesome. And then Malik got up and went into the kitchen, apparently to get a drink of water. I walked in and began to hug him from behind. He turned around and grabbed my arms while I tried to kiss him, but he rejected me," she admits with a nervous, bashful whisper while blinking a mile a minute.

"Please speak up if you can. How did he reject you, Miss Hunt?" the judge asks.

"He told me to put on my clothes and wait for my friend in the other room. I called him queer and I yelled for my friend to leave with me. I was mad and insulted and thought I could go through with this to get back at him, but I can't."

"So you're saying you made all of this up?"

She stops speaking for a moment. With reserve she looks toward a couple in the front row, possibly her parents, and answers, "Yes."

"Miss, do you realize you could be charged with making false accusations and filing a false police report?"

Amber unclasps her hands and begins to wipe away a single tear chased down her face after a quick blink. "Yes." Her eyes shift to Malik as she gives him a timid glance. "Mr. Tolliver, I want you and your family to know I'm sorry. I'm really sorry. I hope I haven't caused too much grief for you. Please forgive me." At first Malik looks down, and then he leans back in his chair and looks up to the ceiling.

"Your Honor, we will want a public apology and a public statement released to the media from Miss Hunt as soon as possible," requests one of Malik's attorneys.

"Miss Hunt, you may step down," says the judge. She vacates the chair, sniffling and looking down at her feet until she returns to sit beside her attorney.

"Mr. Tolliver, please stand," says the judge. Malik and his attorneys stand as well. "All charges are formally dropped and you are free to go. Your attorneys can work out the arrangements for your bail return."

Malik responds, as if relieved yet inconvenienced, "Thank you, Your Honor."

Joy and elation are written on my face. Malik turns to look over at me and motions for me to come to him. He is talking to a tall, distinguished-looking Black gentleman with salt and pepper hair. I assume he is the attorney Malik's grandfather sent to handle the case.

"Mariah, this is my father, Cedric Tolliver. Dad, this is my girl, Mariah!" he tells me with wide eyes, in anticipation of my reaction.

"Nice to meet you, sir." I start to weep subtly as I reach out my hand to shake his. His face is just like

Malik's. Even his full lips and his deep dark eyes are exactly like my baby's. And as I look down at his hand, I notice his fingers are shaped like Malik's too. He pulls me to his chest and hugs me with strength. My weeping turns into full-blown crying.

"The pleasure is mine. So it was your idea to write the letter, huh?" he inquires in an "I'm gonna get you" tone.

With a quivering voice, I answer, "Don't get mad at me, this was a joint venture."

"Well, I'm sorry to hear about your dad. I know it must have been difficult losing him. But now, he is everywhere. Do you know that?" Mr. Tolliver explains.

"Yes, sir!" I reply as I wipe the tears from my cheeks. "Everything happens for a reason, right, Malik?" As Malik pulls out his handkerchief from his suit jacket pocket, handing it to me, his package of Sweet 'n Low falls onto the floor.

"Ahh, right, baby," he says, sounding nervous.

"Boy, are you on a diet? You'll need all the bulk you can get playing in the league."

"No, Dad," Malik replies while he bends over to pick it up.

"That's really what I call bringing your own. Excuse me but I see your coach. I'll be right back. Can we go get some coffee? Will you be around?" he asks me.

"I'm not going anywhere," I answer while I continue to blow my nose and wipe my tears.

"She's an emotional one, son. Just like your mama." Mr. Tolliver walks away as he pats me on the top of my head.

"That was embarrassing," Malik confesses.

"He doesn't know. No one would ever figure that out," I say.

"Shoot, my grandfather told me that one. Believe me, he knows."

"Your grandfather?"

"Just be glad I didn't have my lime greens in my pocket. What about you? You had me worried last night when I didn't hear from you. My dad called me at the hotel and we talked all night. He explained so much about his choices and I thank you for being an example to me about clearing up old issues so one can move on. Your experience with your dad has taught me a lot."

"You know, this experience you just went through has changed your dad's life, my life and your life forever. I'm glad yours turned out this way and that you have the second chance I'll never have."

"You too have one with me. See, I'm willing to forgive you for that little attitude thing over the phone yesterday, so you'd better get with this," he says with confidence.

"I am here just like you asked," I say, still wiping my tears.

"Can you believe she made it all up?" he asks in disbelief.

"Yes. But it's over now. Let's just go ahead from here. And one more thing . . ."

I reach into my pockets and extend my arms out in front of me with my fists closed tight. "Now, this is your relationship fantasy come true. Choose what's behind fist number one or fist number two."

Malik laughs at me and touches my left hand.

As I slowly turn over my fist and open my hand, it is my dad's half of the broken heart charm.

"You chose my dad's half and I want you to have it. It would mean so much to me if you would take it," I encourage him.

"This was your dad's for years. He held on to it for so long. I don't know what I would do if . . . no, I don't want to be trusted with it," Malik says, shaking his head in refusal.

"Are you saying you can't be trusted? Is that what you said?"

"I can be trusted because I am trustworthy," he says after a second thought.

"We know this."

"Okay, you got me. Give it up! Here, put it around my neck."

I carefully clasp the chain around his beautiful seventeen-inch German-chocolate neck, and kiss the heart with a soft peck.

"Thanks, baby," Malik says.

"Thank you for being the exception to my rule. I love you," I say without missing a beat.

"You what?" he asks to confirm, just in case.

"I said, I love your ass, Malik," as I tighten my jaw and move into his face to plant one on his generous lips.

"I love your ass too, feisty one. Hot damn! What a day! I've got my girl and my dad," he exclaims with relief.

"So what did your dad say about my age?"

"Shoot, he said if I won't, he will. He said you remind him of Miss Parker."

"No, he didn't."

"Yes, he did, brought it up himself. Asked me if you had a sister."

"Malik," I say as if I am too through with him.

He pauses and then questions me, "Wait a minute, you flew here?"

"On 'angels' wings,' Malik. If you only knew."

We continue talking as we walk out of the courtroom toward his father.

"So are you and Kyle moving to Baltimore next year after Donovan goes away to Stanford? 'Cause you know that's where he's going. And we will have Kyle with us full-time. Did my uncle call you about that? Don't you slack up!" he reminds me.

"Oh, I didn't tell you. Sarah made me an offer I couldn't refuse. It's a position co-hosting a magazine show on television, but it's in L.A."

"Oh, we do have to talk about that one. Congratulations," he says, almost with a question mark.

As Mr. Tolliver, Malik and I walk away from the courthouse toward the coffee shop, Mr. Tolliver implores, "Son, by the way . . ."

"Yeah, Dad?"

His dad proudly lights up a handmade Cuban cigar with a Sumatra seed wrapper label and affirms, "The answer is *yes*."

We both know this clear and proven answer of yes is in response to Malik's fervent question in his letter of "Will you be there when I need you?"

The sweet, spicy, nutty aroma of his Cuban

cigar lingers in the air, triggering memories of my own father while we walk down the street feeling liberated and carefree. I feel as though I am finally in Shangri-la.

37

BACK IN LOS ANGELES the next week, all three of my girls and I attend our regular controversial relationship seminar. Dr. Singer's assistant passes out a pale pink brochure titled "The Virtuous Woman's Creed."

"Ladies, welcome. Now turn to the inside flap of your handout, hold up your right hand and read along with me," Dr. Singer instructs.

Violet remarks, "She really needs to cut out this Girl Scout shit."

"You'd better put your hand up and smile. You know she will clown you," I whisper from the side of my mouth.

"Oh damn," Violet says, looking straight forward, only barely raising her right hand to chest level.

"I will choose a partner who compliments me, cherishes me, and honors my feelings. One who is interested in receiving happiness in return once I'm happy, who knows that I will keep him mellow when he keeps me mellow, who gives unconditionally so that I am free to give in return, who adds to my life, not takes away from it, and who chooses to lead the waltz if I choose to

follow. If I want a long-term relationship, I will inquire as to his intentions early on and will not complain later if his decision was to just have me as a sexual partner. I will not have sex without a commitment and monogamy, if a commitment is what I desire. I will shut my big mouth and listen to what he has to say, as opposed to dominating the conversation, especially until he has fallen in love with me. I promise that I will not date men who are already spoken for, men who lie, men who cheat, men who do not live up to their commitments, men who abuse me verbally and/or physically and men who violate my moral standards and spiritual beliefs. I will not blurt out my demands and insist that I be heard. When I want to talk, I will respect him by asking his permission to talk first so that he can shift into his proper lobe, and even then I will negotiate, not threaten. I will not expect a man to treat me like I treat him. I will expect him to treat me as I deserve to be treated, like a lady. If I choose to get married, I will not date for more than one year without a ring to show his intentions. I am a virtuous woman who deserves to be cherished and deserves to be loved." She closes her copy and says, "Now that's the 'ladies first' theory!"

"Shit, I've got a lot to learn," Violet admits with a mumble.

We put our hands down, looking around at the other ladies.

"Did you all get that?" Dr. Singer questions. "If you didn't, give me six weeks and you will. Now who wants to share?" I raise my hand. "Come on up here, young lady. I hope you have an update for us. Where's the ring?"

I stand up and approach the stage. "I don't have a ring on my finger, but I do feel like giving myself one." I turn toward the audience as the doctor hands me the microphone.

"Why is that?" the doctor queries, standing to my left.

"Because of you, Dr. Singer, I let go of someone I was not compatible with. I have allowed him seven years of my life on his terms. Now I have met someone who *adds* to my happiness and honors my feelings first. And while there's still so much to be worked out, I've learned that it's all about loving yourself first. Loving yourself enough to make good decisions in your life for you. It's about living for today in spite of the past. I've learned to let go of all things that are not for my betterment. That includes issues with parents, boyfriends, children and myself. Letting go does not mean that I give them get out of jail free cards, it just means that I value the lesson, have learned from it and choose to move on. We must surrender and accept it as it is, not what it should have been. Believe me, I had to learn it the hard way.

"I pray you can learn that now before it's too late. You cannot choose the beginning or the end, but you can choose the in-between. Love comes through us, not to us and what we draw to us is what we are. We need to get as whole and complete as we can in preparation for the journey of continuing to grow. There's something Dr. Singer wrote in my copy of her book, *How to Be a Virtuous Woman,* when I first met her, and I never forgot it. She wrote, 'I want you to love yourself first, and then learn to share it with others.' For me, that's the lesson and I've learned it.

"I've also met someone who accepts me as I am and I too accept him as he is. We care enough to work through the stuff together, yet we do not cross the boundaries of individuality because we want to experience the rewards of evolving. I know that our paths have crossed before; it's just too right to be wrong.

"So my bit of advice is this: in spite of age differences, ethnic differences and other obstacles that should be negotiable, just be yourself, relax, allow yourself to be given to and be *loved*. As Dr. Singer said, ladies, we deserve it." Dr. Singer and the audience applaud.

Dr. Singer sits down and makes a playful gesture. "No, you can keep the microphone, let's just have you offer advice for the rest of the evening. I couldn't have said it better." She then snatches the microphone back from me and returns to the stage. "Just kidding. I have one question," she says, leaning over the podium. "Have you let him in?"

"No!" I admit as I return to my seat.

"Good girl!" the doctor says, walking back toward the audience.

I add, "But I'm about to!" The audience laughs and the girls give me high fives. Vi gives me the finger.

"You ain't shit," she says in jest. "Did she say no more men who are already spoken for?"

"I think so, you hard-headed woman."

"It's the hard heads that make it so hard," she jokes. At least I think she's joking.

"What's this 'shut my big mouth' stuff?" one disconcerted woman inquires from the front row.

"Yeah," Ariana replies as backup.

"That means listening instead of sharing all of your goodies right off the bat. Stop trying to impress him and let him impress you. If you shut up on the first four dates or so, you just might hear him tell you that he's an ax murderer. If you talk through it, you could miss that important tidbit of information. Ask him questions, determine whether or not he's husband material. For him, all you have to do is shut up and refuse to let him in until he's committed. Once he's fallen in love with you, he won't care that you have cellulite, dandruff or that you're thinking about quitting your job. By then, let's pray that the unconditional love has kicked in and you're both willing to negotiate. It's the nonnegotiable issues that should make him and you head for the door," Dr. Singer says.

"That's deep," Carlotta comments.

"No, that's real. That's part of the masculine energy and feminine energy roles that affect every relationship. Some of you are entirely too liberated. Think back to how your grandmother related to your grandfather. There's nothing wrong with being old-fashioned. Marriages lasted a lot longer back then. That's why you're here, to learn those roles because what you're doing is not working." Dr. Singer puts her hand on Violet's shoulder. "Okay now, who wants to know where to meet all of these available men?"

"Now that's what I'm talking about," says Violet. "Where are these single, available men?"

"Well, I'm about to tell you. How about Tom Bradley International Airport? A smorgasbord and melting pot of all nationalities—German, Asian, French, African and Italian. But just make sure you put on a good deodorant and don't wear silk. You'll be sweating for a good ten minutes after giving that three-second stare, smile and look away. Three-second stare, smile and look away. Try it with me, feminine ladies!" Dr. Singer encourages us.

I watch in joy as Carlotta, Ariana and especially Violet practice the infamous three-second stare as we all say in unison, "Three-second stare, smile and look away, three-second stare, smile and look away."

Hot, soulful and fabulous fiction from

Marissa Monteilh

MAY DECEMBER SOULS

0-06-050280-0/$6.99 US/$9.99 Can

Things are good, not great, for Mariah Pijeaux, the mother of three and about to turn the big 4-0. Then she meets Malik Tolliver. He could be the answer Mariah has been desperately seeking in relationship seminars—but he happens to be twenty-one years old.

HOT BOYZ

0-06-059094-7/$13.95 US/$21.95 Can

The Wilson brothers are three famous, sexy, and successful "boyz" who've got it going on. But beneath the surface of their ideal lives are secrets that could shatter three perfect dreams and shake a family to its core.

THE CHOCOLATE SHIP

0-06-001148-3/$13.95 US/$21.95 Can

Delmonte Harrison, an African-American entrepreneur-billionaire purchases three ships from a major cruise line and re-designs them to meet his soulful standards. Then he hires a handpicked crew, including foxy cruise director Tangie Watson to keep the romantic adventure going full speed ahead.

www.AuthorTracker.com

Available wherever books are sold or please call 1-800-331-3761 to order.   MMO 0105

Fiction with Attitude...

The best new African-American writers from AVON TRADE.

because every great bag deserves a great book!

Paperback $12.95
($17.95 Can.)
ISBN 0-06-093645-2

Paperback $13.95
($21.95 Can.)
ISBN 0-06-056449-0

Paperback $13.95
($21.95 Can.)
ISBN 0-06-059535-3

Paperback $12.95
($17.95 Can.)
ISBN 0-06-050965-1

Paperback $13.95
($21.95 Can.)
ISBN 0-06-059094-7

Paperback $12.95
($17.95 Can.)
ISBN 0-06-058709-1

Don't miss the next book by your favorite author.
Sign up for AuthorTracker by visiting *www.AuthorTracker.com*.

Available wherever books are sold, or call 1-800-331-3761 to order.

AAT 0105